A Man to Cross Rivers With

By Richard Davis

Ouray, Colorado

To my wife Christine Knight for all her support and encouragement.

First Edition 1999
Printed in the United States of America

ISBN 1-890437-09-3
Library of Congress Catalog Number 99-61619

Cover and text design by Laurie Goralka Design

Western Reflections, Inc.
P.O. Box 710
Ouray, Colorado 81427

TABLE OF CONTENTS

Acknowledgments

No book such as this is accomplished by a single individual. The author wishes to thank, in sequence: Sheriff Cyrus Wells "Doc Shores", who, at the advanced age of eighty, wrote his autobiography upon which this story is based; Wilson Rockwell who compiled that self-account into Memoirs of a Lawman; my publishers at Western Reflections, Inc., P. David and Jan Smith, for their help and encouragement; Dr. Dwayne Vandenbusche, a mentor and eminent Western Colorado historian of Western State College in Gunnison, Colorado.

Preface

This is a novel, a fictional adventure, based on the life of a real and colorful Western American sheriff, Cyrus Wells, "Doc Shores." I am greatly indebted to both Doc Shores and Wilson Rockwell who devoted themselves to writing the accurate history upon which this story is based. If I were to be asked how much of it is fiction and how much fact, I would have to say about eighty percent, respectively.

I had two overlapping goals when I began writing this book in August of 1997: create a good story which people would enjoy reading and remain true to the character of Doc Shores as a historical figure, a person, a man of great personal courage, ambition, honesty and integrity, and a devoted and tenacious lawman.

The high points of his life are generally accurate: he was born in Michigan and left at age twenty two to follow his brother out west. He worked as a trapper/hunter, bull-whacker, teamster, cowboy, cattleman, and law officer. In many ways he is the personification of the myth of the American frontiersman.

Other characters were simply created. For example Agnes Shores, doc's wife, is mentioned very little in his autobiography. Her creation is an amalgam of characteristics of the pioneer women in my own and my wife's families, historical accounts of American pioneer women, and my personal extrapolation of the myth of the American pioneer women. Other characters were similarly created.

Doc Shores did indeed have contact with Colonel John Chivington, the "hero" of Sand Creek, Wild Bill Hickok, Tom Horn, and the notorious Telluride, Colorado Marshal, Jim Clark, but usually not as created in this story. The characters of John Malcolm Douglas and Stryker McQue, Shores' main antagonists, are purely my own creations.

I heeded the very sensible advice of my publisher to keep the name of the town and river, Gunnison, so readers familiar with Western Colorado could better place them within the story. Details such as the exact location of the La Veta Hotel have been changed to assist the plot.

PART 1

CHAPTER 1

The Old Man's been dead a long time, nearly thirty years. Now I am old, nearly as old as the Old Man when I first met him. He died alone. Alone I now serve his legacy. If stories improve with age, he and I have seasoned his to near perfection.

I met him only once, on a Sunday afternoon in mid-September, when autumn's first cool breath blew down from the rusting oak on Horsefly Ridge and battled with the armored heat of summer still yet rising from the alkali pans of Western Colorado's Uncompahgre Valley. It rattled the parchment-dry poplar leaves in our backyard and portended, some said, an early winter. My father brought the Old Man, my great-uncle, to our house for dinner. We considered it an event. The Old Man had a standing invitation to our home, but for some reason only now accepted it. My father even insisted that I be home from college to attend this auspicious occasion.

As I gazed languidly into the golden heat haze from our porch swing, my father's gray Ford coupe with its large yellow sheriff's star crunched to a halt in the shade of our giant sumac tree. Mesa, my father, got out and trotted around the front of the car to the passenger side. The Old Man waited for him to open the door and to assist his exit with a hand beneath the right arm. Together they shuffled up the cracked walkway to the house, Dad watching the Old Man's every step. The Old Man stepped slowly, with great dignity, and just the hint of a limp. He tapped along with a gold-headed cane in his right hand. In spite of his age, he walked head high, chin up, straight and tall, evidencing a former youth of considerable size, strength, and vigor. Only his shoulders slumped slightly beneath the burden of the years. Thick white hair flowed cloud-like to his shoulders from a head and face appearing more rock than flesh. His high cheekbones were made even more striking by a perfectly sculpted goatee and mustache, the very likeness of Buffalo Bill. He wore an ancient but immaculate black wool suit, in spite of the heat, over a brilliantly starched white shirt with a high celluloid collar and a black string tie. An ornate gold watch fob with an elk tooth dangled from his vest pocket. His boots glistened black.

As he drew closer I could see bright gray eyes illuminating deep, dark sockets. His poise and countenance brought me to attention and drew me to the screen door. I would have moved no more quickly for a president or emperor than I did for this legendary lawman. I held open the screen door and stood aside as they entered the porch. As he passed by me, the Old Man gazed silently into my eyes, a practiced look, honed razor sharp from living and surviving among strong, determined, and desperate men. The look, without menace, stripped me bare and skinned me inside out, leaving nothing of my character hidden. But the look was just, not judging.

"Mr. Shores," said my father formally, when they were standing on the porch, "I would like you to meet my son Raymond. Ray, this is your great-uncle, Sheriff Cyrus Wells Shores . . . Doc Shores."

"Mr. Shores," I said, extending my hand, "it's really a pleasure to meet you. I've heard and read much about you." I stopped short. His wrinkled, brown hand did not move from the golden head of the ebony cane, the penetrating stare not even broken by a blink. My hand was left suspended in midair. My breath caught.

Slowly, carefully, and deliberately, C.W. Shores lifted his cane with his right hand and raising his left arm, rested the head of the cane in the crook of his left elbow. He extended his right hand which I all too eagerly clasped. I was surprised at the strength of the tawny, skeletal fingers. In a deep, strong, and resonant voice, he said, measuring his words carefully, "I hasten to correct Mesa. I am but a former sheriff, one who is all too pleased to make your acquaintance, young Raymond. May I call you Ray?"

"Of course," I said, attempting to adjust my voice to his formal eloquence. "I would be honored. Please won't you come inside where we can sit comfortably? May I get you something to drink?"

A smile touched the lips between the grand mustache and goatee. He replied that he would be pleased to accept a whiskey and branch water . . . preferably with ice. My mother, in her best Denver-purchased apparel and starched gingham apron entered the room and intercepted me. She gushed a greeting so formal I almost expected a curtsey, after which she retired to the kitchen to prepare our drinks. I guided Mr. Shores toward our premier, overstuffed chair indicating that it was the most comfortable seat in the room. He declined in favor of a stiffly woven willow rocker, saying that otherwise, because of his bad leg, he would have to trouble us for assistance in rising from the deep, soft leather. He lowered himself rigidly into the chair with my father still standing by solicitously. He politely objected, saying that if he needed help he would ask for it. "And, please, Ray," addressing me as if an old friend, "call me Doc. Mister Shores is a trifle awkward for easy conversation. Everyone, friend and enemy alike, has always called me Doc."

"Thank you. I will," I replied in my most respectful tone. "I am curious however, how a lawman came by the name Doc. Were you ever a physician?"

My mother brought in the drinks and set them before each of us. The ice cubes tinkled pleasantly in the thin, etched Waterford crystal glasses. The glasses were already dripping with condensation, and Doc politely requested a coaster to prevent leaving a water-mark on our beautiful furniture. My mother, obviously pleased at Doc's gentlemanly consideration, furnished each of us with a cork coaster, excused herself, and retired again to the kitchen leaving the three of us to converse.

He chuckled, returning to my question. "I wish I had a dollar for every time someone has asked me if I were a doctor. No, I acquired the name when, as a youngster in the backwoods of Michigan, I was presented with a sickly, orphaned lamb by the doctor who had delivered me and for whom I was named . . . Cyrus Wells. I nursed that lamb back to health. My older brothers and the other boys at school made great sport of it and began calling me Doc. The name stuck. I suppose I should be thankful that they didn't start calling me Mary instead, . . . as in 'Mary Had a Little Lamb'." We joined him in laughter.

Doc almost immediately put to rest my apprehensions that the differences in our ages and experiences would lead to a lopsided dialog between Doc and my father about law enforcement and the "good ol' days." Instead to my surprise and delight, Doc rocked forward, and leaning intently upon his cane with both hands, began in very soft tones and measured words, to hold forth, comparing the virtues and disadvantages of different types of wood and finishes used in the construction of furniture. From there, he moved to the different chemical composition of a variety of waxes, varnishes, lacquers, paints, and shellacs. All the while he was sipping frequently from his glass of whiskey and water, around which he had carefully wrapped a monographed handkerchief to absorb the condensed moisture. He frequently solicited my father's opinion and occasionally mine, though I was certain he was less interested in our opinions than in encouraging participation. He possessed the remarkable conversational ability to smoothly transition, upon exhausting his knowledge of one topic, to another. I was so taken with the man's oratory, together with the breadth and depth of his knowledge, I scarcely noticed when he had changed subjects. My father sat and smiled indulgently, interjecting comments only when he thought appropriate. Throughout our conversation I continued to wonder why Shores, only now, following years of apparent camaraderie with my father, had come to our house. My question would be answered before the end of the evening.

When mother announced that dinner was served, Doc surprised me by launching himself from the rocker like a spring puppy and skipping lightly across the dining room floor. Mother seated him at the head of the table, a chair normally reserved for my father. Doc, declining wine, continued to sip on a series of whiskey and branch water drinks while commenting unceasingly on the Haviland china, Damask tablecloth, sterling silver, and Waterford crystal, astonishing me, probably my father, and as she stated later, embarrassing my mother, causing her to comment favorably during dinner upon his gentlemanly manners and culinary knowledge. She later confided to my father and me that while priding herself on her own knowledge of tableware she also admitted to feeling inadequately educated in comparison to Doc. We all agreed it contrasted dramatically with, if not contradicted, his reputation as frontiersman, lawman, and even gunman.

Doc raised his whiskey, sipped pensively and said, "I must credit my dear departed wife Agnes, a woman of considerable education and erudition, with impressing upon me the social advantages of such knowledge and good social graces. I possess little formal education, but Agnes, a trained nurse and school teacher, completed my education in our all-too-brief time together. We discovered very early in our marriage I had an aptitude for such things. She impressed upon me how such may enrich life. Agnes, like my mother, was a southern belle, born and reared in the best traditions of the grand Old Dominion of Virginia, and the culture of South Carolina, a woman gifted with beauty and grace. I have consciously attempted to pattern my social, professional, and moral behavior after her."

"My goodness!" exclaimed my mother. "How did such a woman acclimatize to frontier life?"

Doc drew a deep breath and sighed. "She was also a woman of great personal strength and courage who endured gallantly the hardships and relocation forced upon her by the Civil War. She never complained of the discomfort and the danger except when it concerned me as sheriff. I'd be gone on a manhunt for weeks at a time leaving her in Gunnison not knowing where I was, nor if she'd ever see me again. She was indeed a most remarkable person. I miss her greatly." His speech silenced the table, and only through great effort were we able to recapture the earlier light-hearted tone of conversation.

During the course of dinner he questioned me closely about my own education and profession. I told him that I too was influenced by a woman and schoolteacher, my mother, who had directed me toward attending college, for which I would be eternally grateful.

"Yes," he said, "so I understand from talking to your father. Ivy League. Harvard is it?

"Princeton."

"What course of study?"

"Fine Arts. Literature. American literature."

"Have you written?" he questioned. He stopped eating, lowered his knife and fork and was peering at me all the more intently, his gray eyes now wide and brilliant.

"A bit. I would like to do more, but I'm presently employed part-time as an editorial assistant by a publisher."

"Yes indeed!" he exclaimed with some enthusiasm. "So Mesa has also informed me." He seemed poised to ask or offer more but instead fell silent and only peered at me until I became uncomfortable and changed the subject.

Following dinner, Doc so profusely complimented my mother on her culinary efforts I thought she would crawl from the room with embarrassment. He meticulously dressed his flowing mustache with a small tortoise-shell comb that had a scalloped handle and announced that instead of retiring again to the living room he would like me to take him out to see the new gelding my father had recently purchased. As we started from the kitchen out the back door to the livestock pens and barn, Doc surprised us by turning to my father and exclaiming, "Mesa, excuse us, it would please me if I could discuss with your son alone the matter which has brought me here this evening." My father nodded and backed into the kitchen to assist my mother in picking up the dinner dishes.

I waited at the bottom of the steps to assist him, but he waved me off, and hanging his cane on his arm, nearly bounded to the sidewalk. "Your mother's excellent dinner and a few good whiskeys have reinvigorated me. I feel at least twenty years younger." We stood there briefly, both observing the verdant landscape bright as an emerald in the early afternoon sun with its cat-tail ponds and river willows and cottonwoods. The autumn mountain zephyr sang through the goldenrod and ragweed and tangled playfully with the late afternoon translucent heat shimmer. The ponds lay smooth and serene, perfectly mirroring the sky and cotton ball clouds. The tranquillity of their surface jumped into life only infrequently by daddy-long-legs or a bluegill rising from the cool green depths to pluck a fallen mayfly and dive back. I thought I could see his eyes water with nostalgia as he spoke softly, almost reverently. "When I was a youngster in the backwoods of Oakland County, Michigan, I imagined a farm was the worst place on earth. My great- grandfathers, grandfathers, and uncles were all seafaring men out of the Carolinas and Virginia, but I came to think that a farm may have been a great place for a boy to start, but only to start. My uncles, particularly my Uncle Emmit, would come to visit and tell me stories of ocean voyages, foreign places, and adventures with pirates. I never cared to be a seaman, but their stories certainly filled me with curiosity about other places, people, and a longing to travel far away. They instilled in me a spirit of adventure that I have never regretted." Then twirling his cane in his hand, he set off toward the corral where a buckskin horse with a short black mane dangled its head over the smooth, aspen railing and neighed expectantly. Indeed Doc did appear twenty years younger than the man I had seen getting out of the car. I followed obediently.

Doc, hand out, approached the horse speaking softly. "Whoa horse, whoa horse, easy, easy." He maneuvered slightly to one side, knowing, as does an expert horseman, that a horse cannot accurately perceive an object approaching it straight-on at a distance of a few feet and will shy away from the blurred image. His delicate hand moved slowly along the smooth cheek and stroked it gently. The horse's eyelids drooped and its lips smacked in appreciation and contentment. Doc continued to stroke the horse as he spoke. "Never met a buckskin that I didn't like. Best times of my life were spent on a good buckskin named Skip, riding through the dewy sage early in the morning. No fresher scent exists on earth!" He paused, his voice catching slightly, the memory perhaps burning too brightly. He quickly turned to me, almost exuberantly, and asked, "Would you take me riding with you sometime, sometime early in the morning when the sage is fresh with the dew or rain? I would dearly love to go riding and smell the sage one more time before I cross over that last river."

"Of course," I said. "I'd be delighted to if you'll tell me some of your experiences."

The corners of his eyes crinkled and the mustache moved ever so slightly. "Come," he said, motioning with his cane to a planed spruce plank between two cottonwood tree stumps next to the old barn. "Let's sit and talk briefly of such matters." As we walked to the bench I thought he suddenly reverted to the Old Man, as his polished boots shuffled through the adobe dust and straw and his hand trembled on the head of the cane. Taking another neatly folded handkerchief from his hip pocket, he examined the plank, wiped off a spot for himself and examined it again before easing himself down. He leaned forward on the cane with both hands and rested his chin on them pensively.

I sat and prepared to listen.

"I have written," he announced at length, in a very strong, definite voice, "an account of my life, an autobiography if you will, or rather what I could remember of it at the age of eighty." He paused as though to say, "So there, end of the conversation." I half expected him to rise and walk off.

Feeling he needed encouragement, I ventured that I would like very much to read his book.

Sitting bolt upright and stamping his cane on the adobe, "And so you shall," he said very loudly. "As I told you, I am not a particularly well educated man and certainly not a noteworthy writer, although I believe I have done a reasonably commendable job on my memoirs." He arose abruptly, and thinking he was about to leave, I too sprang from the bench ready to follow him, but rather he began pacing the barnyard in front of me, head down. I reseated myself. Three Rhode Island red hens perched on the aspen pole fence near the horse gave audience for a few seconds and then returned to preening their feathers.

"I took my manuscripts, at the behest of a friend, to a publisher in New York City. I was told they were too crude and would have to be rewritten for popular tastes. I refused. I had seen what some of the so-called popular writers like Buntline had done in the dime novels. Made good, honest people look ridiculous, like vaudevillians with make-up and baggy pants." He exclaimed, punctuating his point with a bony finger, "Damn New York

City editors are the last people in the world to know anything about the West and the people and the facts. But," he quickly added with a wink, "be careful of the facts, that they don't get in the way of a good story." Doc stopped and looked at me. "My God! It was an interesting life. Oh, not so much because of me, but because of the people and the experiences. Storytelling is a fine art. It's about folks, what interests folks, captures their imagination and allows them to . . . to . . ."

"To smell the dewy sagebrush in the early morning and listen to the meadowlark on the fence post?" I finished for him.

Doc stopped his pacing, straightened and pierced me with a stare. "Precisely! That's it. To allow them to escape their time and place and problems and travel to places they will never see and do things they will never do otherwise."

"Doc, I agree with you, but writing a story which people will embrace is a different proposition than sitting around a campfire telling one; people read differently than they listen. That may have been what your publisher meant."

The Old Man pondered this for a few moments. "Yeah, maybe," he granted. "But, it's my story . . . they're my stories, and I want them told as they should be. I worked for John Chivington who was considered either the hero of Sand Creek or a murdering bastard, and I knew Hickock and Horn. I pursued desperate men across the West and stood toe-to-toe in gun battles against some of the best shooters of the times. I want that story told, but it also has to be mine."

"I'm sure it can be done. Perhaps if you tried other publishers?"

Doc shook his head solemnly. His shoulders slumped beneath the black frock coat, and once again he was an old, old man who had difficulty reseating himself on the pine bench. "Time grows short young Ray," he murmured. "This is the last great thing I must accomplish in my life, but I fear I may not survive to accomplish it nor do I have the strength any longer to pursue that end. I need to entrust the manuscripts to someone else as I have no living progeny. Will you assist me in this final task?"

"Of course, whatever is within my abilities to perform."

"Unfortunately," he continued. "I did not keep a diary during my life so when the urge to write came upon me — as I've said, I was beyond the age of eighty — I had to rely on only my memory. At times it proved most difficult. I could recall faces, but with no names, or names with no faces, and sometimes I would confuse the sequence. I spent no time researching and cross-referencing except to talk to some survivors who were also older than God and whose memories were even worse than mine. I began writing in the first person but had accomplished no more than a page or two before choking on myself. I am not a vain man. Then I remembered Caesar — The Gallic Commentaries. The thought occurred to me to write again in the third person. Thereafter the writing went much more smoothly. The manuscripts were of course originally all in my own handwriting. Before taking them to the publisher I did engage someone to type them."

I smiled inwardly at the comment about his lack of vanity but said nothing. Together we rose from the bench and strolled back to the buckskin from whose mane Doc combed clumps of cottonwood wool with his fingers.

"Doc, I can't personally promise you that my company will publish your manuscripts nor can I promise you that even if they do it will be in a form to your liking, but I can personally promise you that the spirit of your work, your life, will be maintained."

We walked back toward the house. He sighed, "Perhaps I want too much. Perhaps I'm hoping for too much. Even now, I fear that I may have unconsciously left out some of the bad parts, some wrongs I perpetrated and am seeking to hide. I will deliver the manuscripts to you, and after you have read them we will talk again. But let us make haste, because as I have said, my time on this great green earth grows short."

❂ ❂ ❂

I waited impatiently for several days for the manuscripts to arrive, greeting each mail train enroute from Gunnison. When they failed to appear my father volunteered to pay Doc a visit since he was going to Gunnison on business anyway. I was overjoyed when he returned to see him staggering toward the house carrying a very large, ancient leather suitcase. But then I was dismayed to learn that Doc was in the Gunnison hospital with a failing heart.

I quickly opened the suitcase, exposing reams of expensive white stationery divided into neat thick stacks tied with white cotton string. The top sheet of each ream was numbered according to chapter, and each, I was to discover, had its own explanatory preface.

Time bolted from my grasp. Doc lay dying and I had to be back in Princeton in four days. I hurriedly penned a letter to him saying that I had received the manuscripts and that I was on my way back to school with them and would read them as quickly as possible. I wished him well and said I would be writing to him.

The next day I struggled aboard "The Pioneer" passenger train to Denver, the first leg of my journey to New Jersey, with two suitcases, my own and Doc's. Immediately after the train began moving I set Doc's suitcase on the empty adjoining seat, untied the bowknot in the cotton binding string that held Chapter 1 together and began reading.

Within a week after returning to Princeton I received a long telegram from my father. Doc had returned to and died peacefully in the house in Gunnison in which he and Agnes had lived during the years of his tenure as sheriff of Gunnison County. My father stayed with him until his last few days. On my father's last day there, the two of them had spent the early morning walking their horses through the sage of the foothills. A few days later Doc, probably for the only time in his long life, surrendered.

Stunned, I laid the telegram on the table in front of me and contemplated the autumn sun on the brilliant maple leaves of the University commons. A man whom I'd met only once and I barely knew had entrusted me with his life and I didn't know what to do with it. I was young, distracted. I needed Doc to spur and rein me in the right direction. After reading a few chapters I discovered Doc and the publisher were right, Doc was no writer. Eventually frustrated by the rambling prose I gave up and put aside the manuscripts.

Time and distance began taking their toll. College, the war, marriage and family, the deaths of my parents, the final separation from home, and a career. But wherever I went, Doc's manuscripts, like a family member, followed. They were a benign growth upon my soul, feeding on the decades of accumulated guilt. When finally I too was old, the guilt and remorse of having left behind so little of any consequence in my life overcame the fear and procrastination. I sat down one cold and rainy morning with my orange cat on my lap, coffee cup on the desk, and untied for a second time the bow in the string of Chapter 1, untouched in forty years. I read. Not long thereafter, with Doc as my constant companion, I took up the pen and began writing.

Chapter 2

Doc had resolutely fought the drudgery of farming as though the crops, weeds, soil, and animals were enemies bent upon destroying his life. Oh, never would his father, Jonathan, know of this personal cup of anguish. His enemies surely did not need such an ally. He dutifully, if not cheerfully, tackled the plowing, mucking, tilling, scything, digging, planting, feeding, and harvesting on the Michigan farm all the while dreaming of stalking deer, bear, wolf, and moose through the towering oak and pine.

If the farm chores were for him a war, school was utter hell. No threats nor punishments could compel his imagination to abandon the hunt for the sake of multiplication tables. The teacher moved him to the furthest, darkest corner of the room, away from the windows through which he constantly gazed. But it was to no avail, as the visions of adventure remained stuck to the inside of his eyelids. Doc later admitted, at first with some pride, but ultimately with chagrin, that he sacrificed education for tracking and hunting. He quickly asserted, however, that he had the equivalent of an advanced degree in stalking. On his way to school he would often come across the tracks of some animal and spend the remainder of the day following it through the forest.

His tawny features were accented by a thicket of black hair through which he could pull neither comb nor brush. This made him, he thought, painfully conspicuous amongst his pale, blond classmates. Even his parents, Jonathan and Louise, spoke of a seafaring ancestor rumored to have taken a black mistress or wife. It remained a nearly intolerable inference. Slip Thomas, the school bully, had once committed the double error of combining both the words "Doc" and "Nigger" in a jeer and paid for it by receiving a sharp blow to the head from a sizable piece of school firewood.

Jonathan's brother, Emmit Shores, instilled within Doc a hunger for adventure. Besotted, crazy ol' Emmit introduced him to his first firearm. That ancient military musket came closer to killing him and his friends by accident than it probably "darn near" ever did the enemy on purpose in the hands of a soldier.

Emmit Shores, the older of the two brothers, had indeed influenced Jonathan's move west. He had resolutely struck out and literally sailed away from the family. His home became the rolling, pitching deck of the whaler and merchant ships, his closest companion the limitless horizon beyond the farthest white-capped blue wave. His life's work had been cut short in a careless moment by a coil of anchor rope which wound around the young seaman's right leg pinning him against the inside of the ship's oaken hull. The leg snapped just above the knee. The break required only a stroke or two of the surgeon's knife to sever the remainder. The carpenter fashioned a peg leg for him from a beautiful block of teak purchased especially for the purpose in Bali. Emmit proudly exhibited the wooden appendage saying that it was much better looking than the uninjured leg. Had he known it would be so attractive he would have jumped into the coil with both legs. But the pain of the stump betrayed his lightheartedness. It never completely healed. The wound ulcerated, scabbed, and suppurated. Every waking hour was a hell of fiery pain. After a brave fight he surrendered to rum and opium.

This man one day, without invitation or warning, appeared on the Shores family's doorstep and announced loudly, bottle in hand, who he was and that he would be pleased to "stay awhile."

Their uncouth, unorthodox uncle immediately attracted the three brothers, Cyrus, Nathan and Marcus — the family women less so. Jonathan despaired of his brother's drunken presence. In the evenings after dinner Emmit would enthrall the boys with dramatic tales of tall masted schooners, foaming seas, and ferocious pirates. "My mother's father, your great-granddad, ol' Israel Hands, sailed with Cap'n Teach — that man also bein' called the pirate Black Beard — from the Carolinas o'er a hundred yars ago and was kilt along with the Cap'n at the battle of Ocracoke Inlet. The Cap'n hisself was shot, cut, and stabbed twenty-five times 'fore he was dead. Some say he was ne'er kilt. Then he were beheaded and his headless body throwed to the sharks in the Ocracoke Inlet and away it swum as though t'were still 'live. His head were taken back to Virginee and hung above the Hampton River at a place they named Black Beard's Point, where all that sailed up and down the riv'r could see it as a warnin' to them that might think of bein' buccaneers and outlaws. After yars they took his skull down and stored it in D'vy Jones Locker. But his body still roams the Carolina coast huntin' fer its head and guardin' the treasure what's buried there."

He told of his own voyages to Africa and Asia, the volume of his delivery and drama increasing with his consumption of the local "grog." Jonathan and Louise listened from a distance. Cyrus noticed them rolling their eyes with each new, more fantastic tale. Cyrus's sisters, Frances and Alice, paid little heed to any of the stories and generally retired to their rooms quickly at the first hint of gore.

Emmit gave the boys a book entitled General History of the Pirates which engaged them as much as any book ever had. More than the other two, Cyrus lived the tales. He braced himself against each wave, tasted the salt spray, and first spied land from the crow's nest. He weathered the drenching typhoons in oilskins and piloted the ship downwind before a clear gale. He explored Madagascar and the Ivory Coast, Hong Kong and Macao, Bali and London, resolving somehow to combine his love for hunting and trapping and woodsmanship with travel and adventure.

Then there was the fateful day Emmit successfully persuaded Jonathan to let Cyrus have his first firearm, an old flintlock musket with only part of a stock. Cyrus had received it in return for a hay cutting from an old lady whose entire family had died of consumption. Uncle Emmit helped him fix the gun. They hewed out a piece of soft wood to refinish the stock and colored it black with ink made from witch hazel. Jonathan brought Cyrus some new gun flints from Detroit. The weapon more exploded than fired. After only one shot Cyrus's ears were ringing for hours. It belched fire and smoke enough on a windless day to blot out the target until the next round was loaded. The musket kicked viciously, so one could tell when it went off even during the deafening roar of battle. After only a few shots its recoil often left Cyrus's shoulder badly bruised, his lip cut, and his face pockmarked with powder burns.

On one particularly portentous occasion, he had the gun barrel resting over his shoulder when he accidentally hit the trigger with his thumb, and the gun went off. The vicious recoil somersaulted the musket a good fifteen feet, leaving Doc sitting on the ground burned. Jonathan unsympathetically remarked that it served him right for carrying a loaded and cocked weapon over his shoulder.

Uncle Emmit died as he had lived — drunk. As a mariner, he'd ironically feared above all, a death by drowning. The irony doubled back on him. He drowned, head down in a bog pond. His peg leg had become entangled in tree roots at the water's edge, and he'd fallen over backward into the pond, held to the bottom by the heavy earthenware jug of liquor he carried around his neck. Marcus carved an anchor and cross into Emmit's teak leg and drove it into the ground as a headstone.

❁ ❁ ❁

The War of Emancipation, later called the Civil War, affected even those in the far north woods. Most men in Michigan who attained the minimum age for volunteers quickly toed the line. Cyrus and his brothers had discussed the matter at length, and none of the three felt particularly touched personally by what was transpiring in the South. However, the war would affect Doc in a way that he would never have begun to imagine.

Goaded to action by the school bully, Slip Thomas, and his friends, the three Shores brothers told their parents one fall morning they were going hunting. Instead, they struck out cross-country to the town of Jackson where regiments of the Michigan militia were assembling at the Congregational Church. Doc would later recall that this would be one of the pivotal events of his life.

He'd never mastered that musket, and on the day of their enlistment, just before signing his name, Doc again swung the old gun to his shoulder and again touched it off. The ball passed through Slip Thomas's shoulder.

Doc and Marcus were both knocked unconscious by the somersaulting musket barrel.

"I think that the army's had about enough of the Shores family for the time bein'," commented Nathan. "Doc, you and Marcus ain't gonna be real handy at drillin' for some time and Slip Thomas ain't gonna be real handy at anything."

Cyrus fervently wished the blow from the musket had killed him or had rendered him permanently unconscious so that he would not have to face his father and live the remainder of his life in shame. Although he never really forgave himself for the blunder, over the years he slowly came to realize that, costly as it was at the time, it may well have preserved all of them from a worse fate at Fredericksburg, Gettysburg, or some other distant, lonely killing field.

The brothers' arrival home produced relief and anger. Predictably, it was Louise who ran to the wagon first to ask questions and examine wounds. Then, upon seeing none of her sons mortally injured she chastised them for their thoughtlessness and carelessness. Cyrus took refuge behind his bandages and feigned incoherence. Marcus was truly incoherent. Nathan, the oldest and yet unwounded, bore the brunt of her anger.

They bade farewell to Slip, now sitting beside the private who had brought them home, his shoulder heavily bandaged and pink from his foul wound, his arm in a sling.

Cyrus walked to the wagon and offered his hand to Slip. "Sorry you weren't able to continue on with your soldierin'."

Slip reached down and took the hand. "Well, it wasn't all it was cracked up to be, food wasn't that good, and they's someone always yellin' at ya. 'Sides, can't be much of a soldier with a wooden practice gun." They both chuckled and the wagon creaked back out the lane and disappeared. Later as the soldiers of the Michigan regiments trickled back from the war, Slip never tired of telling how he'd been right in there mixin' it up with the best of 'em but for gettin' shot by a Yankee.

After Slip's departure, the three Shores brothers waited glumly for their father's arrival from town. He arrived on horseback, his face hidden from the setting sun by the broad brim of his hat. He rode up straight and tall, and Cyrus thought him taller and more dominating than he had ever seen him. Jonathan dismounted and walked over to his three sons. His mouth was grim, his eyes wide and bright. He handed Nathan his bridle reins without looking at him and walked to Cyrus, then Marcus, silently examining their bandages. Then he embraced each in turn. Finally he said, "You boys decide to leave — and some day again you will — you come and tell me and your mother about it face-to-face." He paused. "Believe me, there really ain't much good ever come of war, no matter which side wins nor how righteous the cause. If you got to take up arms to defend yourself, home, and family, then don't ever hesitate to do so. If you strike out for what you think's a noble cause, always question what price you may pay for what end. I suppose ever once in a while a man's got to strike a blow for justice, for what he sincerely believes is just, but always reserve for yourself the right to question that — and pray for the right conclusion." He stopped and looked at Cyrus. "I saw the Thomas boy headin' into town. He told me what happened. You still got that old musket?"

"No sir, left it back in Jackson."

"Good. Be a while before you get another; not for as long as you're livin' here." Jonathan squinted into the setting sun. "Time for dinner. Get washed up."

❁ ❁ ❁

Cyrus languished at the farm for the next four years. Nathan packed up and joined Edwin Drake's Seneca Oil Company in Pennsylvania. Marcus drifted to the new Western Frontier to prospect for gold in Idaho.

His school absenteeism and poor teacher reports made for some very heavy weather and would have become a sore point had not Doc come down seriously ill with the croup and been sent away from the fever bogs of Oakland County to relatives at the copper mines of the Upper Peninsula for recovery. Miraculously, he survived the extraordinarily harsh winter of the "UP" as a nightwatchman at the copper mine and by spring had recuperated enough to return to Hickville, but not for long. He had fledged and

wanted to try his wings, and the West beckoned. He clasped his father's hand (for the first time, he felt as an equal), kissed his mother on the cheek, and left on a stagecoach to Detroit. He had $200 in his pocket, a hundred of which his father had given him. Many years would pass before he would again inhabit a place he could name home.

Cyrus stopped only long enough in Detroit to find a hard goods store where he purchased another long-gun, a breech-loader called a Whitney-Howard Thunderbolt, which fired a .44 caliber, copper rimfire cartridge. The rifle was a modern and formidable looking weapon with its twenty-eight inch barrel, hammerless lever action, blue finish, and black walnut varnished stock. Cyrus was enthralled with the heavy, grumbling metallic clicking it produced when he worked the lever. He also purchased a thick-bladed, spear-point knife with ivory grips stamped Booth, Norfolk Works, Sheffield. And lastly, he bought several wool shirts and two blankets. He could neither afford nor carry a trunk or case, so he bought a large canvas bag and stuffed in all his possessions, save the rifle, some cartridges, and the knife. Doc headed southwest toward the Missouri River with the intent of finding Marcus who was with Jim Bridger somewhere around Fort Benton in Montana.

Chapter 3

The way west had no roads as he'd known them, and few trails. Marcus's letters described vaguely his own journey to Council Bluffs, Iowa, and from there to the headwaters of the Missouri River in Montana. They were Doc's only guidebooks. His strategy consisted of simply walking west, keeping close to the shore of the lake, when he could see it, off his right shoulder and asking directions.

In Council Bluffs he learned of a freight hauler named Chivington across the river in Omaha heading west with a mule train. Doc had used horses, mules, and oxen, with both wagons and carts, so he crossed the river and walked to Chivington's camp where he was directed to a large, bearded man seated at a crude, hand-hewn table. A ledger lay open beneath a smoking coal-oil lamp. The man looked up and nodded as Doc entered but said nothing.

Nothing about Chivington reminded Shores of anything pleasant. The man's head size matched his torso. The dark beard was laced with flecks of gray and two gray lines ran from the corners of his mouth below his chin line, giving him, in the dim lamp light, the appearance of two fangs or tusks. The eyes were dark and set narrow alongside a pug nose. The thin line of his mouth turned downward in a perpetual frown and, coupled with the furrows along his forehead, gave him, Doc thought, the expression of a man determined to push his head through a brick wall.

"Mr. Chivington?" Doc inquired.

"Colonel John Chivington," the man corrected him gruffly.

"Excuse me. Colonel, I'm headed west to join up with my brother in Montana and I understand that you're in need of mule drivers."

"Mule skinners," Chivington corrected him again. "Maybe. You got any experience?"

"Grew up on a farm in Michigan and learned to harness and drive about any four-footed animal."

"Hoofed! Mules got hooves, not feet." Chivington thoughtfully picked up the stump of a cigar from where it was scorching the edge of the table. He tested the cigar and finding it dead, relit it over the chimney of the lamp. He drew the cigar smoke deeply into his lungs. "Pay's thirty a month in greenbacks and you find your own keep. If you're any kind of a shot at all with that fancy long-gun, you shouldn't have any trouble at all keepin' yourself in meat. How you fare against Indians?"

"All right I 'spose," said Doc, shrugging his shoulders. "Grew up around 'em, got along fine."

Chivington contemplated this with a grunt and took another deep draw on the cigar. "I mean can you handle yourself in a fight? Have you any problem in killin' the heathen savages?"

Doc was surprised at Chivington's vehemence. Not that he hadn't encountered many men who hated the natives, but Chivington's words fairly dripped with blood. Doc knew instinctively he needed to react quickly and decisively to the man's question as a good frontiersman would, but his words were stopped in his throat by the image of the pitiful Indians who came begging his mother for food. "No," he finally replied, "not if they're trying to kill me, I'd treat 'em same as I would any other man."

Chivington leaned back in his chair and frowned. He appeared to regard this statement with suspicion. Standing abruptly, he said, "You know, my fine lad," he paused as though launching into a sermon, "You know," shaking his left fist, the cigar still firmly clenched between his fingers, scattering ashes as far as Doc's knee, "the battle for the West, for the White Man's rightful place in this land will not be won by indecision and faintheartedness. No sir! The West is being won by Christian soldiers, the army of a righteous God whose will it is that we wrest the land and its riches from the godless red heathen and put it to good use in His name. Kill them if we must, but certainly nothing short of slavery and banishment." Chivington paced the floor behind his desk occasionally bumping it with his leg, splashing ink from the open bottle onto his writing paper. Doc thought he had become oblivious to any objects in the room, including himself. "It is our duty," Chivington raged on, "to either subjugate or eliminate these pestilential, rapacious red hordes from the lands which they have wasted for many years and bring it to fruit. That was precisely my mission at Sand Creek in Colorado Territory, and though vilified for my actions, I will tell you sir," Chivington's voice was approaching to a crescendo, "I will tell you, that I was not without my supporters when I paraded hundreds of Cheyenne scalps through the streets of Denver. I was merely serving the will of God." His beefy right fist thundered upon the table. "The will of God I tell you and the will of the Christian American public — and the will of my government who so ignobly stabbed me in the back after I had done their bidding." Chivington leaned forward over the table, the lamp light catching his face from below and casting shadows that made his already coarse features dark, sinister, and demonic. "Don't you agree?" He growled.

Doc wasn't certain what part of the speech he was expected to agree with. In principle he didn't really agree with any of it, but he was not about to say no. "Yes," he replied weakly.

Chivington straightened and tugged at the front of his grimy vest. He drew a breath and composed himself. "Where you from?"

"Michigan."

"Good, good, Michigan boys performed admirably in the war. Very well, I think you'll do splendidly." Chivington reseated himself, shuffled the ink-stained papers aside, and opened a ledger book with a cracked spine. "Name?"

"Cyrus Wells Shores. Everyone calls me Doc."

"You're not a doctor?"

"No . . . I was named for one."

Chivington scribbled in the book. "Come here and sign next to your name. Then we'll go out and pick you out a wagon, team, and harness. We got some spare tents for shelter or you can throw in with some of the others. Most just toss their keep into a common pot and eat from there. One other thing, no spirits. I catch a man drinking or drunk and he's finished. When we get enough consignments, we load up and make dust."

Doc had no sooner become comfortable in his tent when one of the mule skinners announced that he had heard that Chivington had gone broke and headed out for parts unknown. The mule skinners immediately moved to Chivington's clapboard shack, which indeed was dark and empty. The men roused to an emotional pitch from their liquor, would have certainly chased him down that very day and probably lynched him had they been able to find him. Doc collected his belongings in his bag and recrossed the river to Council Bluffs.

He walked along the shoreline where the shallow draft Missouri River steamboats beached themselves awaiting cargo and crew and decided to simply board the vessels and ask to hire on. After numerous futile inquiries and having reached the end of the line of boats, Doc was about to trudge into town in search of other work when a steamer named the Huntsville scrunched into the sand in front of him. He boarded the boat as quickly as they lowered the gangplank and inquired again. They were indeed short-handed as one of their crew members had fallen overboard on the trip up from St. Louis and had gotten caught in the paddle wheel. Even more fortunate for Doc, their ultimate destination was the same as his, Fort Benton, Montana.

Doc wrote his parents:

> *The trip up the Missouri was fraught with hazards and at nearly every turn in the river we witnessed the harsh realities of frontier life.We are going through 3,600 miles of hostile Indian country. I wouldn't have believed any river could be so long. We have to stop regularly for wood to fuel the boilers. When we do, it is also my job to shoot game to feed the passengers and crew. It is a long trip. To go all the way from St. Louis to Fort Benton often takes three months and demands a skilled captain and crew.*
>
> *Even in calm times, steamboating is hard, dangerous work. Many steamers that start for Fort Benton never arrive. Snags lurking beneath the muddy waters can sink a boat at any time within a few minutes or it can get stuck on a sand bar delaying it for days or weeks. Sometimes when steamers go aground on sand bars the crew will have to unload freight onto yawls or onto the*

shore to lighten the boat and hope it floats free. If this doesn't lighten the boat enough for the crew to pull or rock it off the bar, they try "grasshoppering" it with great long poles carried on the boat to lever it off. Sometimes herds of buffalo, antelope, deer, or elk crossing the river will block passage. Boiler explosions and fire occur frequently, I am told, and they are most feared by the crew and passengers alike because there is often no warning, and the victims are burned badly from the steam and fire. A person injured out here is almost certainly doomed to die a slow and agonizing death as there is no medical help available.

❁ ❁ ❁

On one occasion Doc witnessed a man who was plaiting a splice in the anchor rope become entangled in it, as had his Uncle Emmit, and he was pulled into the river when the anchor was playfully kicked over the side by another. The man's body was hauled up from the depths and he astonished everyone when, after being placed stomach first over a barrel and rolled head down, he coughed and sputtered his way back to life.

Heavy planking and even iron casements in some places protected the pilot house of the steamer from arrows fired by Indians along the shoreline. A four-pound cannon was mounted just forward of the wheelhouse and contained a load of grape-shot for protection against boarding by Indians. Both came in handy during the trip.

From the boat Doc saw ample warning of the coming Western Indian wars. On one occasion the steamer passed a former riverbank settlement which had been overrun by Indians, its occupants killed, scalped, and mutilated, and the stockade burned. Now, as the revolting smell of rotting flesh filled Doc's nostrils, he more easily and kindly recalled Chivington's speech concerning Indians on the occasion of their first meeting than he did the memory of the harmless and helpless old Indians begging for food at his mother's door.

Doc relished leaving the steamer to go hunting until one day he narrowly escaped being cut off from the vessel by a raiding party. Only fusillades of concentrated rifle fire and a shot from the brass four-pounder saved his skin as he sprinted to the rising gangplank.

In the days of calm following the fight, Doc reflected with nearly bottomless guilt on his terror and panic. Though none aboard the vessel chided him for his headlong flight to save his neck, his true fears remained hidden behind bravado. He suspected he was a coward. This thought weighed heavily on his mind for days causing him to question whether or not he was cut out for the life of a frontiersman.

Often, after completing several routine tasks early in the morning, he would be left with little to do. Doc would go to the bow of the boat and hang his bare feet into the chocolate-colored foam of the bow wave. The Missouri was muddy, "Half a common wineglass of mud or ooze to every pint of water." He would watch the passage of the snags and sawyers— uprooted trees with their trunks buried in the muck of the river bottom — and of sawyers. The buffalo grass of the prairie and foothills waved in the wind at him. He watched the redwing blackbirds skip from stalk to stalk amidst the cattails of the shoreline. Sometimes he would yearn for home and the safety and security of the dark, damp forests and sunlit green meadows of Michigan, the warmth and familiarity of the cabin and his bed, the companionship of family, and the smell of his mother's cooking. But he also remembered the interminably long and boring hours spent in the fields and pens of the farm. He remembered without any nostalgia, the suffocating, cramped feeling of perhaps never knowing anything else.

❂ ❂ ❂

The lands of Montana embodied the depths of the frontier. Land of the nomad, both native and settler, it fairly bristled with excitement, adventure, and danger, attracting only those who would push the limits — their own and the land's. Some men, like mythical Titans drew strength and courage from these boundaryless expanses. It sucked the air, blood, and life from others. Like a beautiful, unconquerable woman, men embraced it, loved it, swore at it, hated it, were possessed and driven to desperation by it, tried to leave it, and in the end, were consumed by it. Doc, standing on the shore of the Missouri watching the Huntsville back out into the river and set off downstream, tried desperately to suffocate his fears with excitement and buoyancy. A lump caught in his throat and he hurried to find Marcus.

Fort Benton appeared to Doc to be little more than a transient camp. It reminded him of his father's stories of early Hickville, Michigan — a tent and stick village composed of miners, soldiers, Indians, freighters, and teamsters who patronized an abundance of liquor shops, saloons, whore cribs, gambling dens, and hardware tents. Powdery dust kicked up by crude boots, moccasins, and animal hooves was carried by an incessant wind into every nook and cranny of the town and into a person's every exposed orifice.

Marcus could not be found nor had anyone ever heard of him. Doc became disconsolate. Though he had money for a room, he chose to camp outside of town thinking he might well need it for more important things.

Doc easily obtained employment as a bullwhacker for sixty dollars a month (payment, he learned, to be demanded in gold dust as greenbacks were worth only about eighty cents on the dollar). His equipment, in add tion to the "Thunderbolt," was an old, heavy, but functioning, Colt Dragoon six-shot revolver, his English-made spear point knife, and a "bullwhip." The bullwhip was at least fourteen feet long. The butt, about one inch in diameter, was fastened to a foot and a half long stock intended to be used with two hands. The popper was buckskin or other tanned leather two inches in width at the far end.

Doc thought bullwhacking was the dirtiest, toughest job that he had ever had. Bullwhackers, unlike mule skinners, never rode but walked alongside of the oxen in their dust. It was hot and dry in Montana during the summer, and the dust deepened with each passing day. When it did rain it was most often a brief shower which turned the dust on his skin and clothes into a thin layer of mud which quickly dried in the sun coating him with layer upon layer of baked dirt. There was usually only water enough for drinking, and often not enough for that. Bathing was unknown, except for the infrequent dip in a muddy river or stream. Doc commented later that he wouldn't take anything for the experience of being a bullwhacker, but he wouldn't do it again in a million years. He overheard one time a young boy asking his father what a bullwhacker was and whether they ate grass. "No," replied the father. "They're part human."

But when he couldn't find his brother Marcus, he did take other jobs as a bullwhacker, then as a mule skinner, meat hunter, and trapper, eventually working his way to Hays City, Kansas, where he was to meet two of the most influential people of his young life.

Chapter 4

Doc learned that the Bridger party was camped outside Fort Benton, so he sought out the famous frontiersmen who remembered Marcus but said that he had departed the company some months ago to hunt for gold. Shores had scant time to concern himself either with his brother's fate or indulge in self-pity. Spurred by the urgent need to survive in a strange and forbidding land, he forced such thoughts from his mind. He hoped only that their paths would eventually cross.

When Doc had saved enough money to start his own freighting company, he contracted to haul freight into Kit Carson, Colorado Territory. One of the company's routes took him and several other skinners from Fort Dodge to Fort Hays, Kansas, about a mile from the small town of Hays City. Hays had a reputation as a rollicking, wide-open cowtown with an overabundance of saloons and whore houses which suited the soldiers from Fort Hays and the trail-weary cowboys just fine, except both groups considered it their territory. Wild shots from the frequent gunfights sent all law-abiding citizens fleeing the streets for their shops and houses. It was a situation ready-made for a hired gunman and former scout named James Butler Hickok.

Doc's fellow teamsters were no less susceptible to the town's charms than were the cowboys and soldiers. They had just completed a haul in blazing heat from Dodge to Fort Hays and were looking forward to beds and beer. The town was only about a mile from the fort along a well-cut road thick with dust. Through the shimmering heat, Doc saw a wagon and a rider headed toward them from town. The track ahead passed through an arroyo which would accommodate only a single wagon at a time. Doc pulled off and signaled the wagons behind him to do the same. The driver waved a thanks across the washout and pulled forward. As they approached, Doc recognized cowboy regalia — broad-brimmed sombreros, chaps, six-guns and neckerchiefs. The wagon drew abreast of him and stopped. In the bed of the buckboard Doc saw the outline of two human forms wrapped in white canvas and trussed up with rope. Alongside the canvas figures was a spade.

"Looks t' me like somebody had a turn o' hard luck," said Doc, nodding toward the bed of the wagon. "Where ya headed?"

The wagoneer, a cadaverous man Doc estimated to be about ten years older than himself, sported at least a week's growth of grizzled beard thoroughly stained with dried tobacco juice. He spat a stream of brown saliva into the dust of the road. "Yonder," he said, swinging the stump of a right thumb toward a flat-topped hill several hundred yards away. "Boot Hill, Hickok City."

"I've heard the term 'Boot Hill,' but never heard of a cemetery called 'Hickok City.'"

The grizzled man spat into the dust again and shook his head at this piece of ignorance. "Bill Hickok, Wild Bill Hickok . . . he's what passes for the law in these parts. He sees populatin' Boot Hill as a big part of his job as Hays City marshal. These boys," indicating the canvas shrouds with another flick over his shoulder with his nearly thumbless hand, "ran afoul o' him." The wagon driver then recounted in some detail the story of the shooting. "Well," he said as the sweat trickled from beneath his stained hat, "best be movin' on. These boys'll ripen up quick in this heat. They sure 'nuf had as much fun as they could stand. Guess it be your turn." He snapped the reins and moved off in a cloud of dust with his outrider.

"Glory be!" exclaimed Street Martin, the young teamster sitting next to Doc. "You reckon that story's fair 'nuf true, Doc?"

Doc, although only a few years older than Street, smiled at the boy's youthful astonishment. Street looked just like a new colt or calf, wide-eyed and surprised at everything. "I reckon the gist of it is. I'd like to see this Hickok, but sure as hell not at the receivin' end."

"You know, 'at's sad. Them two fellas that got killed, no family to bury 'em, probably just a pile of rocks to cover 'em and a plank cross."

"Yeah," agreed Doc, snapping the reins. The wagon lurched forward. "Sometimes out here it doesn't pay to get to know a man too well 'cause mor'n likely he'll be gone soon enough."

The boy pondered this in silence as the wagon jounced along the dusty track into town.

In town they parked their wagons outside the livery stable, unhitched the mules, fed and watered them, and hot-footed it for the nearest hotel. Some of the men stopped by a saloon on the way to buy a bottle of whiskey.

"Whiskey, food, and a woman," panted a teamster on the way to the hotel. "In that order."

"Bath first," added Street.

Doc felt an uncomfortable sense of foreboding as he watched his partners in the evening twilight pulling great swigs from the whiskey bottle and drawing their six-guns on each other in mock duels. By the time they decided to eat dinner, all save for Doc were thoroughly drunk. Their drinking continued throughout the meal. Occasionally, a man would bolt from the table to run outside and vomit into the street but then return to his steak and potatoes and whiskey.

After weeks of quiet prairie nights broken only infrequently by a wolf or coyote howl and nothing brighter than the soft silver glow of a full moon, Doc felt assaulted by the din of piano and fiddle music coming from the garishly lit gambling houses, saloons, and dance halls. Individuals and clusters of men staggering through the street were sucked into the glowing maws of fleshpots. Peals of laughter, shouts, and whoops of men cheering on fighters ricocheted like wild gunfire up and down the wide dusty street.

His companions, starved for excitement and women, attacked the streets and houses after they had dinner. Men hollowed by loneliness, devoured like gluttons the lights, noise, food, and sex, hoping to fill every nook and cranny as though they could store the excess to sustain them later through the cold, lonely nights. Frequently one of his men would drop out at the sight of a particularly attractive face and "come hither" wink of a dark eye and reunite later with the group. Doc began to relax a bit himself and even had one or two small swigs from an offered bottle of whiskey that tasted more like turpentine smelled and made his eyes water.

The hands of the clock over the bar of the Lady Be Gay saloon pointed to ten o'clock and already many of his teamsters, up since four o'clock in the morning and drinking solidly since before dinner, dropped in their tracks or returned to the hotel. Looking around, Doc saw that the Lady Be Gay, like the dozen or so saloons and gambling houses they'd already visited, harbored a mixture of trail hands, teamsters, saddle tramps and soldiers standing at the ornately carved red oak bar or seated at tables in groups. A few card tables and a roulette wheel occupied a corner of the room and an unattended player piano tinkled out a familiar tune, its keys moving up and down in a ghostly rhythm. Most of the chairs about the room were occupied so Doc and the remainder of his crew bellied up to the bar. Doc sipped a glass of beer; the others continued to tip bottles. Shores struck up a conversation with one of the bluecoats standing at the bar. Street Martin staggered over to a poker table and seated himself in a chair when its previous occupant passed out drunk. His gaming partners laid him out in a corner of the room, his chips and gold coin being carefully placed on his chest. The dealer, a woman Doc heard someone call Suzy, exchanged Street's few dozen remaining greenbacks for stacks of red, white, and blue chips and the game proceeded. One of the players, a particularly roguish-looking corporal missing most of his front teeth, was dead drunk and losing, a bad combination thought Doc. Each time the fellow lost a hand, usually every hand, he would push his dirty blue cap back on his head, throw his cards on the table and swear loudly at the dealer. Doc decided she must be used to it. All the swearing elicited only a sigh and a tired grimace. Doc made a few side bets with the soldiers standing with him at the bar. Then Street Martin changed for the worse. He began winning.

"Looks like tonight is your lucky night," said Suzy with a wink. Street was a good-looking young man. Suzy obviously thought so. But the corporal glared ominously at the two.

"Street," called Doc over the din of voices and piano, "let's call it a night."

Martin tucked his cards into his hand and turned around with a drunken leer. "Okay Doc, let me finish this one last hand." As he turned back he bumped the table with the hand and the cards fluttered to the floor. Street bent down and began gathering them up. The corporal half rose, folding his own cards to his chest, and watched Street with great interest. Doc was certain that the dealer would call for a new hand, but she didn't. Both Street and the soldier reseated themselves and bet recklessly for the next few minutes as other players dropped away. The corporal raised a last time, sliding his entire pile of chips into the pot. Street, beaming, matched his rival's bet stack for stack.

"Read 'em and weep," gloated the corporal as he lay down a full house. He leaned over the table and wrapped his arms around the pile of chips.

"No so fast blue boy," smiled Martin, spreading out four jacks. "You're short."

The soldier leaned back in his chair again. "Son of a bitch!" he exclaimed in surprise. "Son of a bitch!" He sat red-faced, his jaw working hard as Street counted out his chips to cash in with the dealer. She handed him his money with a wink, and he slid a ten-dollar gold piece back to her.

"Son of a bitch!" the corporal shouted again. "You and that whore are in cahoots." He pointed a finger at the dealer. "You slipped him a card when he dropped that hand."

"Bullshit," Suzy spat back. "I didn't have to slip him a card. You're just a lousy poker player . . . and a lousy loser."

The soldier jumped up, sending his chair over backward, and began fumbling with the flap on his holster. He unlimbered his Colt just as Suzy slid her own chair back. She tried to raise a parlor pistol palmed from beneath the edge of the table. Doc figured she might well have gotten the drop on the corporal and killed him, but as she pushed back, her chair caught in a crack in the floor. Her hand bumped the table as she brought up the derringer giving the soldier just enough time to draw his pistol and fire, hitting her in the neck. Suzy somersaulted over backward beneath a fountain of bright red blood, crinolines, petticoats, and legs looking like a giant red blossom. The derringer spun from her hand and landed atop the table. Street reached for it. A soldier at the bar cried out a warning. The corporal spun and fired again. Street tumbled backward to the floor, his right hand to his left shoulder. The corporal upended the table with his free hand and pointed the revolver again, this time taking careful aim. Doc stepped forward not knowing quite what to do, but before he could advance another step he was brought up short by a tall figure of a man stepping from the shadows directly into the corporal's line of fire.

"Enough!" bellowed the man. Everyone froze. The man walked into the luminescence of the ceiling lamp lighting the poker table. He appeared tall and strong, but that wasn't what caught Doc's eyes. He had long, curly, sandy hair which cascaded below his shoulders making his face look small and narrow. A rather sparse, curving mustache complemented the hair and underlined a prominent, thin nose. His eyes were narrow and deep set. A red silk brocade vest glistened in the lamplight, partially covered by a cutaway black coat which he had tucked behind a set of two cross-draw pistol holsters. A silver badge adorned the left breast of the coat. His black trouser tops were tucked into a pair of highly polished, black mule-ear boots. The man couldn't have identified himself more quickly if he had been carrying a sign saying "Wild Bill Hickok."

"Drop that firearm, mister," growled Hickok.

"This is none of your business, Marshal," said the corporal. "I caught 'em cheatin' me. I just want back what's due me."

"I was watchin', nobody was gettin' cheated. You just shot two people in my town, so that makes it my business. Now, drop the weapon and raise your hands."

The corporal, a dry-lipped smile framing his toothless mouth, straightened, and he thumbed back the hammer of the revolver. He opened the flap of his holster with his left hand and put the barrel of the revolver into it.

"Drop it on the floor," Hickok yelled and positioned his right hand over the weapon on his left hip.

The soldier hesitated then slowly thumbed the hammer on his revolver and slid it back toward its holster. But the second the barrel touched the holster the corporal squatted and swung it up to fire.

Quick as a wink, Hickok's six-shooter cleared its holster and barked loudly. Doc had never dreamed that a man could draw and fire so fast. The bullet slapped a cloud of dust from the chest of the soldier's uniform sending him reeling backward. His weapon discharged in its holster, and an ounce of lead thumped into the floorboards. The soldier caught himself and again struggled to get his gun out of its holster. Hickok cocked, took aim and fired again, this time hitting the man in the head, taking off his cap and part of his skull in a shower of blood and brains. The soldier hit the clapboard wall of the saloon and slumped into a heap on the floor.

Hickok instantly drew his other revolver and leveled both at the knot of soldiers standing with Shores at the bar. "Using one finger," Hickok said firmly, "everyone take their sixguns out of their holsters by their grips and put them on the bar." The men very cautiously lifted their weapons from their holsters and dropped them on the bar. Doc was unarmed so he raised his hands.

"Now, everyone put your shirt on the bar." This revealed a couple more pocket pistols hidden in waist bands. "Now turn your pockets inside out." Coins and pocket knives thumped to the floor but no guns. "He one of yours?" Hickok asked Doc, indicating the supine Street Martin.

"Yeah."

"Where you stayin'?"

"Central House."

"Get 'im back to his room. I'll fetch a sawbones to come around."

Much to the marshal's irritation, Doc stopped long enough to collect the bets due him at the bar. Then he hastened over to Street who was still writhing in pain on the floor. He got the young mule skinner to his feet and half pulled him out the door, down the street, and to the hotel. The desk clerk at the hotel barely registered an expression as Doc hauled the wounded man, dripping blood, across the white parquet floor and up the stairs, pausing only to tell the clerk that the marshal would be sending a doctor over.

Doc put Martin to bed, bound the wound as best he could with strips of sheet, and then went back to his room to get his rifle, pistol, and cartridges. He attempted to wake the others to tell them what happened and warn them the soldiers might come looking for revenge, but they were still dead drunk and sick. He gave up, knowing they would be useless in any kind of a fight. Doc returned to the room and checked the Whitney-Howard to make sure it was loaded and laid it alongside the old Colt Dragoon on the footlocker and waited.

Within an hour Hickok had delivered a disheveled old doctor to the hotel room. The doctor wore threadbare rebel gray and butternut trousers and jacket. "I am pleased to meet you," he said, offering his hand. His accent was slow, well enunciated, and articulate.

"The good Doctor Stevens is an educated gentleman . . . from the Old Dominion." Hickok evidently noted a question in Shores. "Old Virginia," he explained, mimicking the physician's speech. "He had the misfortune to find himself on the losing side of the War of Rebellion and escaped to the West."

"War of Independence! If you please?" the doctor huffed. "It was not a loss, only a temporary setback. The South will indeed rise again. If only the Federals had had more men like the marshal here we would have won unequivocally."

Hickok grinned. Doc could tell both were used to this banter and he thought each was fond of the other.

"Well," said Stevens, with a more serious tone, "to the patient, lest he die for our words. He is a young one . . . much to his ultimate advantage. The younger they are, the more likely to survive. Cheer up lad, I've removed more bullets from the likes of you all the way from Bull Run to Hays City than you have fingers and toes. . . probably enough to sink a ship . . . and most lived as the result. Courage and a good attitude will serve you well in this ordeal."

Street managed more of a grimace than a smile as the doctor approached the bed and opened his small black valise. He took from it scissors and cut away the blood-soaked bandages.

Wild Bill motioned Shores out of the room. "Those soldiers are madder'n if they'd swallowed a horned toad the wrong way. Wouldn't surprise me none if they came around looking for you. How you boys fixed for arms and ammunition?"

"That's it over on the footlocker," said Shores pointing to the Whitney-Howard and the pistol.

"That's all you got?"

"Yeah. Well I got some more men but they're all dead drunk and useless right now."

"My deputies and me will keep watch tonight but you'd better hightail it outa town early in the morning and I sure as hell wouldn't go back to Fort Hays."

"We'll head back to Dodge."

"Milt," Hickok said, addressing the doctor, "can that boy be ready to ride in the morning?"

"Can. Kill 'im though."

"Well, he might have to take his chances."

"We're in luck," said Stevens wiping his hands on the bed sheet. "Bullet went clean through, but tore him up a good bit. Here, heat this spike over that lamp flame as hot as you can get it, and then I'll need both you boys to hold him down while I cauterize the wound." Shores wrapped the end of the spike in a cloth he soaked in water and heated it until the end smoked and turned an oily blue, then he and Hickok pinned Street to the bed while the doctor quickly drove the spike into the wound. The doctor had given Street a soft pine block to bite on, but with the first touch of the hot iron his body convulsed and he fainted dead away. A bandage was applied and the doctor prepared to leave. "Ideally, he shouldn't be moved for several days." Then he looked at the marshal. "But then I've never seen the ideal. Just take care as much as you can that he don't get bounced around too much." The doctor replaced the bloody scissors and still-smoking spike in his bag. "I'll be around to check on him . . . that'll be five dollars."

Doc pulled a five dollar gold coin from his pocket and handed it to the doctor. "Thanks, be seein' you."

"I'll be downstairs in the lobby for a bit," said Hickok. "See you in the mornin'."

When they had gone Doc locked the door and slumped with exhaustion. He didn't want to leave Street. He looked longingly at the bed, but it was only big enough for one. He went back to his room and retrieved a pillow and blanket and tossed them on the floor. Doc looked despairingly at the Whitney-Howard. He then collected his teamsters' guns and ammunition which he piled next to his bed on the floor. He lay down and was almost instantly asleep.

When Doc heard someone banging on the door he was certain he'd been asleep no more than a few minutes. Startled, he grabbed a rifle and scrambled to his feet. "Who's there?"

"Hickok. Barn's afire. Your wagons are burnin'."

Hickok looked at the rifle when Doc opened the door. "Too late for that. You'll have more use for a bucket and some water." They cascaded down the stairs two at a time. "Guess those soldiers didn't take kindly to losin'," puffed Hickok as they ran outside.

Dawn's light revealed only a scene of utter devastation. Wagon hubs, harness buckles, and the metal parts of hames and iron tires were all that was left of the wagons. The ashes of the barn were dotted with the great black and bloated bodies of horses and mules. A reeking black smoke mingled with the early morning fog. Doc, in dark despair, sat on the boards of the walk in front of the hotel, his skin blackened and blistered, clothes nearly burned away. One by one his bleary-eyed teamsters drifted out of the hotel, viewed the carnage, and sat down with him, asking, "What now?" Doc just shook his head.

Finally, he called them together. "Well boys, looks like we've run up against some bad luck. I'd guess we're out of the freighting business as of right now."

"We could pool our money and get a new start," spoke up one. The others nodded in affirmation.

"What money?" asked Doc. "I'll bet there's not ten dollars among the lot of you after last night." This was greeted by silence and downcast eyes. "No, I been ox whippin' and mule skinnin' since I got to Fort Benton years ago, and I'm about ready to try my hand at somethin' else. I won a bit at the tables last night. I'll split with you boys and send you on your way." Doc retrieved his winnings and their weapons from his room. He divided the money equally among his men leaving himself with a little over two hundred dollars, the same as when he left Hickville. He shook hands all around and wished the men well as they drifted off. Then remembering Street Martin, he hastened back to the boy's room. He was now awake but weak and racked with pain.

"Sorry Doc," he offered meekly. "I'd never got drunk or got into that game last night if I'd knowed this was gonna happen."

Doc nodded glumly. "That ain't the worst of it."

"What is?"

"Somebody, maybe them blue coats, burned the wagons and livery stable. We lost everything."

"God a'mighty! Mules too?"

"Mules too."

Street digested this for a few seconds and peered out of the corner of his eye at his bloody bandage. "Whata we do now, Doc?"

"I paid off the other boys. I got about two hundred dollars, a rifle, a pistol, and what's in my poke. We got a few days before you can travel. I'll come up with somethin'."

"Hell, Doc, you don't need to wait for me. I'll be fit and on my way before you know it."

"Maybe . . . I'm in no great hurry. After last night, I could use some rest. How much did you win off that skunk last night?"

"I don't know. . . you're free to go through my pockets and count it up."

"Well, I'm thinkin' maybe we could throw in together, go down south and find us a herd to bring back up here. . . . I don't know, just a thought."

Doc went through Street's pockets and eventually counted out a little over six hundred dollars. That and the two hundred Doc had would keep them in food and shelter until Street recovered a bit more and then maybe take them where they needed to go. He returned to his room, took off what was left of his clothes and nearly passed out on the bed.

When he awoke he pulled clean clothes from his bedroll, thankful he'd had the foresight to bring it in from the wagon along with his weapons. He checked in on Martin again and found him resting, in good spirits, and hungry. Doc went to the hotel's dining room and ordered a meal of steak and potatoes sent up to the room. He solemnly went through the hill of smoldering ashes that had once been the livery stable and kicked around hopelessly trying to recover something of value. Hickok came up and joined him. The marshal was decked out in a sparkling blue silk vest and black velvet coat, white shirt, and tie with a diamond stick pin. The dust and manure of the streets didn't even stick to his highly-polished boots. It was hot and humid, but no trace of sweat appeared on his forehead. "Ain't much left?"

Doc shook his head. "Coyote bait."

"Got any ideas what you'll do?"

"No, thought Street and I might head south, maybe Texas, when he heals up a bit more, and bring a herd back north."

"Boys from the Taylor outfit are camped south of town. They're headed back down to the Pecos area, you might hook up with them. Never did catch your name."

"Doc Shores, C.W. Shores."

The marshal extended his hand. "Bill Hickok. If I can be of help, call on me." Doc nodded in appreciation. (He later learned that Hickok departed Hays abruptly to avoid the Army's idea of justice for shooting the corporal.)

That afternoon Doc rented a horse and tack from a cowboy who had lost all his money at the tables and headed south of town to the Taylor camp. The first person he met was the old wagoneer who'd been hauling the two bodies to Boot Hill. The old man poked at a smoking buffalo chip fire under a blackened coffee pot. He looked up at Doc and smiled a toothless leer.

"Lose your wagon?"

"In a manner of speakin'," Doc said, dismounting.

The old man cackled and stirred up a shower of sparks. "Yes indeed, sounds and looks like you had a heap o' fun since I last saw you yesterday. Care for some coffee?"

"Thanks."

The old man looked around and found a tin cup lying upturned in the dust, brushed it off and filled it with something Doc thought looked and smelled like pine tar. "Name's Moots, Benton Moots — trail cook," the old man said, extending a desiccated hand.

"Doc Shores. Had a bit of hard luck last night, got burned out, lost wagons, mules, everything. Wonderin' if you fellas could use a couple of good hands."

"Probably. If you recall, we planted those two you saw a couple days ago . . . can't say for certain, that's up to the trail boss."

"You headin' back south afore long? I got a friend that's laid up with a bullet wound who can't move for a few days."

Benton thought for a few moments. "I think he's a mind to rest up here a few more days before headin' back to Texas to collect another herd. If you get hired on, tell the boss I'll hang back until your boy's ready to move, and we'll catch up to them later. He's a good man that's usually willin' to help out in a fix."

"Thanks, I appreciate that. Where do I find the boss?"

"I think he's out there lookin' at the remuda. Name's Ed Taylor. Big tall fella with a red beard . . . how's the coffee?"

Doc swirled the black remnants in his cup. "Great, never tasted anything like it."

"Snake shit! But it kills the bugs in the river water."

Doc found Taylor and told him of his situation. "Ever drove a trail herd?" The big man asked.

"Uh . . . no." Doc decided honesty was the best policy. "But did a lot of bullwhackin', and we're both good dependable hands."

Taylor studied him. "Well, you're honest. That might mean you're also dependable. If you been a bullwhacker you're used to dust and you'll be eatin' a lot of that, because I start all new hands out ridin' drag."

Doc had only a remote idea of what that meant but it sounded good for right now. "What's the pay?"

"Forty a month and keep. You get paid at the end of the drive. You leave before the end of the drive you get nothin'. It keeps hands from walkin' off 'fore we finish up. You make it to the end, you may get a bonus per head, depends on the price we get. Oh yeah, and you get all Moots's coffee you can get down, or keep down."

Doc smiled grimly. "That's a real inducement. What about horses?"

"We put a couple of boys in Potter's Field yesterday. They won't be needin' their stock any more. Go over yonder and find the wrangler, tell him to cut out them horses what belonged to those two and leave 'em behind for you. Tell Moots to point out their tack, might as well have it too." Doc thanked Taylor, and after finding the wrangler and Moots, headed back to town to tell Street of their employment.

Shores entered the room and froze with surprise. A slender, dark-haired young woman was seated on the bed with her back to the door. Startled at Doc's unexpected entrance, she quickly looked over her shoulder. In her hand she held a clump of bloody cloth which she dropped to the floor as she jumped to her feet.

Street grinned broadly. "Doc, this is Doc Stevens' daughter, Agnes. She come around to change the bandages. Agnes, this here's Cyrus Wells Shores. Everybody calls him Doc."

Shores recovered sufficiently from his shock to murmur, "Hello, my name's Doc Shores."

"Yes, just as the man said." Agnes laughed and stepped forward extending her hand. "Are you a physician?"

"Huh?" Doc grunted.

"A Doctor of Medicine?"

"Oh! No, no. It's just a name." Now, Doc felt even more awkward. There was a long pause after he took her hand. He had never shaken a woman's hand. It felt so small, soft, and smooth, the clasp gentle and yielding. His grip felt no resistance. It felt as though he was crushing a small bird. He released his grip and drew back his hand quickly, afraid he'd hurt her. Her face made him catch his breath. He could not remember seeing a more beautiful face. Her unblemished white skin was drawn smoothly back over a small nose, high cheekbones, and prominent forehead by her tightly wound black hair. The creation was an almost perfectly symmetrical face. Pale pink lips curved out, around, and upward into a perpetual smile. The perfectly proportioned head was supported by a thin, delicate neck disappearing into the white lace neckline of a plain dark blue dress with a high white collar. A small alabaster cameo accentuated the lace at her neck. Her slight figure flowed ever so smoothly under the tight bodice of the dress.

"Mr. Shores!" she exclaimed in mock horror. "Your head and neck look a fright. Mr. Martin was just telling me how you attempted to save the wagons and mules in the fire last night. You have a seat and when I'm finished changing Mr. Martin's bandages I'll tend to some of your burns."

Doc felt as though he could crawl through a keyhole. Again he had forgotten his burned hair. Over Agnes' shoulder he could see Street Martin smiling and winking. He turned to look in the mirror above the dresser and saw that his face and head were a patchwork of blistered white skin and ash-black blotches. Agnes gently ushered him to a chair and commanded him to stay. He watched as she expertly applied a new bandage to Street's wound. "Are you a nurse?" Doc asked.

"I am," she replied without looking up. "Educated and trained at the Medical College of South Carolina. But here in Hays I am also the town's only schoolteacher, two of the three occupations open to women in Hays. If I'm lucky, I won't have to engage in the third."

Doc felt his face heat up.

The rhythm of her southern accent, deeper, more aristocratic than her father's, soothed Doc. He relaxed in the chair and nearly dozed off. She bathed his own wounds with alcohol and water and lanced the unbroken blisters with a large darning needle heated over a candle flame, and then applied a salve she called "Denver Mud." Her touch, soft and gentle but firm, caused his skin to tingle and twitch with pleasure even through the prick of the needle and the sting of the salve. He had never been touched by a woman other than his mother and sisters in such a way. He closed his eyes and he very nearly sighed. She smelled so clean, of soap and starch and lilacs. Her dress whistled when she moved. Her breath was clean and warm on his neck and shoulders. Though he could not see, he heard her moisten her lips with her tongue. He could hear his own heart beating inside his ears. She finished. He held his eyes shut a few moments longer hoping to capture her touch and smell for later.

"I'll be going now," she said, putting her instruments away in a bag similar to her father's. "But I'll be back tomorrow about this time to look in on both of you." She looked directly into Doc's eyes. "So promise me you'll still be here."

"We'll be here in Hays a bit longer. But I signed us on with the Taylor outfit, and they'll be headed back to Texas for another herd 'fore too long."

❁ ❁ ❁

Shores and Martin rested in Hays City for several more days as Taylor and his cowboys set out south leaving Moots behind to guide the two new hands to Texas. Street's wound healed well under Agnes' care. For the first time since he took ill back home in Michigan, Doc surrendered to relaxation for more than just a few hours. Most importantly, he was able to see Agnes daily, either when she came to dress Street's wound or when she could find chores for him around the Stevens' house. He took no pleasure in the gambling halls and saloons. He and Street regularly took their evening meal with Agnes and Doctor Stevens. On such occasions the Doctor drank copious amounts of a locally distilled whiskey, lamenting loudly that it compared poorly to southern whiskey. After dinner Doc would help Agnes clear the table of dishes while her father settled into an overstuffed leather chair, regaling Martin with war stories until drifting off to sleep. Occasionally, after the sound of gunfire in the town, Hickok or one of his deputies would call for the Doctor, and he would stagger from the house with his bag. Doc and Agnes would leave Street dozing on the couch and walk in the moonlight.

The nights were still and warm. Prairie breezes carried the scents of warm river water and lush grass. The moon illuminated a narrow path to Cheloah Creek whose course followed the contour of a pasture and then skirted on past the edge of town. Its banks were overgrown with wild rye, cattail, and willow, woven together by cottonwood tree roots.

They talked of the town, the weather. "Miss Stevens," Doc ventured tentatively, "there's something I've been meaning to ask you."

"Yes?" Her tone contained a hint of caution.

"May I call you Agnes?"

She laughed with relief. "I suppose that's only fair since I've been calling you Cyrus almost from the beginning. However, everyone calls you Doc. How did you come by the name 'Doc'?"

Doc grinned. "Almost everyone asks me that. I'm surprised it's taken you so long." He hesitatingly told her the name's origin. "And that's why I always hated it, but I must say I've gotten so used to it I scarcely know who someone's talkin' to when they call me Cyrus. You certainly may call me Doc if you want," he encouraged.

"Doc, would you consider staying here, finding work, and settling down?"

Not wanting to discourage her he said, "Well, I plan to come back here with a herd and maybe get a place of my own. But I don't want to just stay here and work for someone else. Besides, those soldiers who I think burned the barn might want to settle the score otherwise, you know — finish things."

"I guess you're right." Then she brightened again. "Will you write when you're away? I'm sorry. Can you write?"

"I can," he puffed proudly. "And rather well if I do say so myself. I'll have you know that I was readin' without any help at the age of six, so I consider myself to be a tad smarter than the ordinary man."

She laughed.

They sat by the creek and talked and listened to the cicadas, watching bats swoop through the moonlight until the moon had passed below the tops of the cottonwoods. Doc returned to the suffocating hotel and tried to sleep but only stared at the ceiling thinking of Agnes. Heart and mind racing, he arose, gathered up his bedroll, and walked to the grass by the creek at the edge of town. There he lay, fully clothed, watching the stars until a cool breeze from off the prairie lulled him to sleep.

❁ ❁ ❁

The hot, soggy Kansas days passed ever so slowly. The two men languished restlessly in chairs in front of the hotel. When Street had recovered sufficiently they rode out to Taylor's camp and talked with Moots. Doc visited Agnes as often as he felt he could without becoming a nuisance. She seemed pleased with his company. They spent many pleasant hours picnicking in the shade of the trees by the stream or riding their horses in the prairie wind. Moots and Street grew impatient with Doc's excuses to delay departure.

Street had recovered well enough to travel if he rode in Moots' wagon part of the time. Doc, sensing their impatience, thought that departure might be less painful if it were sudden. He awoke one morning before dawn and announced to Street that this would be the day. He rode to the Stevens house shortly after first light. Agnes answered the door and apologized for her disheveled appearance. He took her hand at the door and told her they were leaving. She shook off his hand, and wrapping her arms about his waist, put her head against his chest. He, in turn, enveloped her in an embrace and leaned his chin on the top of her head. He smelled the bouquet of the pillow on her hair, and when he felt his resolve weakening, took her by the shoulders and held her at arms' length. Through his heavy twill shirt he felt the dampness of her tears. First, they kissed tenderly and she told him to come back. They kissed again, this time passionately, and he promised he would.

It was mid-morning when Shores, Martin, and Moots piled the wagon with supplies and bedrolls and struck out on the long trail south driving their small remuda with them.

Chapter 5

Doc had written his family from time to time, to let them know of his whereabouts and the state of his health. On arriving in San Angelo, Texas, he found a letter from home waiting for him.

Dear Cyrus:

I hope this letter reaches you in time for Christmas. We think of you often.

I have some bad news. Our father died in August of a fever. Doc Wells came out and did what he could for him, but he took sick as well and died in town a few days after Father. Mother was seized with a such a melancholy that she eats only once every two or three days. She often wanders off and we find her talking to herself beside the stock pond or in the chicken house or somewhere else. It's never the same place and we spend much time looking for her. I fear she will not be with us long.

Marcus returned just before Pa died. He was surely surprised that you were out West looking for him. Nathan, we were informed by letter, suffered injuries and burns in a fire and died of them. He is buried somewhere in western Pennsylvania. I fear we shall never see his grave. I pray such will not be your fate as well. Frances married Sylvester Thomas, the one you called Slip, who sold his late father's farm here, and the two of them moved to Lansing where he bought a mercantile store. She is ever so glad that it was your shooting that got him out of the war but that you were such a poor shot that you did not kill him. They are planning for their first child next summer. I plan to remain here and tend to Mother and the farm with Marcus. My prospects for matrimony are slim as I think the war eliminated at least half the male population of the Hickville area. But, as you can imagine, Marcus is certainly not at a loss for eligible females. Thank the good Lord we had a big family because fate has exacted a heavy toll from us. Write when you can.

Your Loving Sister,
Alice

Doc's eyes stung. He carefully folded the letter and slipped it into his saddlebag. Taking the stub of a pencil and pad of writing paper he began writing, stopped, tore the paper from the pad and crumpled it. He began again.

My Dear Friend, Miss Stevens:

The circumstances of our passage to Texas were such that I was prevented from writing you until now. I have just read a letter from my sister in Michigan and was made aware of how much a letter can mean to a person. I do hope you will forgive my tardiness in writing.

Our trip south to San Angelo was uneventful but took us a laborious twenty-eight days and required almost constant vigilance for hostile Indians. We went from Hays City to Ft. Scott, and from there followed the old trail blazed by General Winfield Scott on his way to Mexico, and passed through the Cherokee Nation, and met many different tribes or bands of Indians. We then struck out south across the Red River until we came down into north Texas. We noticed the cattle as we went along growing poorer in quality the further south we went. These are the longhorns or wild cattle of Texas. The longhorn drivers generally appear to be a pretty wild bunch themselves, all of them wearing wood-handled six-shooters except the bosses who have either ivory or pearl- handled revolvers. The laws of Texas prevent anyone from carrying a wheel gun — or guns at all — but we all smuggle them under our shirts. Most longhorn herds contain only seven to ten year old steers while the stock cattle herds, which are shorthorn or shorthorn Durham are mainly cows and much less dangerous to handle.

Benton Moots, our trail cook, whom you may have met, is an experienced hand who has ridden many a trail north with Charles Goodnight and Oliver Loving. He has regaled us aplenty on our trip from Hays about the trail up the Pecos, until Street and I were more than glad it would not be our fate to travel that route but rather traverse back north the way we came down. You may imagine our dismay upon meeting up with Ed Taylor and the other trail hands at the confluence of the Concho Rivers that he had contracted with the army to do just that. We will be delivering a herd to the army at Fort Sumner, New Mexico. So regrettably, I will be delayed a bit in my return to Hays.

Fort Concho can be seen from the top of a nearby hill. It contains, among others, the Fourteenth Cavalry Regiment and a couple of infantry regiments. Some of the trail hands who had formerly served with the Confederacy make disparaging remarks about the black soldiers of the Fourteenth, but Street and I agree we are glad to have them comfortingly close at hand.

Both Street and I misunderstood what being a trail hand or "cowboy" entails. We were under the misapprehension that one simply rode into Texas, collected a herd and took them back north. Instead, we have become cattle hunters rather than herders. Daily, in all kinds of weather, we chase far afield tracking and gathering unbranded, unclaimed, semi-wild cattle of the long-horn variety and return them to the general area of our camp where they are added to a larger herd. While we are doing that, Ed Taylor travels northern Texas buying small herds for a dime on the dollar that they will bring under the contract from men who don't want to hazard the drive north. The new duds we purchased in Hays before coming down here have been shredded to rags, even the stiff leather chaps, by the catclaw, lechugilla, and prickly pear cactus and mesquite.

I wouldn't want Benton to see these words, but quite honestly, the food is nothing to brag about. We occasionally slaughter a beef from the herd and have a few days of fresh meat, but when you have up to a dozen hungry men swallowing one, it doesn't last too long and none of us want to see the herd disappear before we even start north. We, more often than not, make do with sow-belly, beans, and hardtack or corn pone. It makes me remember your cooking all the more fondly.

I am sending this letter into San Angelo with one of the hands to begin its journey north to you. I hope it finds you well. Ed Taylor has just informed us that we can expect to begin our own journey in that direction within the next few days.

Respectfully, Faithfully, Your Friend
C.W. Shores

❁ ❁ ❁

"The Pecos River," said Moots, "ain't water nor land. Too thin to plow and too thick to drink. It's the devil's own idea of a river." It's clear, cold, and fast where it begins in the snow up in north central New Mexico Territory, but it slows to a sluggish wallow by the time it reaches the edge of the Staked Plains. An Armadillo couldn't dig a hole in it by the time it empties into the Rio Grande northwest of Del Rio. To the trail herds moving north out of western Texas it's salvation and damnation. It's still the only life-sustaining moisture for leagues in any direction but those steep, crumbly banks and great pools of sucking quicksand take a heavy toll from the men, horses, and cattle desperate or foolish enough to cross or drink from it. The Comanche, Mescalero Apache, and Diamond Back rule the Staked Plains.

"Ne'r been on a drive yet that we didn't lose at least one man to Indians, river, snakes, and desert — one each that is. Then there's also stampedes, lightning, blizzards, flash floods . . . and your fellow man. There's no better man than a Pecos Cowboy. He'll ride right through a hornet's nest of Comanches to rescue a friend, only to shoot him down that night over a card game."

❂ ❂ ❂

The men awoke one morning to a cold fog. The dew lay heavily on the hillsides. Even before he opened his eyes Doc smelled the damp sage beneath the blankets of his bedroll. Without exchanging words the men arose. Shivering they rekindled the fire and boiled coffee. Doc hunkered down and wrapped his gloved hands around the burning-hot tin coffee cup to warm his stiff fingers. They sipped their coffee sweetened with honeycomb from a hive they'd found in the decaying trunk of an ancient cedar. The warmth of the early morning sun cut through the drifting fog. Doc inhaled, deeply savoring the smell, the light, even the chill. He watched their hobbled horses searching for the scant blades of Indian rice grass among the patches of mesquite and prickly pear. He was happy with his life, but he longed for Agnes to huddle with beneath a blanket and together watch the dawn. He looked at Street who was gazing fixedly into the fire from under the hood of his blanket. Doc had always preferred the companionship of men. He understood men better. But Agnes had forced to the surface some deeply buried longings. She had caused him to realize the possibility that women, too, could value someone for honesty and courage rather than hair, skin, flesh, or money.

❂ ❂ ❂

"Doc," Street had asked one day on the trail to Texas, right after a harrowing crossing of the Red River, "how was it you stuck by me back in Hays? We ain't kin or nothin'."

"Well, you're a friend and I thought you needed some help. We all need help time'n again, and most of us out here ain't got kin. Out here you take care of that and those what can take care of you . . . friends, horse, boots, guns. You think of those things, that is if you want to stay alive and not end up in a short, shallow trail grave."

Moots, who had been listening to the conversation as the wagon bounced and rattled over the rocks, looked over his shoulder at Martin. "A man to cross rivers with."

"What?" asked Street.

Moots circled the reins around the California brake lever and leaned back over the buckboard seat on his forearm. "One of the biggest dangers on a cattle drive is a river crossin'. To begin with, there's deep, swift water, sometimes quicksand. Most cowboys ain't much for swimmin' . . . or jus' gettin' wet for that matter . . . they're loaded down with boots, shootin' iron, cartridges, knife 'n such like. Sink like a rock. A man to cross river's with is one who can keep hisself from gettin' kilt but also look out fer others. But it ain't jus' rivers, mor'n likely he'll be the one the others look to for help — no matter where. It's a real compliment out here to say of a man that he's one to cross rivers with."

Doc nodded at this bit of wisdom. "I do reckon that 'bout tells the tale all right. Out here it's not how rich or poor a man is or what crimes he's done. What counts is bein' able to look a man in the eye and know you can trust him and he can trust you."

The first brave crimson and gold blooms of the prickly pear had only just appeared when winter's last cold breath broke over the lava rock on the hillsides and cascaded into camp. The men pulled the collars of their slickers up around their necks, their hats low on their foreheads, and tucked the brims of their hats against the wind. Smoke from the branding irons mingled with the early morning fog. Noreasters blew down off the plains and the cattle drifted; days were lost rounding them up. The unessentials — day, date, and time — were ignored. Each man held himself upright from "can 'til can't," often eating in the saddle. Exhausted men who had eaten no more than a mouthful during the day would fall sound asleep at night even as they ate their food. More than one narrowly escaped a serious wound when he pitched forward sound asleep on his knife or fork. Doc thought that he didn't so much sleep as simply fainted into blackness. Then the day came they had all been waiting for — and dreading — the move north.

On the morning they were to begin the drive Moots awakened the camp at four o'clock in the morning by banging on a pot with a long-handled spoon and singing:

"On the rocky bank of the Pecos
They will lay him down to rest
With a saddle for a pillow
And his gun across his chest."

The herd of over two thousand head of cattle oozed like some gigantic slug, west along the Middle Concho, its trickle gradually disappearing as they approached the headwater. As they passed through Castle Gap the chill of spring suddenly turned to the heat of summer. At the western edges of the Gap they gathered themselves for the eighty mile waterless trek through an alkali wasteland littered with the bones of hapless longhorns, the graveyard of luckless cowboys, called the Staked Plains. The sun reflected from pure white alkali salt pans blinded them. They discovered that the thin crust of the salt pans concealed an even deadlier menace, bottomless adobe mud, mean as quicksand. When they skirted the treacherous crust of the pans, a continuous cloud of choking adobe dust engulfed them.

"As if the heat and thirst weren't enough," exclaimed Moots as he dished out dinner after the first day of the crossing, "there's Comanches, Mescaleros, and Kiowa to worry about."

He launched into another lurid story as Doc and the others gnawed their half-cooked beef and beans and gazed apprehensively into the desert darkness. "Back in '67 we were takin' a herd of seven hundred to Horsehead Crossin' when we got jumped by a band of a hundred or so Comanche. They stole three hundred head but we gave 'em a hellova fight from a breastwork of wagons, dead horses, and cattle. They's some what tried to escape in the dark that night — one fer sure didn't make it. We heard him screamin' most of the night. Near drove some of the men mad. Next mornin' we were figurin' for another fight but the Comanches were gone. Left us a present though — scalped from head to foot, wasn't morn' a few patches of skin left on his whole body — and he were still alive! The rest of us, we were lucky. Made it to Fort Supply and sold the cattle for next to nothing and were glad to be out of it."

"God, Moots!" Doc exclaimed, looking around him, "the only thing worse than your coffee is your timin'." Moots cackled in glee. Most of the drivers had stopped eating and were just moving the beans around on their plates with their spoons. Martin scraped his onto the ground and walked into the night. Doc ate a few more bites, sipped the thick coffee, and walked to the chuck wagon to get his bedroll. He remembered all too clearly hideously tortured settlers and the stark terror of nearly being captured at the sand spit on the Missouri.

Taylor had a plan for crossing the Staked Plains. He'd lost nearly two-thirds of a herd, not to mention cowboys, on his last crossing, and now he planned differently. "We'll form up tomorrow mornin'. Around noon, after the cattle have drunk 'bout all they can hold, we'll drive 'em to sundown. Let 'em eat in the early evening and get ready for the big push. We'll use the moonlight to 'squeeze' the herd, narrow it, by putting more riders on swing and on the flanks, pushing harder in the rear, slowing in the front. We can control a tight herd better and move faster. The last day'll be the most difficult. After we let the herd rest the last morning we'll squeeze 'em again and drive 'em solidly for the next twenty-four hours or so until we make it to the Pecos. Men and horses'll survive on what's left of the Concho in their canteens and the barrels on the chuck wagons. Horses come first; without them neither men nor cattle will make it. The cattle'll have nothing until the Pecos. They'll get desperate, along with the horses, and will try to graze on the goldenrod which are filled with alkali. There's tons of bleached bones out there of 'alkalied' animals. So don't let 'em. Beat the piss out of 'em if you have to but don't let 'em eat anything."

Doc remembered his assertion that there was no more miserable existence than that of a bullwhacker, but his journey across the Staked Plains far exceeded those worst recollections. No sooner than they started, thirst drove the men to drain their canteens, which they attempted at every opportunity to refill from the barrels on the wagons, over threats from Moots and Taylor to shoot any man doing so without permission. With darkness came relief from the sun and heat but not parched throats and swollen tongues. Conversation became words and grunts. For the first two days the cattle bawled incessantly, but then they too surrendered to the silence of thirst and exhaustion. No one attempted to revive or rescue the stock that fell by the way beneath gathering clouds of vultures. By noon of the final day the barrels had nothing remaining but a thick layer of damp mud on the bottom. Some scooped it out by the handful and attempted to wring or suck the little remaining moisture. Doc and Street gingerly cut the needles from prickly pear and chewed the tough, fibrous pads into a cud. They sucked it dry. The horses' heads drooped closer and closer toward the burning hard pan. A dizzying heat shimmer fairly sang upward into the cloudless sky.

Toward evening of the final day a Mexican Vaquero riding drag next to Doc looked around through the milky dust and pulled a whiskey bottle from his saddlebag. He pulled down the dust-caked neckerchief from his mouth and drank deeply. The Vaquero coughed, sputtered, and retched, but the liquor stayed down. He handed the bottle to Doc who attempted a small swig. The moment the whiskey touched his raw throat he coughed violently and spewed it into the dust cloud. He handed the bottle back to the laughing Mexican. It was better to die of thirst.

Men attempted to eat from the saddle but most could not swallow the tallow-like fatback or bricks of hardtack and gave up in frustration. Their thirst and hunger transformed the baked clay into lakes of ice-cold water, the alkali pans into fields of snow, the saguaro into shady saloons. If lucky, the stronger herders would haze them back. But more often, no one had the strength to care. His horse's rocking gait lulled Doc into a nightmarish sleep. He awakened abruptly when his horse stumbled, nearly pitching him from the saddle. Once he awoke and in the moonlight saw the Mexican's horse missing its rider. In his stupor he thought himself still asleep and rode on.

Only in the gray light of dawn did he see that Mexican was, in fact, gone.

Taylor relayed back encouraging news from his point position. Horsehead Crossing could be seen only a few miles away, but also the message warned of a probable stampede as soon as the cattle scented the river. He motioned to Doc to ride point and pointed inquisitively to the Mexican's empty horse which followed Shores forward. Doc tried to speak. He just shrugged. Taylor nodded grimly and urged his weary horse back toward the flank of the herd. He returned bringing with him three other men. Now, he rasped barely above a whisper, they had to control the herd by bunching them in a tight semicircle. The wagons were moved to the right rear flank.

Not until the sun had almost cleared the horizon could they make out, a mile or more distant, a thin line of scrub on an otherwise parchment-like wasteland. The men were weakened beyond rejoicing. Their mounts' heads came up, ears pricked, nostrils flaring. The cattle again began bawling hoarsely. The cowboys wearily closed ranks and began trying to turn the leaders. Doc fixed his gaze on the horizon and rode only by instinct. He rode according to the sound of the herd and what he could see through the dust of the man immediately next to him. He knew that were he to make a single mistake and fall from his horse there would be no stopping the herd leaders from trampling him into the dust. Panic rejuvenated him. He welcomed the cool morning breeze from the west — until he could smell the river on it. Sure enough, a crescendo of bellowing swept back like a wave over the herd, and the leaders surged forward into the point riders. Taylor yelled the order to circle the herd to the left but the thirst-crazed cattle were not to be so easily turned. They pushed even harder against the horses despite lashings from the cowboys' ropes and quirts. Horses panicked, and within seconds the struggle at the front of the herd became a grand melee. Doc forced his horse into the shoulders of the steers while trying futilely to avoid the four-foot-long horns.

He heard the thunder of hooves behind him. Turning he saw the remuda stampeding pell-mell over the top of their wranglers. Taylor dashed past him toward the panicked horses. Shores instinctively dashed off in pursuit of Taylor. He had galloped a scant hundred yards when he again heard thunder. As he looked over his shoulder, the dam broke. Lead steers burst out through the unfortunate cowboys and horses who hadn't escaped to the sides. Men and horses screamed. There were scattered shots from within the herd and then only the thunder of hooves. Doc frantically spurred his exhausted mare hard to the right perpendicular to the front of the herd in the hope of skirting the edge of the moving wall of horns and hooves, but he could quickly see that it was useless. The cattle in the rear of the herd, frantic to free themselves of the chaos and get to water, burst the flanks and surged forward spreading over the desert floor like water from a bucket. They would be on him before he could outrun their furthest edge. He reined left toward the river where the remuda was bunching. Drawing closer he could see Taylor laying his quirt across the backs of the horses, no longer to try to turn them but to urge them on. He rode alongside Taylor who hadn't seen him.

Taylor turned toward Doc's yell. "The herd's broke!" screamed Shores over the din of the milling horses.

"What?" yelled Taylor.

Doc pointed frantically in the direction of a sea of horns quickly closing the distance between them.

"Can't out ride 'em," yelled Taylor. "Jump! . . . take your chances with the river!" The trail boss pulled hard on the reins and spurred his horse over the bank. Horse and rider disappeared over the edge.

Shores hesitated. Damn Moots and his river stories! He rode to the edge and looked down to the river. Taylor and his horse had surfaced a few feet from the shoreline, the horse swimming hard for the opposite side, Taylor holding its tail. Doc quickly glanced back at the oncoming herd and thought again about escape. Just then one of the panicked remuda horses stepped into a prairie dog hole and fell against Doc's buckskin mare sending horse and rider hurtling over the edge. Doc, boots still in the stirrups, left the seat of his saddle. He thought he floated for an eternity above the saddle. The mare cannonballed into the water. Doc crashed down into the saddlehorn with the force of a kick from a Missouri mule. He sank convulsing for air beneath the chocolate-colored water. His horse thrashed beneath him and he hung onto the saddlehorn as it fought upward. Stomach, ribs, lungs — all burned fiercely. Then suddenly, he felt the sun's heat on his face again and opened his eyes into a muddy film. His horse struggled. Doc vomited muck. His eyes cleared. Sliding from the saddle but keeping a tight grip on a stirrup he flailed for the opposite bank. But something downstream lodged in his left side and held him tight against the river's current — a sawyer, an uprooted cottonwood or cedar, its trunk buried in the muck of the river bottom. He and the horse were trapped in the forks of its branches and in danger of being sucked under. Doc grasped about frantically for a limb to pull himself above the current. Something grabbed his left arm and pulled him back down. He looked around to see Ed Taylor's face sinking away. Taylor, too, had been caught on the branches of the snag. The two men struggled violently, each trying to pull himself up. Doc felt himself being torn apart by Taylor, the river, and his horse. He locked a branch into the crook of his right arm and pulled with all his might. The men lurched back and forth, occupying a no-man's-land between light and darkness, life and death. Doc felt Taylor's grip on his left arm loosen and slip. He reversed and grabbed the sleeve of Taylor's shirt. Doc's horse kicked itself free of the entangling branches and struck out for the far bank. Doc let go of the branch with his right arm and sank into the tangle of branches. As he disappeared into the brackish water for a second time he reached out instinctively, desperately hoping to find something to hold on to. His hand slipped along and over the seat and cantle, skirt, saddlebags, and strings, onto and down the horse's rump to where its tail flared out in the current. He wound his fingers into the streaming tail. The swimming horse pulled him onto his right side. His left hand still clutched Taylor's shirtsleeve.

Doc, feeling his grip slipping, was surprised at how quickly the river had robbed him of his strength. He prayed to feel solid ground under his feet once again. Suddenly, the horse surged forward and Doc's hand slipped from the tail. He went under for a third time and instinctively put down his hand. To his relief and amazement he touched mud and through the mud, rocks. Drawing his knees to his chest he thrust down hard with his legs. They struck the bottom and shot him up through the surface. He stood waist deep, but at least he stood.

Doc remembered with a jolt that he still had a hold on Taylor's sleeve with his left hand. Summoning all his strength, he heaved the body up from the water and pulled it by the armpits to the shoreline where he fell back gasping with exhaustion, holding the big man's head and shoulders out of the water with his legs. The first of the herd, those not killed in the fall or carried downstream by the river, were wading ashore upstream from him. Some, overcome with thirst, paused in the shallows to drink. The others crowded toward them. Doc, fearful of being trampled, looked for protection. A copse of tamarisk caught his eye. Half carrying, half dragging Taylor, he lurched inside the thicket. Remembering the man who had fallen overboard on the Missouri steamer he rolled Taylor onto his stomach with his head downhill and began pumping on his broad back with the palms of his hands. Water from Taylor's mouth and nose darkened the white alkali, but there was no sign of life. Doc leaned harder on his arms. Finally, the flaccid torso pushed back, a cough, a choke, brown water spewed forth. Taylor pushed himself up and vomited again, gasped a few times and then collapsed back onto the adobe.

The two men, totally spent, lay on their sides and helplessly viewed the carnage and confusion. The once vertical east bank of the Pecos had been transformed by the bodies of cattle into a gently sloping ramp that covered half the span of the stream. The cattle, oblivious to the plight of their comrades mired in the mud, continued to press down the ramp and into the river. Those injured or too weak to swim against the sluggish current were carried downstream, their bodies already tangling on the branches of the driftwood.

"Shit!" exclaimed Taylor. "What happened?"

"You got hung up on that tree yonder in the stream. I'm 'fraid your horse and riggin' are lost."

"How'd I get here?"

"I pulled you over, my horse pulled both of us."

Taylor nodded weakly. "Obliged to you."

"I fear we lost a real crowd."

"I reckon." Taylor staggered to his feet. "Fetch your horse and regroup the boys, then get back here as soon as you can with another horse and rig for me. I'm afraid you're gonna have to cross this thing more'n once. Got any idea where Moots and the wagons are?"

"Over there, I reckon." Doc said, indicating the far bank. "He might have made it all right. Last I saw of 'em he was high-tailing it outside the remuda. If he made it past them he may have cleared the herd."

"I wasn't planin' on crossin' here. Thought we'd water 'em and take 'em north to Pope's. Now, it 'pears we got more on the west side than the east. Let's get the rest of the herd and the wagons 'cross."

"Right."

"Shores . . . "

"Yeah."

Taylor coughed and cleared his throat. "You're a man to cross rivers with."

Doc smiled. "Thanks." He struggled to his feet and unwound his hat which still dangled from its stampede strings around his neck. He turned and left.

Doc easily caught his horse but the animal was completely jaded. He led it to the remnants of the remuda and lassoed the first horse he came upon, a roan gelding looking like he'd suffered less than most in the crossing. He captured a second horse with a hackamore from some spare latigo in his saddlebags and returned to Taylor who rode off bareback to assess damages. Just as Doc confronted the river again he heard Street calling from the opposite shore. Doc yelled back to him to tell the rest of the hands to start crossing. He was relieved that he wouldn't have to face another river crossing so soon.

Moots appeared with the chuck wagon on the east bank just before noon. It required the remainder of the afternoon to dismantle the wagons, construct float bladders from canvas and fix ropes on both sides of the river, upstream and downstream, to float the wagon across.

"Coulda been worse," piped Moots that evening while handing out soggy biscuits and jerky. "We now got water and only lost a couple men."

"Three," said Shores. "The Mexican."

"Who?"

"The Mexican who was ridin' drag with me before the stampede."

"Don't count . . . Mesi-cans don't count."

Taylor, still bareback, rode into camp. "I want every man in the saddle. There's an oxbow a couple of miles upstream where we can pen the cattle. We'll tally up our losses in the mornin'."

"An oxbow?" Martin looked at Moots.

"A bulge of land between two bends in the river. If it's a good one the neck of it may be so narrow, where the river nearly meets itself, that one or two men can keep the herd penned up while everyone gets some rest."

Brightened by food, water, and the prospect of a good night's sleep, Doc choked down the last of his hardtack with a big gulp of alkali-flavored coffee and hurried to his horse. None of the men had slept at all and had eaten very little in almost thirty-six hours. That and the chaos of the stampede had left most of the men with what Moots called the "mile-long stare." They didn't see anything, just stared. Although tempers were on edge, even the worst of the bunch would not go for a weapon in that condition.

The cattle, their fiery thirst slaked, exhausted from the stampede, were docile to the point of being nearly immovable. The vicious, mean-tempered steers that would have charged at the drop of a hat a few days ago, now had to be beaten to their feet and driven steadily to keep them from lying down again. Cows which had lost their calves in the melee bellowed hoarsely and constantly turned back in search of them. Doc thought it was the longest two miles he had ever ridden. Once penned into the balloon-shaped peninsula the cattle dropped and grazed lying down on the salt grass. The men saw with great relief that the neck of the peninsula was so narrow that the sleeping herd could be successfully confined with just the two wagons and a picket line of rope. Shores took his bedroll from the wagon and put it next to the campfire but didn't have the energy to unroll it. Instead, using it for a pillow, he dropped to the ground and was instantly asleep.

When he awoke the men were lining up for their coffee, mostly chicory. Moots again handed out stale biscuits and promises of fresh ones later. No one complained. Others checked their pokes, clothing, bedding and weapons. Doc examined his revolver. Only where it had rubbed against its holster was it free of rust. His rifle and knife would be in equally bad shape.

Taylor returned to camp and announced that they would remain at the oxbow for the next couple of days. "We'll regroup and take 'em on north to Pope's Crossing and hope to find some grass on the way. At least we'll have water now."

"Water hell!" Someone chimed in, "You'd have to add water to this river just to have damp."

As they herded north along the Pecos the men in turn fell sick from drinking the roily goo. Many could barely ride and none could walk more than a few hundred yards. The wagons became overcrowded hospitals. Some took to filling their canteens in the morning from the coffee pot. Canteens were unplugged and placed bottom-up overnight to allow the black muck to drain from them.

Always coarse and monotonous, trail rations became nearly inedible from the heat and maggot infestation. After the loss of so many cattle at the crossing the occasional slaughter of a steer for fresh meat ceased. Sowbelly, beans, and soda bread became the staples. The sacks of smoked and heavily salted Missouri sowbelly oozed yellow fat. Sour and strong, usually edible only when cooked with beans, it had been a staple of only the most desperate and intrepid explorers, soldiers, sailors, and pioneers for centuries.

The soda bread or biscuits when available, were unleavened. Moots baked it in large, iron Dutch ovens, on the days when they stopped the herd to rest and graze, and then just stacked it in any available space in the wagon. Within a day or two they became stacks of bricks and could only be eaten by breaking them into small pieces and mixing them with the sowbelly, beans, and water. After weeks of such a diet the men's gums bled painfully, and almost nothing could be eaten without losing teeth. When he could find them along the river, Doc stopped and devoured the hard kernels called "hips" from the wild roses there, to fend off the ravages of scurvy.

The weather could, on alternate days, produce searing heat and freezing, drenching rain. One brought choking dust; the other flash floods. Ed Taylor, one evening after such a rain, while they were all drying out around the campfires, told the story of another drenching years earlier. "Late in the afternoon as I was ridin' flank a sudden gust of wind brought the smell of rain. Lookin' up I saw directly ahead, in line with the herd, the blackest cloud I've ever seen in my life. The direction and flavor of the wind told me that we were on a course to cross paths with that storm. Lightning flickered in and out of the black folds of the clouds and thunder rolled down the creek beds and arroyos like hundreds of runaway wagons. Even though it was still hot and the sun was shining where I stood, I put on my slicker and tightened the stampede strings on my hat. The wind picked up quickly and soon began to howl. The herd backed up on us. The leaders were tryin' to get their tails into the wind. I could see a line of rain like a black curtain movin' back over the herd toward me. Then, the full fury of the storm hit. It was the damnedest thing I ever seen, balls of lightning about the size of a fist rolling along the ground everywhere. One would roll along the ground and hit a bush and just explode, 'Bang!,' and sparks would fly out into the rain. I was lookin' to avoid gettin' hit by one of them when I noticed the horns and ears on the cattle all lit up with a blue light called 'Saint Elmo's Fire.' Then I noticed my horse's ears both lit up the same way. Well, the lightnin' commenced to poppin' and crackin' all around and hittin' some of the cattle and breakin' up the herd. Wonder they didn't stampede. I put my hands on my horse's neck and they blazed up like a flame, but I couldn't feel any heat. I quick got off the horse and backed away. No sooner than I did, that horse got struck by lightnin', blew him saddle and all to bits right on the spot. Knocked me off my feet and snatched the breath plum out of me."

Doc never forgot that story. Afterward, whenever he was caught in a thunderstorm, he dismounted and led his horse by lariat from a considerable distance.

❁ ❁ ❁

Fort Sumner offered much the same to the drovers as Hays — a bath, a shave, drinks, dinner, gambling, and women. "Good God! Do I know you?" Doc said to the man in the hotel's bathroom mirror. Three months on the Concho and six weeks on the trail had taken their toll. Sunken red eyes peered back at him from beneath and behind a tangle of black hair and dirty beard. The pants and shirt he'd bought in Hays, then so uncomfortably stiff, were now faded rags hanging from his skeletal frame. His stiff felt hat slouched from sweat, sun, weather, and water. He plucked a louse from one of the thick tendrils of hair escaping from beneath his hat and popped it against his filthy, broken thumbnail. His underwear had disintegrated, now more hole than fabric. He silently resolved that he would not spend the remainder of his life as a cowboy or bullwhacker. Nor would he spend another Christmas in the company of only men.

❁ ❁ ❁

A bath, dinner, a night's sleep in a bed, and new clothes renewed his good spirits and stiffened his resolve. He found Martin and suggested they partner their cash, buy a few head of cattle and return to the Hays area to ranch. Street readily agreed, and they set off to find Taylor and inform him of their plans. "Well, I can certainly understand you wantin' to do it. I'm lookin' forward to the day when I can go back to my own ranch on the Canadian. But you get used to life on the trail — as bad as it can be at times. Lost my wife and children a few years back to the smallpox. Guess I really haven't felt like goin' back since then, will some day though. Gonna miss you boys, you was good troops. Doc, if not for you, I wouldn't be here right now, and I guarantee you I'll remember that. I'll hold back as many head as I can and still fill the contract. Have to sell 'em to you at destination price though — well, maybe not quite that much."

Martin and Shores provisioned themselves during the course of the next two days and said farewell to the friends they had made during the drive. They invited Moots to come back to Kansas with them. He wished them well but declined saying that he also had developed a strange fondness for the cattle trail. On a hot August morning the two men, six horses, two mules, a wagon, and 140 head of cattle began the lonely trek back to Kansas.

Come all you true-born shanty-boys, wherever you may be,
I hope you'll pay attention and listen unto me.
It's all about some shanty-boys, so manly and so brave.
'Twas on the jam on Geary's Rock they met their watery grave.

'Twas on one Sunday morning as you shall quickly hear,
Our logs were piled up mountain-high, we could not keep them clear,
"Turn out, brave boys," the foreman cried, with a voice devoid of fear,
"And we'll break the jam on Geary's Rock and for Eagletown we'll steer."

Some of the boys were willing, while the others hid from sight,
For to break a jam on Sunday, they thought it was not right.
But six American shanty-boys did volunteer to go
To break the jam on Geary's Rock with their foreman, young Monroe.

They had not rolled off many logs before the boss to them did say,
"I would you all to be on your guard, for the jam will soon give way."
He had no more than spoke those words before the jam did break and go,
And carried away those six brave youths with their foreman, young Monroe.

Now when the news got into camp and attorneys came to hear,
In search of their dead bodies down the river we did steer,
And one of their dead bodies found, to our great grief and woe,
All bruised and mangled on the beach lay the corpse of young Monroe.

Chapter 6

"Cyrus Shores!" Agnes intoned as though disciplining an unruly school boy. "You are certainly not the most prolific writer I have ever known. I did expect more than two paltry letters from someone who is obviously very literate."

Doc blinked. He stepped back and almost fell from her porch.

Her aristocratic Virginia accent was thicker and had more of an edge than Doc remembered. In a sentence or two Agnes had shattered his dream, cultivated over the many hours and miles of the last year, of being welcomed with open arms.

"Well I . . . well I," he began.

"Well you . . . well you, well you better come in so I can shut the door before the flies take over the place."

He meekly entered the familiar hall, still cool with night air and fragrant with furniture oil and breakfast coffee. The red oak floors, polished to a brilliant luster, creaked rhythmically beneath his boots. He hung his hat on the hall tree and tried to slick his thick, coarse hair down with the palms of his hands. When Agnes turned back to him her face had softened.

"Cyrus," she said smiling, gently laying a hand on his arm, "don't look so serious. Put yourself at ease." She took his hand. "I'm only teasing. I am truly grateful that you have returned in such apparent good health — and so well dressed I might add."

Doc, relieved, instinctively braced to attention the better to show off the new suit he'd purchased the previous day. He'd made tracks to the same dry goods store where, a year before, he and Street had outfitted themselves in cowboy garb. Now the high celluloid collar was beginning to chafe his neck. He feared it and the new boiled shirt were already becoming sweat stained. When Agnes turned toward the kitchen he quickly ran his handkerchief inside the rim of his collar.

❁ ❁ ❁

"To say you've lost some weight would be an understatement," she commented. "I've seen fence rails with more meat on them. Well, that's easily corrected." She took his hand and tucking his forearm next to hers led him into the kitchen. "Come, I'll fix you a nice breakfast of ham and eggs and some southern grits with red gravy, and in return you may relate to me the adventures you experienced during the course of your journey and your plans."

"I am relieved," he stuttered, "that you aren't . . . mad." Already he found himself mimicking her southern accent. "I apologize that I didn't write more often, but the demands of the trail imposed great hardships —

not the least of which was the lack of reliable mail service." He allowed her to direct him toward a small round table covered with a red and white checked cloth. Agnes filled a white porcelain mug with steaming coffee from a blue and white enamel coffeepot. Without asking, she added a spoon of sugar and a large dollop of sweet cream from a crock immersed in water. She stirred the combination vigorously and handed him the mug.

"Well," she said as she turned to the stove and began assembling a variety of carbon-encrusted cast iron skillets, "I do understand. Please forgive me for my earlier brusqueness. Do tell me of your adventures. I have heard often of the dangers of the cattle trail. Did you find it so?"

He wanted to blurt out that she'd never been out of his mind for more than a few hours the whole time he was gone. The way she scuttled about the kitchen distracted him. In spite of himself he imagined the shape of her body moving beneath the outline of her dress, and he felt ashamed, as though she knew what he was thinking. He wanted to relate to her how he'd passed the innumerable hours in the saddle daydreaming of the time when they'd be reunited. He wanted to tell her that she was the reason he'd suffered danger, hardship, deprivation, and travail.

Instead, he launched upon a recitation of events, places, and people that he'd encountered since leaving Hays. He felt very brave and manly when he told her of the stampede and the rescue of Ed Taylor, of the days and nights of torturous thirst and hunger, of the disappearance of the Mexican vaquero.

She encouraged him with an occasional gasp or exclamation, "Land sakes!" or "My goodness!"

Often he stood and dramatized scenes from his stories using the table and chairs as props. He gestured animatedly. She shrieked and giggled at his acting. They both laughed heartily at his self-effacing description of his reflection in the mirror in Fort Sumner. "Had I met that rascal on the street, I would sure enough have had one hand on my six-shooter long after he was past me!" She laughed into her hand and tears fell down her cheeks. He sighed blissfully. They returned to the relaxed conversation enjoyed before he'd left Hays.

She responded solemnly, "It is truly a tenuous, fragile existence in the West, fraught with many deadly hazards. Tell me Doc, do you ever stop to think of the danger?" She pointed to her own hand. "One could die of an infected hangnail, or at the very least lose a hand or arm from it."

Yes, he thought, I do.

Instead, he said, "Nope, don't have time. I reckon if you let yourself think about such you'll just hole up in a room, lock the door, and never come out. No, I think it was the good Lord's intention that man . . . and woman," he quickly added, "strike out in search for a better existence. Where'd we be now if the great explorers hadn't done so?" He caught himself, the memory of Chivington's speech echoing in his head.

"In the garden of Eden?" she offered, her cheek bulging with her tongue.

It produced an uncomfortable pause in the conversation.

"Cyrus, after I read your letter in which you mentioned your family back in Michigan I wondered," she asked gently, "do you get lonely?".

Lonely? Had she been reading his thoughts?

No, he answered her to himself. A man doesn't get lonely, and if he does he has other men. One can't get lonely if he has other men to talk to, work with, eat and drink with. Loneliness is a weakness, like a disease or injury or cowardice which by itself can kill you, either that or distract you and something or someone else can kill you. Loneliness drives men mad until they walk off into the desert and die from it. A lonely man is a vulnerable man, a man doomed to an early death. A man who would admit to another that he is lonely is making a weakness obvious and inviting victimization. Men shun men who are weak and lonely or victimize them. They know this disease is contagious; they too are susceptible. It is also in the nature of men to hate, torture, and kill men or animal, which they perceive as weak and vulnerable.

"Yes," he said quietly. "Yes, I do. "

She asked, "Doc, now that you have returned, what are your plans?"

"Well, my partner and I . . . you remember Street?" She nodded.

"Well, we plan to graze some cattle on the land down toward the Solomon and start buildin' up a herd. Maybe also do some freighting. Frankly, we'd both like to build a life here, you know, have a home and family and such."

She teased, "I can just imagine there are innumerable women around here who would jump at the chance to make the acquaintance of young, good-looking, ambitious men. Why, the church pews are full of such available young ladies. I would be more than happy to introduce them to you."

"Oh! no, no, I didn't mean that. Well, . . . maybe Street would be interested; he's lookin' to find someone and get married. I could pass that information on to him. I got plenty to do without involving myself with some woman right now. Besides, I don't fancy goin' to church all that much."

"No," she grinned. "I'm certain you are not a regular."

As if rehearsed, the conversation tapered off into another awkward silence. Doc intently studied the coffee grounds remaining in the bottom of his cup. Agnes quietly stood and began picking up the breakfast plates and cups from the table and depositing them in a washbasin beneath the pump. She drew more water from the pump and added it to the water already boiling on the stove.

He watched, concerned again that he might have offended her. Summoning his courage, he rose and stepped up behind her. He reached an arm around her and boldly took from her hands the plate she was washing and set it down on the counter. She appeared not to be too surprised. She turned slowly and looked up at him. He grasped her small muscular waist in his rough hands and pulled her to him. She quietly yielded to his grasp and turned her face up to him. He kissed her gently and felt the pressure of her lips back against his. They stood in a lingering embrace, and then backing away, looked in each other's eyes. He picked up the plate she'd just washed and began drying it. She smiled and fell to washing again. Doc would never before have guessed a man could be so blissfully happy washing dishes.

❁ ❁ ❁

The long hot days of summer all too quickly disappeared into the long, cold nights of winter. The Kansas prairie, Shores and Martin discovered, offered no more protection from the fierce, frigid gales than from summer's suffocating heat. They had no sooner built themselves a windowless hut of cottonwood logs and settled their livestock along the river than the first snows arrived. At first, it was little more than a pleasant respite from the shimmering heat waves. Then rain and sleet. Then snow. Then horizontal snow. Doc yearned to ride into Hays, but there was no chance of it. Hours, days, and dates sped by, filled with work. Doc stopped only to eat, and then only out of necessity. Their four hours of sleep began when they nearly fainted from exhaustion and the day began when the first one staggered from his bedroll to fix coffee.

The cattle drifted with the storms. Doc and Street were both amazed at how far a steer could drift downwind in the dark. Days often began and ended in storms. A day might be spent tracking and rescuing one steer. The next, another. At camp their lives depended on ropes stretched from the cabin to the outhouse, to the corrals, to the sheds. They now believed the stories of men freezing to death within yards or even feet of shelter. Fortunately, the wind most often pushed the herd downstream toward the grass remaining on the flood-plain. They could then easily return upstream, even when the wind obliterated their tracks, by following the river bed.

Earlier that autumn, Street adopted a mongrel black pup with a white patch around one eye. He named her Catfish. She now regularly shared the buffalo robe that served as a mattress for his bedroll. They were inseparable. Doc watched the pup plunge shivering through the broken snow in the wake of Street's horse until, exhausted, the animal collapsed on its haunches and howled. Street turned back. He put the pup inside his coat with only her head sticking out and continued until after dark, the dog warm and sound asleep. In the evening they sat eating and dozing together next to the red-hot stove. In the dark the dog barked at the whisper of a wind or the scuttle of a mouse and Doc pitched a boot in her direction from his bed.

Deep in December, the weather steadily worsened. Doc had spent Thanksgiving at the Stevens' house. Both he and Street were invited for

Christmas. As the date approached both their excitement and apprehension grew with the clouds on the horizon. The closer it came to the date the more spindrift whistled from the cabin down toward the river. The wind brought with it again the smell of snow.

"Doc, you go ahead, beat the storm. I'll hole up here 'til you get back. Just bring me something to eat," Street offered.

Shores protested but he remembered his vow to himself to be with Agnes for Christmas. He let Street persuade him.

Two days before Christmas Doc set out in the early morning with a pack horse loaded with a small tent, food, extra blankets and two Christmas gifts. They trudged off for Hays beneath leaden skies and a stinging wind. Street waved farewell from the door of the hut. Catfish was standing next to him wagging a stump of a tail.

The skies filled Doc with foreboding, but his mood lightened with the overcast. In fact, Doc noted his shadow from the sun which waxed and waned from behind scudding clouds. At first, though unpleasantly cold, he experienced little more than the usual snow squalls. Hours later, however, he retreated. His backtracks had disappeared beneath the drifting snow into the gloom of dusk. The wind cut through his heavy buffalo robe coat and mittens. His eyes watered from the wind; the water froze in the corners of his eyes. Nose, toes, and ears numbed. Doc unwound the scarf from around his neck, tied it over and around his head like a peasant woman, then drew his hat down tightly over it. He dropped his chin to his chest so the brim of the hat flattened against the gale, offering more protection to his head and neck. He knew that to fall asleep now would almost certainly mean death. What he wouldn't give for just five minutes of that Pecos River heat right now. He wondered, would he live to complain about the heat again? . . . Maybe just a moment's rest?

Stupefied, he dreamed he lay in the warm cabin heated by the stove beneath his heavy robes listening to Catfish bark at the wind. The dog's incessant barking irritated Doc, and he reached for a boot and nearly toppled from his horse into the snow. His reverie broken, he groaned with despair. But the damn dog would not stop barking. No! he wasn't imagining things. Somewhere in the dim furthermost corners of his mind he realized that there was a dog barking — barking and howling. Somewhere in the blizzard Street's fool mutt Catfish was yapping her fool head off. Holding his breath, he listened. No barking. "Bark! Bark! damn you," he yelled into the wind. "Bark and keep on barking. I'll never complain about your barking again!" The horses, he was sure, had heard the barking and now could sense home. He spurred his mare forward blindly, stumbling and tripping over bushes and through snowdrifts, in what he thought had been the direction of the barking. Several times she tripped and almost fell to her knees but somehow managed to recover. The barking sounded only a few yards away. Something appeared out of the darkness causing the horse to shy. He dismounted stiffly and groped into the blackness. Relief flooded his mind as his hand encountered a pile of logs, a shelter, the cabin. He felt his way in the opposite direction and began yelling, "Catfish! Catfish!" The barking and howling stopped. The whimpering pup nearly knocked him over as he came abreast of the opposite end of the cabin. He knelt down and hugged the whining dog. Her warm tongue lapped at his ice-encrusted face.

"Catfish, Catfish, it's all right, it's me." He lunged forward tripping over the dog, grasping for the cabin door. The opening was covered with a frozen, snow-drifted, buffalo hide. Shores pulled off his mittens and tore at it. Beneath it he felt the leather hasp and pulled its antler keeper. Throwing his weight against the timber door, he and the dog tumbled inside to the dirt floor together. Energized by his sudden turn of luck, he leaped back to his feet and pulled the buffalo hide and the door back into the frame. He fell gasping for breath onto the floor. The overjoyed pup licked at his frozen mustache.

"Street!" he called out. "Street." No answer. Where's Street? He groped blindly until he located the shelf holding the matchbox. His fingers were no more than dead twigs. He dropped the matches. Cursing loudly he swept his hand through the dirt on the floor but could feel nothing. He stuck the fingers of his right hand in his mouth and sat back waiting for the pain. When he could again bend his fingers he returned to searching the floor. After several attempts resulting only in broken matches, one finally flared to a cheery brightness. He huddled protectively around the match and devoured its light no less than if the brightest sun had suddenly appeared in the corner of the room. It so captivated him that his fingers were burning before he found and lit another, then a lamp. Sure enough, there was no sign of Martin, and he set about building a fire in the stove. Within an hour the stove was glowing a dull red. But Shores, instead of basking in the warmth, prepared to return to the gale. He had two horses somewhere outside that needed tending.

He found the horses in the lee of the cabin, and following one of the fixed ropes, led them to a dugout in the river bank which served as a barn. In the dim light of a lantern he unsaddled them and fed what few morsels of hay and grain he could find. He returned, hand-over-hand to the cabin.

Doc fed himself and Catfish, who was still shivering on Street's buffalo robe mattress, jerky and brick-hard corn pone, which he washed down with frequent gulps of whiskey warmed in a teapot.

"Catfish," he inquired of the dog, "where's Street?" The pup pricked her ears and cocked her head. "Damn! I hope he didn't go after the drifters alone."

The dog wiggled her stump and rested her chin on his knee. After hours of torturous concentration, the whiskey and exhaustion crumbled his mind. Knowing nothing could be done before morning, he surrendered to it. He stoked the fire high before heading to his own bed. Martin must be in big trouble, but there was little he could do about it before morning, and maybe not even then, depending on the storm. He left a candle burning and curled up half-drunk and still half-frozen under his own robe and let the purple glow of the stove soothe him into a black and dreamless sleep.

Shores awoke before he opened his eyes, indulging in the warmth of his heavy robe with its lingering odor of animal fat and prairie dirt. His fingers, toes, and face were still hot from thawing. Gradually, the remembrance of the urgency of his situation brought him upright, and he hobbled to the stove in the dim light which leaked in from the edges of the door. It was day, but he had no idea what time. In the half-light he fumbled with matches, paper, and kindling, finally just soaking some fatwood with coal oil and setting a match to it before rushing back to the warmth of his buffalo robe. Catfish awoke, and although whimpering, made her way over to him. She lay down with her back nestled against him. He stoked the fire three more times, until the room was nearly hot, before finally dressing. As he dressed he carefully checked each appendage, much relieved to find each unblackened by frost. He carved a peep hole in the ice surrounding the door frame and squinted through it. Nothing but a cottony grayness. The wind no longer whistled through the logs. They had either frozen together or drifted over.

He paced, arms folded, face to the floor. He knew Martin might still be alive. Every minute counted, but he could do little alone in the teeth of the storm. The cattle, he guessed, had probably drifted miles downwind again. Hopefully, that would be either downstream or upstream from the cabin. Martin could follow the streambed and trees, even in a storm. If the storm hadn't let up by tomorrow morning he'd try again to make it to town for help. Town! My God! It's Christmas Eve day. A year ago I swore I wouldn't be spending it in the company of men. Well, I'm not. He looked at the pup and grinned sourly. The cabin's welcome damp warmth reeked of wood smoke, dog, and hides. Catfish looked up from contentedly gnawing on a shard of horse hoof. Doc collapsed, frustrated and drained, on one of the crude stools. He rested his elbows on his knees and watched the dog gnawing on the shred of hoof. It produced a surprising queasiness which made him shudder with revulsion. He did not consider himself to be a weak-stomached person. While preparing some beans and sowbelly he sipped at a tin cup of whiskey. It only caused his stomach to cramp more. The sight of the rancid, yellow sowbelly floating in the pot of beans caused his stomach to roll. "Catfish, maybe this'll be more to your likin'." He pitched the yellow fat to the dog who sniffed it and returned to the sliver of hoof. Suddenly, his head caught fire. Stripping to his dingy woolen underwear he quickly sought out a cooler corner of the room, then opened the door to a frigid blast which froze the sweat against his brow. Then he began trembling uncontrollably. Slamming the door back into its frame he rushed to feed the stove and then to the comfort of his buffalo robe.

Doc drifted in and out of a restless, troubled sleep. He alternated between torrents of sweat and convulsive shivering. Nightmares of Street and Agnes assaulted his fevered mind. He awoke yelling. He heard the dog scurrying away in the darkness.

Doc descended into a hell of elemental survival, knowing neither night nor day, light nor dark. In his scant waking moments he thrashed about fueling the stove and eating shreds of frozen jerky, corn flour mixed with melted snow and salt, dried navy beans, or rolled oats. The dog and he lapped together at the melted water trickling down the corners of the cabin. Almost mercifully, the waking moments became fewer. In his delirium his hunger pangs and stomach cramps were driven from his mind by an almost sedating weariness, an exhaustion so complete that survival and surrender merged. He simply let the immensely heavy buffalo robe force his waning body further into the straw ticking.

In his delirium, Doc's mind instinctively grasped onto the barking of the dog as it had done that night in the storm. In the distance he heard someone banging on something wood, and a voice . . . no, two voices, calling his name. A crash, the splintering of wood, and suddenly he was aware of light and shadows moving in the cabin. The dog barked and growled frantically and someone quieted it to plaintive whimpers with a few words. Someone stroked his hot face with cold hands. Relief pulsed through him. Now, he thought, it is safe to surrender to sleep.

From deep within his sleep-drenched mind he heard familiar voices . . . Virginia accents. Am I still dreaming, he wondered. An arm, then a leg moved. A moan escaped his throat.

"It 'pears our patient is alive and coming around." A man's voice! Milt Stevens!

Shores suddenly felt hot and suffocated. He mustered all his strength and heaved at the robe covering him, but instead sheets and quilt leaped from his body and over the foot of the bed. He tried to rub his eyes with the back of his hand, but someone pulled them away.

"Agnes, get a mild boric acid solution to wash his eyes. You're a mighty lucky man, Shores. Had we been an hour later in getting to you, you would most likely be crow bait by now. After the storm when you didn't show up by Christmas Day we suspected something untoward, but it wasn't until the storm had let up a good bit, until two days after Christmas, that we could come looking for you."

"Any . . .," Doc squeaked and cleared his throat. "Any sign of Street?"

"Not a thing. I'll get up a rescue party for another look now that I've got you to safety. You got any ideas what might have happened to him?"

Doc croaked, "The only thing I can think of is that he lit out to keep the herd from drifting and got caught when the storm deepened."

"Where's the herd from the cabin?"

"I'd have to guess downstream but it depends on which way the wind was blowin'. How far depends on how weak they got and how long the storm lasted. We've chased 'em up to twenty or so miles. There's a flood-plain on the lee side of a bluff five miles or so down where the grass is higher. It sticks through the snow some, and the bluff keeps it from drifting so deep. I'll borrow a horse and go with you."

"No!" Agnes said firmly as she re-entered the room. "You're in no shape to be going anywhere."

"I'll be fine."

"No," said Stevens. "Ag's right. In your condition we'd end up carrying you back in less than a day. If we can't locate either him or the herd, we'll come back for you."

Doc conceded that they were both probably right, and the thought of a few days being waited on in bed was too enticing. "What day is it?" He asked Agnes.

"Wednesday."

"No. I mean the date?"

"Um . . . second or third."

"Of January!"

"Yes."

"My God! I started out for town on the morning of the twenty-third and turned back that afternoon. That means I made it back to the cabin early in the morning of the twenty-fourth. I've been out pretty much for eight or nine days."

"And you look it. I'll get out the bathtub and some soap and a razor and we'll begin honing off those rough edges tomorrow," laughed Agnes. Shores, always sensitive about his appearance, even standing on death's doorstep, apologized.

Stevens pulled the stopper from a crystal decanter and poured each of them a strong drink, saying that good southern whiskey was the preferred medicine for right now, and should he awaken during the night he might want to take another dose. Agnes poured herself a drink, and the three of them toasted Christmas and Doc's good health, and Shores nearly choked as the fiery liquid passed down his dry throat.

Stevens departed, leaving Agnes seated at the bedside. Doc willingly let her take his hand in hers as they talked on softly in the waning evening light which filtered in through the lace curtains. He fought the drowsiness brought on by the alcohol and warmth, wanting to capture the moment and hold onto it for eternity, but in the end succumbed to sleep.

CHAPTER 7

"I'm feelin' fit," Doc affirmed each morning to his reflection in the mirror before breaking the ice from the basin on the dresser and washing the sleep from his face. He then fell to a regimen of exercises which left him famished. Each morning he shaved, combed the tangles from his hair, dressed in clean clothes and went downstairs to the kitchen where Agnes had breakfast waiting for him. Each morning she went off to school, and each morning Catfish watched him pace the floor throughout the day waiting for some word of Street Martin and their herd. Repeated searches had found no sign of Martin and only a handful of starving stray cattle. Days which should have been bright with happiness and contentment instead were dark with guilt and depression. If it hadn't been for my selfishness, he thought, Street Martin would still be alive. If I hadn't abandoned him for my own selfish pursuit we would still have the herd.

A wagon approached one afternoon, not Milt Stevens' light runabout, but a heavy buckboard. From the window he saw the steaming horses stop in front of the house. A man descended from the wagon and slogged through the newfallen snow to the front door. Before the man had a chance to knock Doc opened the door. He was tall and dour. His shoulders were weighed down with a buffalo robe coat. A gray, wide-brimmed sombrero covered his head. The man took a quick step back when Doc opened the door.

"Excuse me," said the man, "I'm looking for Agnes Stevens."

"Miss Stevens is at the school."

The man raised his eyebrows and looked over Shores' shoulder questioningly.

"And you are?"

"Oh! Sorry. Name's Cyrus Shores. I'm staying with the Stevens. Got caught in the storm of several days ago and barely came through alive. Come on in." Doc extended his hand, and the man took it as he strode inside.

"Name's Bridges . . . Marshal Jack Bridges," he said, removing his hat. "I guess you're why I'm here."

Shores felt an ominous nudge from the marshal's tone. "What do you mean?"

"I got some real bad news. Your partner and Doc Stevens are out there in the wagon." Bridges jerked a thumb over his shoulder and Shores looked out the window at the empty wagon seat. "They're in the back. We found your partner . . . what was his name?"

"Street Martin."

"Yeah. We finally found him down on the Solomon, 'bout fifteen miles from your hut, froze stiff 'long with most of your herd I'd guess, although we didn't bother to count 'em. He'd evidently tried to hole up in an undercut in the riverbank. Didn't make it. We were tryin' to get the body out when the Doc collapsed. His heart gave out I reckon. Weren't much any of us could do about it. He was gone too in a matter of minutes. Had to truss both bodies up like Christmas turkeys and drag 'em to where we could get 'em in the wagon. No need to tell Miss Stevens that I reckon."

Doc, only beginning to recover from the surprise, shook his head and murmured, "No, I reckon not."

"What would you like me to do with the bodies?"

"Um," Doc scratched his head, "durned if I know."

"Well, how 'bout if I take 'em over to Tisdale's Lumber Company and Funeral Parlor? You and Miss Stevens can decide what you want to do. They'll keep good this time of the year. Can't bury 'em until spring when the ground thaws out a bit. Warms up too much in the spring, there's an ice house we can put 'em in for a spell. Probably cost somethin' for storage though I reckon." The marshal started for the door, then stopped and cleared his throat. "You plannin' on stayin' here with Miss Stevens?"

"I don't know, don't really have anywhere else to go right now. Why?"

"Well, some folks is bound to talk now that her father's gone, 'specially her being a schoolteacher and all."

Doc straightened combatively and his brow furrowed.

"Don't matter none to me," said Bridges. "None of my concern what you two do, but you need to be aware that this here's a small town and people need something to talk about in the winter."

Doc relaxed a bit and nodded. "Thanks, marshal. I'll break the news about her father to Agnes and tell her of your concern."

Shores and Bridges shook hands and the marshal departed in a swirl of condensed breath.

Doc methodically plodded through the remainder of the day hoping that the accomplishment of some small task would also provide insight on how to break the news to Agnes. He'd enjoyed no such revelation when she tramped through the door, red-faced and shivering. She pecked him on the cheek and turned to hang her coat and hat on the hall tree while she talked exuberantly about the issue of the day — absenteeism caused by an epidemic of whooping cough. She walked back toward him with open arms but was brought up short by his somber expression.

"What's the matter?" she teased. "You look like you just lost your best friend . . . " She gasped, her hands coming up to her mouth. "Oh! I'm so sorry, Doc. I saw the wagon tracks and wondered who they belonged to. They found Street didn't they?"

Doc nodded and directed her to the couch. He poured them each a glass of the imported brandy the old man had kept for special occasions in a finely-etched Irish crystal carafe on the fireplace mantle. Doc had reverently never before taken such a liberty. He downed his in a single gulp. She sipped hers and tilted her head with curiosity. Slowly, measuring his words with an unnatural precision, he related Bridges' visit and the news of the discovery of Martin's frozen body. As he talked, she sat down on the edge of the couch and rested her elbows on her knees holding the crystal goblet in both hands, studying it intently.

"What else?" she asked. "There's something you're not telling me. Why was it Bridges? Father should have been the one to tell you."

"Your father's heart gave out," he said with a dry mouth. "They were trying to move Street and he collapsed. He was dead before they could get him to the wagon."

Doc went to her. He sat next to her on the arm of the couch and put his hand on her shoulder. "Ag," it was the first time he'd used her father's pet name, "I'm so sorry." She quietly placed her hand on his and leaned her head into the curve of his waist.

"I know," she said.

"It's my fault." He stormed across the room to the bottle of brandy and sloshed his glass to the brim. "If I hadn't left the ranch that day to come into town, neither of 'em would be dead."

"No," she said quietly, so quietly he barely heard her. "No — it wasn't your fault. If we're to trace cause and fault, then it was my fault, and Father's, for insisting you come for Christmas. It was no more your fault than I killed my father or he committed suicide. Doc, it's a world filled with tragedies which are no one's fault. Sometimes it's just a person's time to go." She sighed heavily and also drank the contents of her glass in a single flick of the wrist, offering it back to him for more.

"I miss him already. I will miss him terribly. I want him to walk through that door right now and start work on a bottle, have dinner, rant about the injustices of the war, and hear him snoring in his chair while I wash dishes. But Doc, we all have to die. It's part of the human condition. What's important is what we have done with our lives up to that point, however long or short the life. Father may have been luckier than most. He died a quick and noble death, an end to a noble life spent in service to others. He died on a mission. He died trying to save someone else. It's better than I expected for him. I was always afraid he would simply drink himself to death in the chair. Which reminds me, could I have another?" she asked handing her twice-drained glass to Shores.

She continued, "He often said that by all rights he should have been killed in the war. Father believed that doctors should not be spared from the dangers of combat and often took up a musket to fight alongside those he would later give succor to on the field and in the hospitals. One would hope that such a man should be delivered from any further pain after the cessation of hostilities. Instead he returned to our home in Virginia to find my mother left mindless, and myself living in a shelter I had constructed from the remnants of our burned-out house. Our stock had been killed and fields burned by the great Army of the Potomac." Agnes lifted her glass to her lips and drank the third as quickly as the others. "I'll have another," she said, holding her glass out again. "Mother could do no more than stare for hours at our pitiful few remaining household ornaments: a candlestick, the Irish crystal, a quilt made by her mother. Then, one morning she was gone, left. We searched for hours. Found her sitting against a hickory tree staring out across the Shenandoah not far from where she had buried three of my sisters. She had a fever from the cold night and died within days. No, her death was in no way noble nor ironic. Her life was pitifully short and unproductive, save what she provided me and Father."

Shores remembered with a pang the line of graves in the Michigan forest, brothers and sisters, some of whom he'd never even known.

"We buried her there with them. Father sold what was left of our farm, bought a wagon; we moved west." Her eyes brimmed but no tears fell. She smiled at Shores. "God may be loving, but it's a mean trick He plays on us, Cyrus. If life is to be such a struggle, we should all have been constructed of sterner stuff." She rose abruptly from the couch and flung herself at Doc with open arms.

He'd never expected such a speech. Her strength surprised Doc but he was grateful for it. He wrapped his arms about her tightly. They stood immobilized in an embrace for what seemed to be an eternity. Then she released him and looked up into his face. He bent and kissed her tentatively, tasting the salt of her tears and smelling the brandy upon her hot breath. She returned the kiss with a passion that made his heart race. She dropped her arms and retreated a few steps, then she reached to him through the diagonal bars of twilight streaming in from the western windows. He took her hand in the light. He allowed her to lead him up the creaking staircase to her bedroom.

❁ ❁ ❁

The following months revealed the truth of Bridges' comment. Frontier savagery compared favorably to the righteous wrath of Hays, Kansas' Christian brothers and sisters. He'd been right, an unwed couple living together, especially if one were a schoolteacher, attracted attention from a corps of moral defenders. Hays, the defenders deemed with the departure of Hickok and the trail herds, should now be molded into a respectable farming community. The townspeople cast a wide net and holding their upturned church-going noses, culled from their catch gambling, drinking, and whoring which they ceaselessly worked to cast from the town. But also they carefully examined the lesser fish of the catch for any disturbing flaws. They discovered with joy that flaws could be found wherever they wanted to find them. They found flawed shopkeepers, ranchers, farmers, preachers, cowboys, blacksmiths . . . and teachers. One of the flaws, though it was doubtful that either the righteous or victims alike would have recognized it, was the victims' nearsightedness — they didn't see the net.

❁ ❁ ❁

The days lengthened, the snow receded and then disappeared. Crocuses and tulips fairly leaped from the warm, fertile soil on the south side of the Stevens' house. With the budding of the trees appeared more visitors to the Stevens' home, paying their respects they said, to the town's late, beloved physician. They stumbled and stammered through regrets and excuses that they were months late in their condolences. It was an odd assortment of individuals and groups, none of whom had graced that particular door with their presence when the old doctor was alive, except to seek his services. Preachers, parents, the mayor, and even the school principal now paraded in and out of the house. Between words their eyes darted about the rooms, or if Doc were present, between him and Agnes. Though bristling inwardly, Doc also secreted a lump of guilt deep in his stomach. Yes, he and Agnes were in fact, sharing a bed. He remained mutely discrete. Agnes, less inhibited, on occasion actively defended their living arrangement, and even at times went on the offensive indicting the intruders for hypocrisy.

Shores proposed marriage and Agnes accepted. The ceremony was performed, but the damage had been done. As Agnes said, "One cannot unring the bell quietly." With the end of the school year came news from the chairman of the highly principled school board that she would not be asked to return the following year.

In May they buried Dr. Milton Stevens and Street Martin. Shores regretted that Street had no relative to send his personal effects or obituary to but took solace in the fact that Street had been buried in a cemetery, with a marker, a preacher and two close friends standing by rather than beneath a pile of rocks along some remote trail.

Shores daily made the rounds of farms and ranches looking for work, but in the land of the Jayhawk a man could be tainted by a Virginia wife. He busied himself repairing the Stevens' house and property which the alcoholic doctor had let fall into disrepair, but it provided no income.

He rented a horse and rode south with Catfish to the Solomon on the chance that he might be able to collect and sell remnants of the herd which had survived the winter. As they passed the old cabin Catfish flattened her ears and veered away from it. He stopped long enough to rescue some of their possessions. Along the Solomon he found nothing but bleaching bones and scraps of hide, some with his brand. The live cattle he happened upon either had another brand or were unbranded. In either case, he avoided them, knowing that the Jayhawk cattle barons would like nothing more than to ride down a rustler. He and the dog headed back to town, retracing the route of that fate-filled cold December day.

The verdant prairie now welcomed him. Doc thought it nearly inconceivable, watching the sunflowers on their tall stalks waving in the hot wind above the buffalo grass, that he had nearly frozen to death here scant months ago. Intercepting the road to Hays, Doc urged the horse into a slow, rocking-chair canter. As he crested a hill he could see a buckboard in the distance. Drawing closer he could see no driver. Prodding his horse he soon overtook the creeping wagon. Now, Doc could see someone lying stretched out on the seat. A victim of Indians or highwaymen he thought . . . something familiar about the figure. He guided his horse alongside the wagon. The sound of his horse spooked the team causing the wagon to lurch forward.

The driver jerked upright. "Ho!" he yelled, hauling back on the reins and spraying the horses' hind quarters with tobacco juice. "Ho, God damn it!"

"Pull up or you're a dead man!" yelled Shores.

The driver yelped in alarm and threw his arms above his head knocking his greasy, cratered hat to the ground beside the wagon.

"Pull up and don't turn around."

The shaking driver hauled back on the reins again, applied the brake, and returned his hands above his head.

"Your money or your life."

"Then I'm a dead man for sure 'cause I ain't got no money."

"Then how about some of your stinkin' coffee?"

The driver cautiously peered over his shoulder just as Doc, laughing loudly, drew back alongside him. "Moots, you're sure enough a sight for sore eyes."

"Shit, Doc, you scared me outta a year's growth. I thought I was a goner fer sure."

"What the hell you doin' back in these parts?"

"Well, fact of the matter is, I'm lookin' for you. Let's light a spell. I'll fix some stinkin' coffee and tell you about it. Where's Street?"

As they dismounted Doc told him of Street's misfortune. "Sad to say, as close as we were, I didn't know a damned thing about him, where he came from, or if he had any family."

Moots nodded. "I know. Much as you want to at times, seems like it just don't pay to get too close to a feller. Here today — gone tomorrow."

Moots built a small fire of sage twigs and boiled coffee while he told Shores about his mission and fed Catfish strips of jerky. "After you left we headed back down the Pecos to pick up another herd but we got ambushed by the Comanches at Pope's Crossin'. Made a hell of a fight of it, but there was less'n dozen of us and twenty or thirty of them. Half our boys panicked and skedaddled in the night. Don't think any of them made it though, lot of yellin' and shootin' in the dark. Then things quieted down just before mornin' . . . that's always a bad sign. Taylor got hit pretty bad, gut shot and couple other places. We was laid up in a hole on the river bank. Wasn't long 'til our red friends started crossin' the river up and downstream to get at us from the opposite side. We dug down into the adobe with our rifle butts. Wasn't any scrub on t'other side of the river so we had a clear field of fire goin' back a quarter mile or so, but it worked both ways. We couldn't make a move without them seein' us. Taylor knowed he was a goner and 'fore it was dark gave me a oil-skin poke that he kept sewed up in his shirt. Said he trusted me to get it to where it belonged if I lived. Taylor died jus' before dark. Those of us who were left sure 'nuf knew that if we didn't get out of there early at night our hair'd be decoratin' somebody's lodge pole by mornin', so we lit out for the river just a bit after dark. It helped that we had some rain and wind too. Most of the boys was intent on driftin' downstream, but I thought that was just what the Comanches expected so I started makin' my way upstream by pullin' myself against the current with roots and grass and branches and the like. Sure's hell, I hadn't been gone an hour but what there commenced a real ruckus downstream — shootin' and shoutin' and all kind of carryin' on. If any of 'em boys made it, there truly is a God. I stayed in the river all through the night and holed up the next day in some tamarisk on the bank. Didn't have nothin' to eat and only river water to drink, and you remember how good that was. I still had my rifle and six-shooter but couldn't take a chance on shootin' somethin'to eat and havin' my red friends hear it. Next night I hightailed it until I saw the lights of a ranch. Walked right up to it, must have looked a sight. Surprised a lot of folk and sent the hands reachin' for their shootin' irons so I commenced to hollerin', 'Don't shoot, it's a white man.' Place was owned by some of the old Two Bar K boys who knew Taylor. They formed up and went backdown stream for him. I was too tuckered out to join up with 'em, but I think we all knew it was too late. They gave him, or what was left, a proper burial, no rocks, actually dug a grave. I borrowed a horse and made my way back up to Fort Sumner and told the blue boys what had happened. I doubt if it did much good." Moots paused and poured another round of his infamous coffee.

Shores expressed his sadness at the fate of Taylor and said that he had been a good and honest boss, and they had shared some high ol' times together, both good and bad.

Moots brought up a finger. "And that's why I'm here. Taylor didn't have much of a family. A sister, I think, down in New Mexico or some place; I wasn't able to find her. That pouch that he gave me before I went swimmin' contained his will, five hundred dollars in gold and greenbacks and a bank account in San Angelo. The will said any money was to be split between his sister and you . . . "

"Me?"

" . . . for savin' his life that day on the Pecos. Said you were truly a man to cross rivers with and deserved mor'n just thanks. Anyway, I went to San Angelo and found you had to hire a blamed attorney to help do something called probate. Well, like I said, me and that lawyer tried our damnedest to find the sister, but she's plumb disappeared. That left you, and I wasn't 'tall certain how to get hold of you 'cept ride out here and hunt you down. There's a fair piece of cash waitin' for you in San Angelo, 'bout seven thousand dollars — save for the cost of the lawyer."

Doc could barely believe his ears. No more than an hour ago he'd been nearly penniless. The two of them headed for town, Doc's head swimming from the news — and about four cups of Benton's "Patented Potent Pecos Putrid." Moots angled for an invitation to stay with Doc and Agnes, but Shores had already been downwind of him and noted that Benton hadn't changed clothes since the last time he'd seen him. "The man'd make a coyote sick," Taylor once commented.

Doc lied instead. He told Moots that Agnes had the ague and it would probably be a better idea if he got a room at the hotel. To salve his guilt however, Doc did tender a dinner invitation. Perhaps a table set outside in the cool evening breeze — with Moots downwind. In the end, since neither of them had any money, Doc offered Moots a bunk in the barn.

❁ ❁ ❁

"Whata we got to lose?" Moots questioned over top of a mouthful of steak, beans and bread. Doc squirmed as Agnes dodged to the side of the table when the old man tried to wash the mess down with a big gulp of warm beer, choked and sprayed in their direction. " 'Scuse me," he gasped while drying his face on the edge of the tablecloth. He continued, "It 'serves some serious consideration. After all, what's holding you here? 'Tain't like you both got well payin' jobs."

The Shores looked at each other. "Well," admitted Doc after an embarrassing silence, "maybe not a whole hell of a lot. But we . . . Agnes does have the place here. We could buy a ranch and herd with the Taylor money."

"Sell out! That and what you got from the late Ed Taylor will buy you a new start in Colorado. That's where the fortunes are to be made these days, the Colorado gold fields. I heard tell of men fillin' their pockets so full o' nuggets in a day that they could barely walk away from the creek."

From the corner of his eye Shores could see Agnes' eyes again roll toward the heavens. He sympathized with her expression. But he also felt the tug of a new country and new adventures.

Later, when Moots had staggered off to his bunk in the barn loft, Doc broached the subject again. "I think we'd agree that Moots may be dreamin' about all the gold, but let's consider other things. You know the people who got rich in California after '49 were not the prospectors and miners, it was the freighters and suppliers." Agnes frowned at him over her shoulder from where she was piling dirty dishes into a dishpan. "And, he's right about one thing, there's not much holdin' us here."

"What about buying a place, like you suggested?"

"We could do that. But do we really want to live here after what's happened in the last few months?"

She folded her arms across her chest and leaned against the cabinet. "I don't know . . . no! I feel as though I don't have a friend left in this town. I certainly don't know of anyone that I can trust here anymore. But even at that, it'll be hard to move. When Father and I left Virginia I wasn't sure that I would ever have a real house and home again. I was scared to death. We did make a home — this is it."

"I know," he said, "maybe that's a point. This house, Hays, and Kansas were home to you and him. Maybe we need to strike out and make one for ourselves. Yeah, it was tough, and it will be again, but you did it and we can do it."

Agnes looked out the window above the dishpan and sighed. "I guess I just wanted so badly for it to be different. For a long time, even before you asked me, I thought we'd get married, but I thought we'd have our own place here, or somewhere around here. It'll be hard to sell out and move, if for no other reason than I just wanted to be settled."

"We will be, I promise you that, and somewhere even better than here."

"Go easy. It's going to take me some time to get used to the idea. I don't want the two of you pulling the rug out from under me."

Shores cautiously broached the subject with Moots the next morning being careful not to start a stampede. Even then, his old friend took the bit in his teeth.

"I 'spect our best bet is to head farther southwest into the Sangre De Cristo and the San Juans. The hills ain't as played out down there. Not many willin' to put up with the winters."

"You been there?"

"Naw! Talked to enough people who have though. Seems like I been there. I fig'er we head for Fort Garland and maybe head into the mountains west of there. Can't dally here too long though, would want to get where we're goin' afore winter sets in. You think winters here are bad . . ."

Doc raised his hand and turned his head. He cringed at the thought of any winter, and certainly he would not be mentioning that to Agnes.

"Agnes and I talked it over. We'll give you a thousand dollars to go ahead and get things set up, buy wagons and such, and scout out the territory. We gotta sell the place here, and I have to make a trip to San Angelo. Shouldn't take too long. I expect we'll be there before the first snow."

❂ ❂ ❂

Nowhere in the probate instruments did the word "haste" appear. Both Stevens' and Taylor's wills languished for another cycle of seasons. Doc took a series of temporary jobs: cowboy, teamster, shop clerk, stable hand. Agnes devoted herself to the house and home. But even she grew restless in a friendless town. They wrote or telegraphed Moots almost weekly in Pueblo. Each succeeding letter or telegram canceled plans and set new deadlines.

A summer later they walked together in the pink-gray early morning fog to deliver a handful of purple iris to two graves. They stood in silence above the white marble stones as the sun broke over the horizon and flashed through the trees.

Agnes caught his hand in hers and looked up at him. "Take me to Colorado," she said. "Let it begin."

Doc Shores as a young man.

Photo courtesy of P. David Smith

Doc Shores at an advanced age.

Photo courtesy of P. David Smith

The first cabin built in Gunnison.

Photo courtesy of Denver Public Library — Western History Section

The first post office in the Gunnison Valley.

Photo courtesy of Denver Public Library — Western History Section

Two Gunnison Valley cowboys circa 1880.
Photo courtesy of Denver Public Library — Western History Section

Gunnison's LaVeta Hotel circa 1880.

Photo courtesy of Denver Public Library — Western History Section

The Alonzo Hartman house in Gunnison.

Photo courtesy of Denver Public Library — Western History Section

Gunnison Main Street looking North.

Photo courtesy of Denver Public Library — Western History Section

Main Street and Tomichi in Gunnison.

Photo courtesy of Denver Public Library — Western History Section

PART 2

CHAPTER 8

The same summer the Shores brothers trekked to Jackson intending to join the Michigan militia, there were other men, prospectors and frontiersmen, camped along the banks of the Platte River in Colorado Territory who talked of quick riches. They excited each other with stories of mountains of gold. Then they flooded through the passes to camp in the high mountain valleys and canyons. A few trickled into the Gunnison Valley, named for the early day explorer John Gunnison.

The valley was a mountain citadel occupied by inhospitable Utes. It was surrounded on three sides by peaks which shot upward to 14,000 feet, and a 2,000 foot canyon on the fourth. Even the Utes, these hardy "People of the Shining Mountains," every autumn abandoned the valley and its arctic-like winters for the milder ranges of the Uncompahgre and Tabeguache fifty miles to the west. The lowest of the mountain passes remained choked with snow until midsummer when passage into the Gunnison Valley, other than by foot, involved hundreds of complicated and dangerous detours hindered by an impossible maze of crosshatched deadfall lacing the densely wooded slopes. Icy cascades from the thawing snowfields pounded down vertical-walled canyons.

The Black Canyon of the Gunnison was so narrow and deep, people unfortunate enough to find themselves in its depths on even the longest day of the year caught only two or three hours of direct sunlight. The canyon could not be directly crossed and circumnavigation funneled explorers, frontiersmen, prospectors, and settlers north and south of the valley. The valley of the Gunnison therefore remained relatively pristine and unapproachable — until the white man's lust for land and the shining metals it contained overcame nature's hardships.

Bertram Smith, asserting direct descendency from Joseph Smith, claimed that he, not Brigham Young, was rightful heir to the Mormon leadership. Usurper or not, he attracted a following who he persuaded to settle a farming community in the rich bottomland of the Gunnison Valley. The trek began in Denver in the humid heat of late August — immediately preceding a particularly harsh winter.

The Smith party crept through Buffalo Pass and into the snow-laden valley just before Christmas, their plan having been to subsist on a meager supply train and the local game and fish until crops could be grown. But the game, like the Indians, had sought out lower, more habitable ranges before the onslaught of winter. And the lakes were frozen nearly solid. Those spans of the Gunnison River not covered with thick blue ice remained only a sluggish frozen gruel grumbling and hissing its way through the valley. Efforts to build log cabins from the trees along the river were thwarted by hip-deep snow and temperatures so low that ax heads broke like crystal against the frozen tree bark. Everyone in camp suffered from at least one frostbitten limb.

By early January food had all but disappeared, even under severe rationing. Horses, oxen, and mules which had been intended for spring plowing, were now frozen and starved and all were slaughtered for meat. Bark, leather, wood, paper, and cloth were boiled into a glutinous, foul-tasting mess and consumed. Rumors of cannibalism caused some to abandon the lowly camp shelters for certain death in the deep snow.

When the first leaf buds appeared on the aspen trees in late spring and there was less snow than grass on the ground, the Smith Party was but a handful of pitiful, living skeletons. Prospectors returning to their summer diggings stumbled in amazement upon humans who grazed on all fours like elk and deer. All those who survived into the summer and regained their strength cursed the valley and Smith and walked out vowing never again to darken this part of the earth with their shadows. All save one man. Were it not for him, the tragic story of the Smith Party would have ended with the last person vanishing to the southeast over the top ridge of Buffalo Pass and the history of the Gunnison Valley and Doc Shores would have been written much, much differently.

❂ ❂ ❂

John Malcolm Douglas, descended from Thomas Douglas, Fifth Earl of Selkirk, who founded the Red River Colony in Manitoba, Canada, couldn't have been more different from Doc Shores. Never were two men more destined to join in conflict. John Malcolm's father, Malcolm, the Earl's bastard son, had become disillusioned with the Red River settlement project and had taken his family south into the United States. A talented blacksmith by trade and training, he easily found work wherever he directed his family. Bedeviled by his illegitimacy, he'd become a voraciously ambitious man driven to travel and acquire the wealth and power denied him by his birthing. He successfully plied his trade in St. Louis for nearly ten years, establishing a foundry which manufactured horseshoes, nails, and wagon tires. Prosperous, other than in his own eyes, he heard stories from his clientele of overnight wealth in the California gold fields. Leaving the care of family and business to his oldest son, Ian, who had more of a taste for whiskey and river-front brothels than either family or business, he struck out to the west. Malcolm returned two years hence richer than when he'd left, but he also found his previously prosperous business without customers and drowning in debt. Ian fled his father's wrath and died a year later, killed in a gunfight on his way to New Orleans.

Neither Malcolm's genius nor his new wealth could salvage the damage done by Ian's incompetence. He moved his family further west to Kansas City where he again took up blacksmithing, until one day a wagon painted with the words "Pikes Peak or Bust" pulled into his shop. Malcolm inquired. The owner told him gold in quantities that would put California to shame had been discovered in the Colorado mountains. Within days he and his family bumped along in two wagons along the trail to Denver.

Malcolm settled his wife and younger son, now his only child, John Malcolm, into a cabin on the banks of Cherry Creek and quickly departed for the gold fields in the Arkansas River drainage below Leadville. After a few letters his family never again heard from him. Decades later, John Malcolm would devote tens of thousands of dollars of his personal wealth and years of time to a fruitless search for his father. Malcolm Douglas, like so many nameless, faceless miners and prospectors of the time had simply been devoured by the granite teeth of the Colorado Rockies.

Young John Malcolm had been his father's apprentice and had become renowned as a skilled farrier and wheelwright. His mother, Eileen, supplemented her son's wages by selling butter and eggs, baking, and doing mending. John Malcolm quickly discovered that he possessed his father's gift for inventiveness and entrepreneurship. He further developed his father's idea for mass-forging iron wagon tires and mechanically fitting them to the wheels rather than laboriously hand forming them. Soon he was supplying tires and wheels to blacksmith shops and wagon makers throughout Eastern Colorado Territory. When he delivered his wheels and tires to the wagon makers he noticed that each wagon was constructed individually by hand by a crew who made each piece separately and hand fitted them. The finished wagon was sold on order, and the buyer might have to wait weeks for delivery. He returned to his shop and built jigs into which a stockpile of previously finished parts could be immediately fitted, thereby cutting the time of completion in less than half. He, too, prospered. He moved his mother into a new house in downtown Denver. This tall, handsome, sandy-haired and aggressive young man quickly became a person to be reckoned with in the Denver business and political communities.

But John Malcolm, being his father's son in business, hungered no less than he for wealth, power, and notoriety. He grew restless, constantly susceptible to change. Then he met a visionary, Bertram Smith. Ever the model of confidence, the idea that he too could become a member of this new nation's wealthy and powerful landed gentry appealed to this descendent of a Scottish earl. He and Smith struck a deal in which Smith would recruit for and organize the expedition, and Douglas would initially fund it. The two would share equally as well in the profits gained off the sale of corporate lands to those that followed them into the hinterland. Smith's interests were strictly agrarian. John Malcolm was welcome to pan and mine all the gold he could find and pay Smith a commission. John Malcolm sold his businesses, and with such uncharacteristic foresight that he was later to regret it, funded a large trust for his mother. She warned him of burning his bridges. He kissed her good-bye.

❁ ❁ ❁

Most men alone, in such a precarious predicament as the one in which John Malcolm found himself when he awoke the morning after departure of the last survivors of the Smith Party, would have been sick with fear, failure, and remorse. Instead, he looked not at the path beaten eastward toward the summit of Buffalo Pass, but rather at the thick, wavy grass along the broad banks of the meandering Gunnison River, and he saw opportunity and felt exultation. Now, he alone possessed and would own forever through his descendants, the wide fertile valleys, their rivers, lakes, and surrounding hills up to the escarpments of the distant lofty peaks. His realm would put to shame any Scottish lord's. His mountains were higher, his valleys broader, his land richer. Neither he nor his issue would again bow to anyone. As the morning sun warmed his wide-ranging domain he had only a vague idea what he would do with his holdings, or how he would even hold on to them. But no matter, not for now. He was giddy with conviction. With no more than a hardtack biscuit to sustain him for the day he strode down from his hilltop viewing station, picked up a battered washbasin and knelt into the river gravel. He began washing sand. By dark he'd collected several good-sized nuggets and half a palm full of dust. That night by the light of fire and lantern he took a scrap of board from one of the abandoned wagons and carved with his knife the words: "Douglas Colorado." The miners and prospectors who passed the sign chortled. He pulled the sign and replaced it: "Gunnison Colorado Pop. 1 Douglas."

The Gunnison River Valley and its tributaries contained a half-dozen independent communities whose foundations were only as strong as the malleable metals upon which they rested. In a land notorious for its hard men, no special notice was taken or at least mentioned, of the tall, wiry lad furiously sluicing gravel. When the aspen leaves turned yellow and tinkled in the breeze, Douglas bought two mules, tack, and packs from one of the miners. He loaded his packs with jerked venison and buckskin bags heavy with dust and nuggets and set out for Denver.

❁ ❁ ❁

"My God!" Eileen cried upon greeting the buckskin-clad, bearded giant at her door. "You look like something the cat dragged in."

"Or coughed up," John Malcolm laughed.

"I was 'fraid you were dead for sure. Newspapers were full of the Smith Party for nigh onto a week. People couldn't talk about much else." She wrapped her small frame and short arms around her son, and he lifted her off the floor. "Put me down! Whew! You smell like a freshly-skinned skunk! You ever bathe?"

"Sure 'nuf, a year or so ago. Haven't needed to since then. But I'm fixin' to right now. Then I'm goin' t' treat myself to some of your cookin' and go out and buy a brand-new suit of clothes. I got a lot of business to tend to over the winter and I need to look proper for it."

"What kinda business?"

"Cattle, land, minin' and railroads."

"Sound's like you plan on bitin' off a heck of a chunk — and that's aside from the fact you don't know anything about any of 'em."

"Nope." John Malcolm went to the kitchen and busied himself boiling water for a bath while he talked, his diminutive mother trotting along. "Nothin' true enough, but I'm not about to let that stop me. You can bet your last dollar that a year from now I'll know everything there is to know about at least one of them and in two years most of what there is about all of them, and in five . . . I'll know all there is to know about all of them."

"You're pretty dern cocksure of yourself."

"I came by it honestly . . . I had a hell of a teacher." Then he noticed his mother's crestfallen expression. "I'm sorry, Ma," he said, softening his voice and coming back to embrace her gently. "I'm sorry. I didn't mean to dredge up bad memories."

Eileen daubed her eyes with a linen handkerchief. "No, no . . . it's all right. I just been afraid I'd lost my last man these many months. To see you again is a bit of a shock. You settle in and I'll draw you a bath and fix you somethin' to eat."

"I won't leave like Pa did. You'll be with me every step of the way . . . well at least after I get started and get some kind of a respectable house built." He brightened. "Wait'll you see it, valleys full of grass and water and mountains full of gold and silver. And one day we're goin' back to Scotland and build our own castle, bigger and better 'n his and we'll look down on it from high upon a hilltop." He noticed her smile wasn't back.

"Johnny, that was your father's dream, his obsession, not mine, and he killed himself chasing it. Back in Scotland the old earl's long dead and nobody else, here or there, gives a tinker's darn who you are nor what you've done."

"No matter, I'll know. You'll know. Maybe the old man'll know."

"Whew!" she said, fanning her palms toward him. "You don't smell any better for all your highfalutin' ideas. You go 'head and bathe and shave and maybe you can give me another hug then."

He turned to go, but she stopped him with a word. "Johnny! . . . try'n'-muster up some self-confidence. I think you'll find it helpful in whatever you decide to do."

He laughed. "What I'll find more helpful is minin' equipment and a herd of cattle."

"Cattle? I thought the Gunnison was minin' country."

"It is, but there's damn little in the way of fresh meat up there. The game's mostly hunted out. Any supplies have to be hauled in."

"From where? It's locked in by the mountains."

"Buffalo Pass. Up the river and then southeast to San Luis and Fort Garland. It's even passable in winter some years. There's a dozen or so minin' towns within a hundred miles just beggin' for meat. The second thing to do is to tie up the pass with a toll road and freighting monopoly. There's no railroad, so no competition."

Eileen shook her head. "You've inherited your father's overheated imagination."

"I could stay here in Denver and be rich or I can go back to the Gunnison and be wealthy . . . and when I am, I'm goin' back to Scotland and have a castle dismantled stone-by-stone and brought back for us to live in."

"And how and where do you plan on gettin' the money to start this venture?"

John Malcolm held up a finger and pointed to the canvas carpenter's tool bag he'd struggled carrying in. "Right here," he said, hefting the bag onto the dining room table. It creaked and groaned under the weight. He unlatched it, and his mother pried the satchel open further. "Nice rocks and sand" she commented dryly. "You'll get a pretty penny for those I'll bet."

"Right you are. Those and many more like 'em. Look more closely." He took one of the rocks from the bag and held it in the sunlight coming through the window. "You see that?"

Eileen leaned closer. "I see a mess, nothin' special."

"Ha! Mother dear, that rock and the others are so special they near defy description. That's gold-bearing quartz. Here, feel the heft of it. The thing's pregnant with gold and silver. My guess is that it will assay out at near a thousand dollars a ton, which would make this one of the richest mines since the Comstock in Nevada!"

Eileen looked at the rocks and back to her son's face. "Might be the richest vein in the world; you still need a bath and a shave."

❁ ❁ ❁

Simon Levits placed the enormous black cigar he was smoking in an onyx ashtray and leaned back in his high back leather chair resting his fat, white, manicured fingers on his paunch. "Can't be done. The bank will not, nor will any bank finance such a venture. Jack, that might be the richest vein in the world and still not attract any investors. From what you describe it's just too difficult to get to and then too difficult to mine. First, there's no railroad, or even a road into the valley to bring in mining equipment and supplies and food. Then simply climbing up to the mouth of that slot canyon would be no picnic. Then how are you going to get men and equipment into the canyon and the grotto, beneath a waterfall, to mine? Then, how are you going to get the ore out and smelt it?"

Douglas leaned forward on the banker's desk. "If not the bank, then you — and others like you — interested in becoming wealthy, perhaps wealthier than the Bonanza Kings in Nevada. Remember Sutro? They're still pulling millions out of the Comstock because he did the impossible. He knew he could engineer a drain tunnel and divert the water flooding the mines. The stream creating the falls in front of this vein is not all that big. We can do any number of things including tunneling an upstream diversion and damming the flow or building a hanging flume." Douglas rose from his chair and flailed his arms dramatically, the ashes from his own cigar showering his new suit and the oriental rug beneath his polished boots. "As for the material and logistics problem, we build our own toll road, man it with our own freighters and teamsters, then build our own railroad and tunnels and our own smelters. We grow our own beef to sell to our workers and tradesmen and other cities in the valleys." John Malcolm's voice boomed with passion. Privately he thought, the lode won't last forever, but by the time it plays out we will have control. Then I will have control.

Levits remained expressionless and thoughtful, but the fuming ember at the end of his cigar and the swirling plume of smoke about his head told Douglas that he had captured the banker's attention. "J.M., it's risky, very risky but also very interesting. But what would be your stake in this — other than taking the money and heading west?"

Douglas considered this. "There's my businesses, the foundry, the wagon shops I could put up for collateral."

Levits shook his head again. "Do you forget I'm the one who put it all in trust for your mother?"

"Can the trust be dissolved?"

"Perhaps. She'd do that?"

"If I need her to."

"I'm skeptical. If you're insistent on this scheme — you'll need her to give permission. There's no one out there who is going to buy into this thing — including yours truly — unless you're willing to assume a like risk."

"What about others?"

Simon studied his immaculately manicured nails silently. "A thought came to me, even as we have been discussing this. Are you familiar with General Russell?"

"General Maxwell T. Russell?"

"The same."

"Only by name and reputation. He's majority stockholder, and for all practical purposes, the owner of the Denver and Colorado Western Railroad."

"Among other things. He's hosting a minor soirée. I can only imagine the crop of potential investors who will be in attendance. I might be able to arrange an invitation for both of us."

"Marvelous! We'll tie up the financing over cigars and brandy."

Simon arched an eyebrow at this. "I caution you, Douglas. Do be discrete. These men are nobody's fools and will have you drawn and quartered in the middle of Larimer Street should they smell a rat."

But Douglas was already bolting for the door, cigar ash flying. He stopped at Simon's admonition. "Well then, I should fit right in — wouldn't you say so?"

Levits grinned and nodded at the young man's confidence. "Oh, this crowd dresses for dinner."

"Of course," said Douglas with a tilt of his head and impromptu Cockney accent. "I'll be in me best bib and tucker, straight off the shelf from Charlie's Mercantile and Dry Goods Emporium, and on me best behavior."

Levits winced as the large oak doors slammed shut behind the brash Scotsman.

❁ ❁ ❁

Maxwell Russell, the scion of a prominent New Hampshire family, had overcome a childhood plagued by rheumatism and home tutelage by sheer force of will and a regimen of strenuous physical exercise to become one of the Union's most decorated officers in the Civil War. A wound brought him near death, so debilitated that the army thought him better suited for a staff position in charge of logistics. He was placated with a promotion to the rank of Brigadier General. A man of action addicted to combat, he sullenly accepted his new tasks, but true to his nature, threw himself wholeheartedly into perfecting the supply and transportation of Union material. He observed the future of railroad transportation from his perch atop the logistics command. Even before the conclusion of the war he'd begun planning and connecting himself to the political and financial powers-to-be. He made it a point to consult frequently with General Grant and General Sherman. At war's end he hastened west to carve out a personal niche and preempt such powers as Gould, Fisk, and Vanderbilt.

He staked out the formidable Rocky Mountains as his territory. He assaulted them with powder and pick as though they were rebel forts. The original "easy-pickings" of the '59 rush had been replaced by the deep tunnels and shafts and permanent towns and settlements that needed to be served by wagon and rail.

From the turrets of his granite mansion perched strikingly on the slopes of Denver's Capitol Hill he administered his expanding empire like a feudal baron. The man once obsessed with wealth and power, in his later years became equally obsessed with marriage and propagation. He had taken as his wife the youngest, most beautiful and most socially prominent woman he could find. It was a marriage of convenience and position for her. She immediately conceived and they had been blessed with a girl, Christine. Further pregnancies resulted only in bitter disappointments — miscarriages and infant deaths. By the time of Christine's sixteenth birthday it was very apparent that if the general was to gain a male heir it would have to be through another marriage.

Christine, a strikingly beautiful girl with glossy brown hair and emerald eyes, was on the occasion of that birth date, ceremoniously and almost literally lifted from her cloistered cradle and put on the auction block. Stunned, the best she could hope for was a mate so cowed by her father's wealth, power, and the promise of a life of the same that she would be left to her beloved horses and needlepoint and brought forth only for childbearing and ceremonial occasions. She aspired no higher. Thus commenced a parade of suitors, most of whom wilted and died under the general's withering inspections and heated interrogations.

Neither father, daughter, nor John Malcolm Douglas perceived the least glimmer of precognition at the Scot's inauspicious entry into the hall of the mountain king at the side of banker Levits. At first, aside from his handsome features, he created no particular stir, being bound on oath to Simon to curb his natural tendency toward assertive ostentation. He dressed in the most conservative and conventional white tie and tails with silk top hat, doffed along with gloves and white silk scarf at their entry. His manners were immaculate and beyond reproach as Simon guided him carefully through the throng of homage payers and their courtesans toward the emperor himself.

"This is absurd," groaned Douglas. "We're acting like a pack of coyotes circling a bear for tidbits."

"Patience, Dear Boy," replied Levits in a soft voice. "One must observe convention in such circumstances. We must wait for the proper opening so that we are not just two more in the greeting line but neither so we attract too much attention. I must also make certain, a mere nod of the head will do, that the general remembers me and that I may address him familiarly."

"And who is that lovely creature at his side? Certainly not his wife I should hope, perhaps a paramour."

"Most certainly not!" hissed Simon. "His daughter, Christine. Do be careful J.M., an incautious remark like that could put us out onto the street in an instant."

"I will be careful. Though she does have the longest legs — I can only imagine. Convention be damned!" growled Douglas who broke straight for the general with Simon left sputtering protests.

Douglas brushed through the astonished crowd surrounding the general and extended his hand. "General Russell, I want to thank you for inviting me here this evening." Russell's eyebrows arched in surprise. "I hope you will forgive me sir," Douglas said, leaning close to the general's ear, "for being so forward, but my associate, Simon Levits and I have an urgent business matter to discuss with you."

"And," said the general stiffly, "you would be . . . ?"

"John Malcolm Douglas, Sir. Of course, you're already familiar with my associate, Simon Levits, of the First National Bank of Denver." He turned and pulled the pale plump Levits forward by the shoulder. He thought Simon was going to kiss the general's hand.

"General Russell," Levits spoke, "It's an honor to have been invited this evening. I hope you'll forgive my friend for being so forward."

"Well, . . . yes. I can always appreciate an audacious young man. Was one myself once." He signaled to a waiter to bring a tray of drinks. "Hope the two of you will enjoy yourselves here tonight."

The general's daughter, Douglas noted from the corner of his eye, reached out and touched the shoulder of a woman a couple of steps away and whispered something to her. The woman looked over her shoulder toward Douglas and whispered something back. John Malcolm wished to catch her eye once more, but he was too late. The general spoke. Introductions were made according to prescribed protocol and courtly manners. Simon made appropriate references to John Malcolm's business accomplishments and ended with a vocal nod toward recent "adventures" in the Gunnison Valley.

"You don't say?" asked the general, peering intently at Douglas. The general was a very tall man who held himself militarily stiff so as to appear even taller but now would have had to stand on his toes to match John Malcolm's height. "The Valley has always interested me. What business were you there on?"

"I had the misfortune to be a member of the Smith party."

"Indeed? Yes, a most tragic quest. But why on earth were you with them? Homesteading?"

"Not precisely, I was the primary investor. My business was land speculation."

The older man nodded thoughtfully. "Well, you're lucky to have survived the experience."

Douglas sensed the conversation might be ending with that comment, except Simon, probably sensing the same, injected, "Mr. Douglas has stumbled upon quite a mineral find."

"Minerals? Have you indeed? I was under the distinct impression that the basin's minerals were insignificant or had largely played out."

"Yes, Sir; that is probably correct — those to be found on the surface anyway."

"You've staked a claim I take it?"

"Yes, that and I own patents to most all of the valley by default from my deceased partner, Bertram Smith."

Simon placed a quieting hand on John Malcolm's back. Then directing his suggestion to Russell, "I thought perhaps we could discuss this business in more detail over brandy and cigars this evening."

Russell considered this for a moment and shook his head. "Too much company and commotion. I'd prefer just the three of us meeting initially, say lunch here tomorrow?"

"Yes," said Simon, "that will be most satisfactory."

"Now," said Douglas, "that we have that out of the way, could I impose upon you to introduce me to your lovely daughter?"

"Douglas, really!" Simon sputtered and began directing an apology toward Russell.

The general waved aside Levits' protests and looked Douglas squarely in the eyes. "It's all right, Simon. I rather like a man who knows what he wants and is direct about it. Yes, Mr. Douglas, come along and I will introduce you to my daughter — upon your solemn promise not to steal her away, at least not tonight."

The three men approached the young lady. She looked demurely toward her mother. Malcolm thought her eyes were the deepest green he had ever seen. His heart pounded in his chest.

"My Dear," General Russell said," I would like to present Mr. Simon Levits and Mr. J. M. Douglas. Gentlemen, my daughter Christine."

Malcolm discreetly stepped aside for Simon who bowed courteously. He scarcely lifted the fingers of her proffered hand. "I am very pleased to finally meet you. Your father has spoken so often of you in the years since I have known him."

"Thank you, Sir," she replied with a curtsey. "I too have heard your name mentioned frequently. You are an officer with the First National Bank of Denver, are you not?"

"Vice President of Trusts."

"It's most pleasing to know Father has such well-placed friends." Then turning to Malcolm, "I'm afraid I don't know Mr. Douglas either by name or reputation." She looked at Malcolm and it seemed to him that her eyes fairly bloomed. Encouraged, he lifted her hand to his lips, his eyes never leaving hers.

"I am truly enchanted, and I do hope that I may have the opportunity to make you more familiar with both my name and reputation."

"You are direct, Sir, and perhaps a bit crude."

"Perhaps, but my father always said, 'Faint heart never won fair maid'." Turning to the general, "May I call upon your daughter, Sir?"

"You have my leave to do so, but perhaps she'll take a bit more convincing."

"Well," replied Malcolm, returning to Christine. "No time like the present to find out. May I attend you with a glass of punch, Miss Russell?"

Christine glanced at her father, then in the direction of her mother who, Malcolm thought, pretended to be overly engaged in a conversation with Governor Evans. "You do take one's breath away, Mr. Douglas. Well, yes, I suppose so."

Later, as they collected their accessories from the cloakroom maid, Simon remarked: "My God, Douglas, you narrowly missed being uncouth tonight."

Malcolm grinned broadly as he adjusted his silk top hat to a more jaunty angle. "It's uncouth only if unsuccessful. I rather think I'll wed a late lunch tomorrow with the father into early tea with the daughter. Dear me, did I say 'wed'? A mere slip of the tongue."

❁ ❁ ❁

"I'm most impressed," said General Russell laying aside the magnifying glass that he had been using to view the ore sample on his china lunch plate. "But certainly before I or any of my associates would consider investing in a venture we will need a similar good faith effort on your part."

"Agreed. I will match the amount of the highest single investor." From the corner of his eye Malcolm saw Simon's eyebrows arch skyward.

"You'll maintain controlling interest?" asked the general.

"Yes, but we'll draft an agreement which will provide you with options on any future stock issue up to parity. Together we will possess the controlling block."

"I see you've given this some thought."

"Much thought. I knew you wouldn't buy into it if I was to have sole controlling interest and I wasn't going to buy into it if you did."

The general nodded pensively and referred to some scribbled notes. "The vein's not going to last forever, maybe not even a year or a month, but it's rich enough that I'm willing to gamble on that, and I'm almost certain the others can be similarly persuaded, right, Simon?" He nodded in the direction of the banker who sighed and bobbed his fleshy cheeks. "But what consideration have you given to other economic prospects?"

"I own the patent on most of the valley and its tributaries by virtue of my investment with Smith, and his death. I will provide you capital-free access for both rail, road, and freighting rights-of-way."

"In return for what?"

"A fifty year agreement for five percent gross revenues of all freight into and out of the valley, excluding mining equipment and ore, and I get free haulage for livestock when the railroad is built." And otherwise, thought Malcolm, as I have it planned, I will inherit your shares when you're gone.

"Very well, but I will pick the subordinate investors."

"Acceptable, as long as my interest is not endangered by a voting block."

"We can work out the wording."

"Then let us drink to the success of our venture." The three men raised their glasses in unison. "Perhaps," said Malcolm, "we can discuss other matters this afternoon over tea."

"Tea? Well, yes, I suppose so. Normally, I leave tea to my wife and daughter."

"Yes . . . precisely," said Malcolm allowing the comment to hang over the table like his cigar smoke.

"Ah! Yes," replied the general. "I do hope you will take tea with us this afternoon, say four o'clock?"

Malcolm tilted his head and winked. "Yes . . . yes I gratefully accept your kind invitation."

He returned that afternoon with a box of imported Swiss chocolates and a stampeding imagination. I have no spur to prick the sides of my intent, save vaulting ambition, he thought to himself, as he bounded up the mansion's steps two at a time. True perhaps, but also true that he intended to make them all unimaginably wealthy and powerful and surely that justified some machination.

Malcolm left his cape and hat with a comely maid and was ushered by a butler into the parlor where Christine Russell and her mother sat on a high-backed divan. In front of them, on a polished pink marble table was a porcelain tea service and plates of cakes. He approached the two women, "Miss Russell, I hope you and you mother will receive this small gift in the spirit of friendship in which it is given," he said, bowing slightly and handing her the chocolates.

"Thank you, Mr. Douglas. May your friendship with our family be most happy and profitable. Have you been formally introduced to my mother?"

"I have not and I beg her pardon for the oversight. Mrs. Russell, I am charmed," he said taking her extended hand. "Your daughter's beauty and charm are exceeded only by your own."

"Thank you, Mr. Douglas," she said pouring a cup of tea for him.

"RS Prussia?" he asked indicating the tea service.

"I beg your pardon?"

"The service set, RS Prussia is it not?"

Mrs. Russell could barely disguise the surprise in her voice. "Why yes it is. How did you know? Other than my close personal friends I've never had anyone else recognize it."

"I gave my mother an almost identical set for her last birthday."

"Is it true, as Simon tells us, that you are descended of English nobility?"

"Ah no, he's being too kind . . . Scottish, Thomas Douglas the Earl of Selkirk."

"We're most impressed, aren't we Christine?"

"Yes, we certainly are. My father says that the two of you may be concluding a business arrangement?"

Douglas glanced up at the old general who had just entered the room and replied, "I fervently hope so. I believe that it's a proposition which could bring us all immense good fortune."

"Let us drink," interrupted General Russell, "to the ultimate success of our joint venture and mutual interests."

After tea, Russell and his wife discretely exited the parlor for the adjoining study to ostensibly discuss arrangements and staffing for a midwinter charity ball. Malcolm noticed the double doors connecting the study to the parlor were left slightly ajar. At their exit, he quickly seated himself next to Christine on the love seat. She reacted equally as quickly by repositioning herself to the other end.

"I hope you don't think me too forward," he said, turning toward her on one haunch and bringing his legs beneath himself to spring from his seat if demanded by decorum, "but I do so hope that my alliance with your family can be even more securely joined by an amiable association between you and me."

"Possibly," she said, looking down demurely. "But you do realize that such things take time and must be comported with dignity."

"Yes, of course. I had nothing other than that in mind."

"If true," she said, raising her eyes to his, "then I'm sure my family and I would welcome you to our house . . . ah . . . frequently."

"I assure you, my intentions are strictly honorable," he said, sitting forward and placing his hand on hers with a tenderness that made her catch her breath ever so slightly. Malcolm noticed the tiny gasp. Her eyes darted toward the door of the study from which they could hear her parents' voices.

"Do be discrete, Mr. Douglas."

"Of course," he replied with a boyish grin. "Forgive me, your beauty evokes in me a nearly uncontrollable passion."

Christine blushed and giggled but also drew away her hand and stood. She turned her back to him and walked to the bay window. "I've never known any man as forward as you. Are you so passionate about everything?"

"No, only those things that truly matter to me. But, I see life as either a daring adventure or nothing at all. When we breathe our last breath we have nothing left but the experiences. One must attack the challenges of life."

"Am I a challenge?"

"Romance is the greatest challenge. All else in life is either leading up to it or away from it." He went and stood beside her. He stroked the lace cuffs of her dress and then let his hand fall around her waist as he leaned forward and quickly touched his lips to hers. She pressed back with her lips then gasped and retreated toward the door of the study.

"You're much too bold. Perhaps you should leave."

He shrugged but rang for his coat and hat. "I shall for now, but I give you fair warning, you've captured my heart and I possess great powers of resolve." He walked to the door where the maid stood with his garments.

"I'm giving a small party for some close friends Friday evening . . . could you come?" she blurted as he started through the door.

He stopped and cocked his head at her. He tipped his hat slightly and said, "Delighted."

❂ ❂ ❂

Douglas, true to his nature, made quick work of both Russells. By early spring he had secured a party of investors through the general, formed the MaxDouglas Mining and Transfer Corporation, and most importantly to his ultimate design — proposed marriage to Christine. They were married on the first day of June and on the second, Malcolm set out with the first wagon train of mining and construction equipment, supplies, and provisions and a small herd of twenty cows and heifers and a prize bull.

Before they had reached the site of his first permanent camp, he toppled the Gunnison town sign and erected a new and bigger one which read: "Town of Gunnison Colorado Population 20." By midsummer his crews had damned and diverted the stream above the box canyon falls which veiled the quartz vein and had begun mining operations. The diverted water disappeared into a fissure which, Douglas and his engineers thought, must join somewhere with one of the Gunnison River tributaries. No matter, it no longer inhibited mining operations.

❁ ❁ ❁

The town of Gunnison grew quickly from a cluster of white canvas tents to log cabins and then, thanks to the mine's sawmill, to clapboard houses and store facades. General Russell commanded, from Denver, a logistic and supply system which provided a steady stream of wagons carrying basic food supplies, whiskey, and mining and milling equipment into the valley during the summer and transported out tons of high grade ore. Malcolm's prized herd grew fat and flourished on the valley's thick grass. In the late summer he left the mine to personally lead a crew of grumbling miners into the heavy bottomlands to scythe and glean mounds of grass for winter fodder. His normally lithe body became piano wire taut. Trousers which had fit snugly in Denver now hung loosely from his suspenders. On the infrequent occasion when he shaved, he barely recognized his own visage. His face had become narrow, burned dark from working in the sun without a hat. He resembled a bird of prey. His thick sandy hair was now sun-bleached light blond and, uncut for months, surrounded the face like a lion's mane. I'd not be welcome at the royal court looking like this, he thought and smiled at himself. "Good God!" he could hear the general sputtering, "the man looks like a common laborer." He looked at his hands, callused and scarred from pick, shovel, and scythe and could imagine his young, tender wife's reaction to their touch. She would be repelled. No matter, there were others on Larimer street who for a few dollars wouldn't be. The thought reminded him that he must be making preparations for his return to mollify his fat investors.

For the men who would remain behind for the winter, game needed hunting, the rivers fished, the meat smoked and dried. Remembering the catastrophic experience of the Smith Party, he sent word to Denver to freight nothing to Gunnison other than food for the winter from now until the snow closed the pass and to recruit men willing to spend the dark days of winter in the mountains. To his laborers he offered a premium for those who would brave the cold and doubled the wages of those willing to become cowboys for the duration of the season to protect the precious herd.

Happily, the first light snows didn't arrive until early in November, providing them with almost an extra month to prepare for departure. Wagons were loaded with trail supplies and the all-important crushed gold quartz. Only the strongest and healthiest mules were selected for the trip. They left on an early mid-November morning beneath a leaden sky pelting them with snow granules. At the foot of Buffalo Pass the granules changed to wet flakes. An attempt to cross the pass in the darkness, relying on the mules' memory of a journey most of them had made often, ended in failure; the moonless night and driving snow punished them to a halt. The mules were fed by torchlight, and the men clustered beneath blankets and oilskins around small fires or candlelight under wagons and gnawed on elk jerky.

Near panic strangled Malcolm's normal exuberance. He choked on the vivid remembrance of being trapped in the snow, his body being devoured by its own gnawing hunger, no food, fuel, or shelter. He thought of frozen limbs and cannibalism. He huddled, buried beneath his blankets, awake and shivering, searching the black night sky for the glimmer of a star which might mean clearing weather.

Dawn broke cold but fair, and the troop jubilantly boiled coffee and downed hardtack and jerky before harnessing the mules and winding their way along the ruts through the willow-tangled ravine leading over the pass. "Weren't an easy night," remarked one of the skinners to Malcolm, a man nearly as young as he was.

"I've seen worse, a lot worse," retorted Douglas caustically. "If such scares you, perhaps you should endeavor to find a safe, indoor job."

The young man blinked at the attack. "I reckon that's true enough. I'd probably be better off working inside."

Malcolm's chin fell to his chest in embarrassment. "If you'd like, I'll find you a job in one of my wagon factories when we get back to Denver."

The boy brightened and grinned. "I'd like that jus' fine Mr. Douglas. I do thank you."

Chapter 9

My Dearest Sister:

Please forgive me for being remiss in my correspondence to you. If I can recall correctly, I haven't written since the drive north from Texas, and certainly a lot has happened since then. Savage death lurks around each bend in the trail out here and I am lucky to have survived when others close to me did not. Moreover, I have been doubly blessed. I am now married to a wonderful, beautiful woman possessing great vigor, endurance and an adventurous spirit.

I recently came into a small sum of money, through no effort on my part, which we are using to move to Colorado where it is my intention to set up my own freighting business. We had planned originally to go to the San Juan Mountains in deep Southwestern Colorado, but my partner wrote me just before we left Hays, Kansas, saying that because of possible Indian trouble we needed to go farther north, to a mountain valley town called Gunnison. We are in fact, on our way there even as I write this. I will mail it at our next stop. Please be patient. I will write again as soon as I can.

Your Brother, Doc

About the same time Doc Shores had been struggling to survive the rigors of the frontier between Montana and Kansas, John Malcolm Douglas was fighting a much different, but equally important battle in Denver, Colorado. The ultimate outcome of both contests would be a fateful meeting between the two men in the Colorado mountain town of Gunnison.

"No! I won't dissolve the trust." Eileen's eyes flashed white-hot. "I'm shocked you'd even ask, Johnny." Her chin jutted out pugnaciously. "I'll not go back to livin' in a cabin on Cherry Creek and takin' in washin' for a livin' if you go back up there and get yourself killed."

"I'm not goin' to get myself killed. Without that money there'll be no mine and no ranch." He took his mother's hand and led her to a couch. "I'll will all my holdings to you before I go. I'll build you a castle on a hill."

"Johnny," her eyes softened, pleading, "I don't need a castle on a hill, I don't need half of Colorado Territory. I need my son. Come back to Denver and pick up on your business. They're all good profitable businesses. Be happy with your wife and raise a family. Johnny, your father died to atone for bein' a rich man's bastard; don't let that be your legacy."

"I . . . we could be rich, wealthier, and more powerful than your wildest dreams."

"I don't need, I don't want to be rich and powerful . . . and I don't want to see your ambition destroy you."

"Mother, I need that money. I've made promises, commitments. . ."

"Yes! And one of them, your first commitment, was to see to my welfare, my care. I'm not going to let you run out on that promise. Johnny, come here." She patted the couch next to her, but he remained standing. "What about your wife, Christine? For God's sake, don't take her up there; it'll be the ruin of both of you. Stay here in Denver and buy your own house and move out of that mausoleum Maxwell Russell calls a home. It's time the two of you had your own home and started a family. It's not good, the two of you living there."

He waved her off with a flick of his wrist. He continued pacing about the room with his head down. "Children and a family aren't in the cards right now. I've got other things to do first."

"Have you talked to her about your plans, I mean to move to Gunnison?"

"No, not yet."

"Don't you think you should?"

Another wave. "It's of no consequence. She'll do what I tell her."

"Such talk! And you barely married."

"Mother, spare me. It's a marriage of convenience. I need the general and his connections, and he needs an ambitious son-in-law who will provide wealth and power for his daughter and progeny." Malcolm saw the pain in his mother's eyes and weakened. He sat beside her and put his arm around her shoulders. "I'm sorry. I don't mean that I don't love Christine too, but realities have to be addressed."

"Have you ever considered what she wants or needs?"

"I know what she wants. She wants to go on living as she is accustomed to living and have wonderfully smart and beautiful children who will grow to be rich and powerful as well. She wants that for her grandchildren too. I can give her, give them all that, but first I need the trust money."

Eileen dodged his embrace. She stood and walked across the room. "No," she said, "just no. That's my final word."

❁ ❁ ❁

"No! I'll not move! Castle or no!" Christine bolted naked from beneath the bedclothes and then realizing it, tried to cover her breasts and tiny black thatch with her hands and arms. She turned her back and edged toward a robe lying on the floor. Malcolm barely heard her. The amber glow of the fireplace reflected from her white body distracted him. He propped himself up on the pillows and took a large gulp of brandy from a glass on the night table.

"You'll move," he said matter-of-factly.

"Not on your life." Then pleading with him, "please, do be reasonable. My family and friends are in Denver. I have social obligations."

"You have an obligation to your husband that supersedes all else." The spell was broken and he too rose and dressed. "I won't expect you to move immediately. It will take some time, perhaps a year or two, before construction of the initial phase of the manor can be completed. It will provide you with sufficient time to draw yourself up to the occasion, get used to the idea, so to speak."

"Not likely. Not in years. Not in centuries, nor eons," she yelled.

Malcolm stopped dressing. His heart raced when he saw her long legs outlined by the firelight through her diaphanous robe. His breaths came quick and shallow, from both anger and passion. He felt flushed in the heat of the room. He was upon her in two quick strides, and reaching out pulled her to him with a handful of her long brown hair. When she attempted to call out he crushed his mouth against hers and silenced her. She attempted to struggle. Her arms flailed helplessly against his cable-taut shoulders. He whirled her around and forced her, face down onto the bed. In seconds he was inside her. She gasped and cried out in pain which only produced greater brutality. He was disappointed when, at last, she surrendered and went limp in his grasp.

Christine defied all Malcolm's attempts to draw her into conversation at the dinner table that evening, looking down at her plate and answering simply "yes" or "no." Instead, Malcolm carried on an animated conversation with the general about the mine and next season's plans while the two women eyed each other in solemn silence. After dinner, over cigars and brandy, the general winked at Malcolm and leaning close whispered, "What think you about a trip to Mattie Silk's?"

"Yes," Douglas whispered back. "Yes, I suppose I could do with some recreation." The two women excused themselves and bustled from the dining room. The men called for their coats and hats. "Don't forget," Russell reminded him, "we have a stockholders meeting of the MaxDouglas Mining and Transfer Company tomorrow evening. I do hope you'll have many good surprises for them."

"Surprises aplenty," assured Malcolm. "The ore has been certified at over $400 per ton. The Consolidated Virginia, which was considered to be almost ten times as much as the average Comstock assay, was assayed at $380 per ton."

The general's eyes widened. He raised his glass. "To my exceptional son-in-law."

Malcolm saluted the general with his brandy snifter. Your exceptional son-in-law indeed, he thought. I can only begin to imagine the pariah dog I would have been had I delivered anything less. But your descendants, to whom this bounty will flow, will carry the name Douglas, not Russell. He felt the old general slipping. Maxwell had spent his allotted amount of time basking in his wealth and power, very little of which, Malcolm observed, he had acquired honestly. Now it was Douglas' turn, and he would be no less ruthless.

❁ ❁ ❁

Winter still lay heavily upon the Colorado's Front Range when Malcolm began receiving the first rail cars of steam engines for the mine hoists, cable, pipe, explosives, and drills. He carefully catalogued each item and stacked it in a corner of the nearby stockyards. He rented a warehouse where he stockpiled flour, corn, lard, candles, lanterns, whiskey, nails and hand tools, coffee, beans, and bacon. His own factories produced dozens of wagons reinforced with iron and hardwoods to make them sturdy enough to plow though the late mountain snows and rocky trails. Miners, carpenters, and mechanics were recruited from the Denver streets. From the ranches he handpicked a select group of cowboys, barroom brawlers, and jailbirds for their physique, endurance, marksmanship, and loyalty. He armed them with the latest Winchester rifles and Colt revolvers. Douglas knew that once the word about the rich strike in the Gunnison Valley made its way along the Front Range and then back East, the valley would be under siege and he would need a personal army to fend the carrion eaters off.

"I don't know if they'll scare anyone else," Simon remarked to Malcolm as they viewed the men collecting their weapons, "but they sure as hell scare me. I'm damn glad it's you what has to keep 'em in line and not me. I wouldn't want to be 'tween a one of 'em and any gold, or anything else of value for that matter."

Douglas agreed that he had never seen a scruffier bunch in his life. While he wasn't exactly afraid of them he also knew that not a one would hesitate to kill him for the nickel in his pocket.

"Not to worry Simon. I've found another who's more'n a match for the lot of 'em."

"Indeed. Well then, I'd say you've recruited no less than the devil himself."

"Close, an Irish pugilist named Stryker McQue. I saw him give O'Ryan the licking of his life at Muldoon's a few nights ago. Never seen a man so handy with his fists. If he's half as good with a gun we'll have no problems with this bunch. Looks the part too. Black Irish, made of piano wire and tram cable. The man's stare alone could kill. If I'm the shrewd judge of men that I think I am, he'll tame the lot of 'em quickly."

"And what does he get in return for bein' thrown to the lions?"

"A magnificent salary plus concessions for the gambling, saloons, and whores in Gunnison." Malcolm continued, noticing Simon's raised eyebrows, "I consider him worth every penny of it."

"Well, I'll certainly leave you that part of it." Simon shifted uncomfortably. "The real reason I'm here . . . some of the stockholders . . . not me, you understand, but some of the others, have been querying about your share of the investment."

"What of it?"

"Only that there hasn't been any. You've invested nothing and still are listed as the majority stockholder. Are there problems with your mother?"

"No, of course not. By the way, did you draft my mother's will?"

"The department's attorney."

"You have seen it?"

"Yes."

"In substance, what does it state?"

"Not much really. You're the sole heir."

"Well, just curious. I won't detain you any longer."

Simon maneuvered his ponderous weight toward the staircase. The banisters shuddered and creaked in his hands. "My regards to your lovely young wife. How is she?"

"Marvelous," Malcolm replied dryly. Barren as the badlands, he thought. I've mounted her enough to spawn litters, and she still shows me nothing! "We'll have you for dinner some evening."

"Not dress I hope. I fear I've outgrown even my most recently acquired dinner costume." Simon wheezed as he lowered himself one step at a time.

"Always — the Russells always dress for dinner."

The rains came early, often, and heavy that spring in the head waters and tributaries of the Platte and Cherry Creek. The mountainsides, denuded of their grass by herds of cattle and of their forests by mining and lumbering, quickly became saturated. The sandy soil with no roots left to hold the water tumbled into the drainages. Creeks became streams, streams became rivers and rivers became muddy, raging torrents. The MaxDouglas men worked day and night, ankle-deep in muck and pelted by a cold drizzle, preparing for their departure, and they watched apprehensively as the Platte devoured its banks and crept ever closer.

Malcolm, foreseeing disaster, ordered equipment and supplies transferred to the west side of the flow. Soggy mules, oxen, horses, and men were marshaled to pull or carry the tons of lumber, pipe, steam engines, stamps, food, whiskey, and personal belongings across the flooding river before the bridge was swept away, trapping them on the east bank unable to move until late summer. The closest bridge was composed of two spans of approximately equal length and supported in the center by pilings planted precariously into a gravel bar. The bridge swayed, creaked, and groaned ominously as each wagon load of equipment crossed. The rain-swollen cascade beneath it was now filled with tons of debris, trees, animals, and even an occasional person. Men ran and whipped their animals across the first span to the center pilings and stopped to catch their breath and rewind their courage, all the time Malcolm's shouts and curses hurrying them along, although he took none across himself.

Stryker McQue, his coal black hair hanging across his forehead in wet ringlets, called out, "The bridge'll not hold much longer. It's like walkin' the deck of ship in a storm." Instead of caution and hesitation, it provoked Malcolm to further urgings. The last of Stryker's cowboy crew had gathered the few remaining items into a wagon and started across when the span on the near bank began collapsing, and they ran for the other side only to be confronted with the same thing on the far bank. Within seconds men and mules were isolated on the center of the span waving and yelling for help.

Douglas, who always considered himself the man of action, watched paralyzed with indecision. Stryker sprang forth. He tied a rope about his waist and headed upstream of the deadly flow ordering Malcolm to tie the other end to something solid downstream. He ran as far as the length of rope would allow, and dove in, arms and legs churning a chocolate froth. Malcolm recovered from his astonishment at being ordered into action by an employee and raced for one of the last remaining railroad tie fence posts at the top of a slight rise abreast of the island. He drew the rope as taut as he could around the post and tied it off. Stryker had already reached the island and tied his end of the rope to what was left of the bridge railing. He began ushering men to the rope. Some he had to push and kick from their platform, but one by one they scrambled over the raging water. McQue paused only long enough to cut the stock from their harness and then went hand over hand to the bank. When he reached it the men he'd saved caught him before he'd even let go of the rope and carried him to safety. Douglas stood watching the remainder of the bridge and mules being swept downstream as the bridge totally collapsed.

"I couldn't find a bridge intact all the way up to the Cherry Creek confluence," Malcolm told Stryker that evening when he returned. The men had built a bonfire from what dry wood and railroad ties they could find and were sitting or lounging about it in their steaming underwear while their clothes and boots dried on a forest of forked willow branches. "I fear we're stuck on this side for a bit. About all we can hope for is that the storms to the south let up so the bridges can be rebuilt or solid footing for a ford can be found."

Stryker nodded. "I'll shelter and provision the men on this side. Those on the other side have all the tents and food supplies so we won't have to be worryin' about them. I'll get word to them somehow what we're up to."

As he spoke, one of the men, a black cowboy who Stryker had earlier saved, approached in his grimy and drooping woolen underwear. "I'd be pleased if the two of you wou' join me in a drink." He offered the two men tin cups of whiskey. The black cowboy turned toward Stryker and raised his tin cup in a salute. " . . . To a man to cross rivers with."

The three downed their portions in single gulps. Malcolm choked back a gasp, eyes watering profusely as the nearly pure alcohol seared his throat. "I'll second that," he coughed. The cowboy lurched back to the bonfire waving over his shoulder.

"I'll be guessin' that's a compliment?" Stryker asked.

"I'd say so," replied Douglas. "I thought you'd have to beat that bunch into submission one by one, but I dare say that now they'll follow you into Hell and spit in the Devil's eye."

"Well, I'll be gettin' back to the fire," said Stryker.

"Were you able to save your personals?"

"Nay, on t'other side — if I'm lucky."

"Come home with me, at least for the night. We'll get everyone outfitted again tomorrow."

"I'm beholden to you, Mr. Douglas, but I think it's best if I pass the time and share a wee drop or two with the lads here." Stryker turned and walked back to where the men were now singing. Malcolm braced himself against the cold wind and the sting of envy. "Perhaps then you'll dine with us sometime!" he yelled.

McQue looked back over his shoulder. "I'll be happy to do just that."

❁ ❁ ❁

"He will not. Out of the question! I won't hear of it!" Christine spat. "I will not have a common Irish saloon fighter in my house."

"For once I must agree with her," said General Russell blowing a smoke ring toward the ceiling of the parlor. "Wouldn't do anything for our community standing to let it be rumored we were on social terms with the downtown riffraff, and what's more, we don't need our fellow investors thinking it."

"Not likely," replied Douglas. "A quiet dinner, just the five of us."

"But, what in the world for?" asked Mrs. Russell, her hand quivering as she refilled her tea cup. "Why would you want to invite him to dinner?"

"Rapport. This man will be my closest and most trusted associate when we're in the mountains. We will be living, working, eating, and drinking together."

"And whoring," interrupted Christine.

Malcolm shot her a withering glance but continued within the same breath. "We need to establish close ties."

"Goes against the basic principles of military command to fraternize with one's underlings," huffed the general. "Disrupts the chain of command and undermines authority. When I was a commander . . . "

"When you were a commander," sneered Douglas, "Napoleon was at his mother's breast and the cavalry charge was thought to be tactically sound. This is not the army, and times change. His invitation stands." Russell glared. Douglas knew that only a few years ago the general would have personally thrown him out the door, but age and ill health now weighed him down. Russell glared but threw up his hands in a sign of resignation. Christine rose and bustled from the room. Malcolm knew he'd won an important round.

When the members of the Russell household gathered for breakfast the following morning the servants told them they had served Malcolm earlier, and he'd left saying that he was heading to the warehouse to assess the damage there. However, shortly after lunch a carriage arrived. Simon Levits rolled from it and puffed up the steps where he was greeted by the general himself.

"Simon, what a surprise, but slow down old fellow."

"Is Malcolm here?" the banker gasped.

"No. Went to the warehouse I believe."

"Curious," Simon gasped, "I was just there. His men hadn't seen him today. No matter, I bring bad news. Earlier this morning I went to his mother's house. He'd asked me to drop by some papers for her to sign. The maid who met me at the door was hysterical beyond comprehension. I finally got out of her that Eileen had apparently suffered some sort of seizure. I hastened to the bedroom where I found a doctor already in attendance, but too late. He informed me she had died, probably her heart."

"Good God!" sputtered Maxwell. His wife's and daughter's hands flew simultaneously to their mouths.

"So, you see I must find him." said Levits.

"Yes, of course," said the general. "Try the warehouses at the railroad yards. If he returns here we'll tell him."

The Russells had just seated themselves for dinner when the butler entered and announced there was a message for the general from Malcolm. Apparently Simon had found and informed him, because the note said that he was on his way to his mother's house.

The general had just gone to the door to hand the messenger a tip and send him on his way when Simon's carriage again pulled in front of the house and disgorged its portly passenger.

"Come in and calm yourself," said the general. "The messenger just arrived with a note from Douglas that he's heading to his mother's house."

"Oh! Thank God! Well, I won't go back there. If he wants the solace of company he knows where to come. Some prefer to be alone in their grieving."

"True enough," said the general, ushering Simon into the dining room. "Won't you stay and have a bite with us?"

"Very kind of you. I haven't eaten all day — maybe once or twice." He bowed to the two women. "Mrs. Russell, Mrs. Douglas. I may now stop long enough to offer my condolences."

"We are so glad you caught up to him."

"But I didn't, I have no idea how he received the news."

Malcolm, after deciding upon a firm date for crossing the Platte and beginning the trek west to the mountains, declared their last evening in Denver the proper time for the postponed dinner. Stryker, no more inclined to accept than the Russells were to invite, eventually acquiesced. He arrived promptly, carefully shaved with only a meticulously trimmed military mustache. When McQue removed his bowler hat and handed it to the maid, Malcolm was nearly shocked to see his long, black locks shorn and parted with pomade. The thin white remnants of ill-sutured fighting cuts scattered about his face still advertised his profession. Malcolm thought him particularly handsome and dapper in his rather crude tweed suit. Douglas had been put on notice that his employee would be politely but coolly welcomed, nothing more. But, introductions accomplished, none in the room were prepared for the pugilist's chivalrous, almost courtly manners.

"General," he said, his words nearly dripping with sincerity and missing entirely their Irish brogue, "I'm one of your most ardent admirers. I practically memorized your treatise on the development and protection of extended supply lines. In fact, it and your exceptional tactical presence at the Caldron in the Iron Triangle were the subject of my own graduate essay at Sandhurst."

The general, eyes wide, sputtered his thanks. Malcolm discovered his own chin practically resting on his chest. McQue turned unhesitatingly to

Mrs. Russell, commenting for some length on her youthful beauty and her diamond and emerald necklace which he correctly identified as having been designed and crafted by Karl Gustavoich Faberge. She breathlessly confirmed his assessment.

Finally arriving in front of Christine he bowed slightly and lifted her hand to his lips. "Mrs. Douglas, your husband talks ceaselessly of your beauty and charm, and I must say that he is a master of the understatement. Would you grace us tonight with a harpsichord piece or two?"

Christine was flustered. "Mr. McQue, I am charmed and would be honored to play for you later." Malcolm turned his back to the couple upon hearing an unusually melodic tone in his wife's voice. McQue turned to Douglas and asked if he might accompany Christine to the dining room. But before Malcolm could even nod his consent she had placed her hand on McQue's arm and together they entered the dining room.

"You did say you attended Sandhurst?" asked the general a bit incredulously during the soup course.

"Yes, Sir, I did indeed, not only attended but matriculated and served in Her Majesty's Fifth Royal Irish Lancers." He glanced around the table, and appearing to have everyone's attention, he continued. Gone was the accent and reticence that marked Malcolm's first conversations with him. "You'll be wonderin' how a callow Irish farm lad came to graduate from Sandhurst, become an officer and a gentleman and end up fightin' in Casey Muldoon's Saloon? Not all that complicated really. My father served nobly with Cardigan at Balaclava and was awarded an Earldom in Ireland."

"You're an earl!" exclaimed Christine.

Malcolm came abruptly back in his chair, his soup spoon suspended in mid-stroke.

"No . . . but I'm brother to one. The firstborn males may have inherited the empire, but it grew because of the second, third, and fourth. I suppose we latter succeeding progeny might consider ourselves more fortunate in a way. We were forced from the nest to explore the world and colonize, much more interesting than sequestering oneself in a dreary old manor. I probably would have retired a squire with a high commission, but I engaged in a contest of honor with a fellow officer and gentleman."

"A duel?" inquired the general.

"Aye."

"Over a woman?" blurted Christine now wide-eyed.

"Nay, nothing that romantic, a wee bit of name callin." Anyway, I advanced my personal cause but was forced to exit the country to save my neck. I'd developed a talent for fisticuffs as a lad and later at Sandhurst so I decided to profit by it in America. The land of opportunity eh, Malcolm?"

Unaccustomed to such familiarity, Douglas frowned in reply. "I would never have guessed your lineage from our first conversations," said Malcolm dryly.

"No, in my trade I've found it wiser to resume my more humble mannerisms and speech, at least until I know to whom I'm speaking."

"Quite astounding!" Maxwell bellowed, and raising his glass toward Stryker, toasted, "to the latest and perhaps the most incredible member of the MaxDouglas partnership." The ladies raised their glasses in unison. Malcolm hesitated and then mutely raised his glass to his lips.

"Well," said Christine gaily, "we are indeed blessed to be in the company of so much nobility, or rather," turning an eye to Douglas, "near nobility."

"How so?" inquired Stryker.

"Why my dear husband of course. Are you not aware he too is descended from nobility?"

Malcolm felt his face grow hot and heard his heart pounding in his ears. He leveled a dark scowl at his wife. He hoped it would forestall her commenting further.

"Yes." she continued. "Malcolm's father was the son of Scottish nobility. Who was it dearest?" Her voice fairly dripped venom.

Silence blanketed the table as Malcolm studied his wine glass. Stryker looked at him, head cocked inquisitively.

"Thomas Douglas, Earl of Selkirk," he muttered.

"Father of the Red River Colony," chimed in McQue. "But as I remember it, he died in Scotland without a male issue."

"Or," offered Christine in a tone that fairly tinkled, "at least without legitimate male issue."

It was Stryker's turn to be taken off guard, and he quickly averted his gaze from Douglas to Christine and then to his soup. "Excellent mushroom soup," McQue commented to Mrs. Russell. "But where are you able to obtain mushrooms this early in the season?"

Mrs. Russell, a woman accomplished at smoothing over social contention, as were most society matrons, quickly responded that they were grown in a basement room adjacent to the wine cellar under closely controlled temperatures. Picking up on the theme, Stryker inquired further about the care and feeding of mushrooms, Mrs. Russell's greenhouse/herbarium and a variety of horticultural topics while the general gulped wine and the Douglases exchanged burning stares.

When the company had finished dessert Malcolm expected, as was customary, the general to rise and invite the men into his study for cigars and brandy. But tonight the old man complained of gout and asked to be excused early. As he departed the room he motioned to Malcolm with a shift of the eyes and a slight tilt of the head. Malcolm excused himself as well and accompanied the old man to the study. Once inside Maxwell closed the heavy oak door and settled himself gingerly on the settee. "You're a shrewd judge of men Douglas. I think this McQue could prove invaluable to you . . . to us."

"Could?"

"He's strong and smart, maybe even smarter than you." The corners of Russell's eyes crinkled. "I and my colleagues have many vested interests in this venture, a mine, a railroad . . . my daughter and progency."

Malcolm stared a hole through the general's forehead but said nothing.

"You've got damn near everything tied up in this as well. McQue will serve our interests but he's no fool and the time may come, if you give him the chance, that he will look you straight in the eye while stripping you naked."

"He'll die tryin'," said Malcolm evenly.

Maxwell nodded thoughtfully. "Or you will . . . Tell me then, what are your plans for tomorrow and from there on?"

Malcolm told him of the plans to cross the Platte early the next morning, mobilize the men, animals, and equipment without delay on the other side and head for the Gunnison, first south and then west through Buffalo Pass. He wanted to move quickly and begin building, mining, and smelting before winter closed in again come October or November. "I hope to have enough progress made on my own house that I can move Christine there the following season. We should also have the foundations of a town laid."

"For my part," said Russell, "I will be sending out several surveying parties within the next few days to reconnoiter a rail route. Christine? Moving out with you? What did she say to that?"

"She was quite excited. Couldn't wait to be off."

The grandfather clock in the atrium chimed ten when there was a knock at the study door and Mrs. Maxwell entered. Malcolm rose and addressed the two of them. "I'm sorry, time escaped me. I didn't realize the hour. I should be seeing to my guest."

"Needn't hurry," Mrs. Russell said coolly, "Your wife is entertaining Mr. McQue." With that she vanished into her private boudoir adjoining the bedroom. The general cast a meaningful look toward Malcolm who excused himself and quickly departed.

From the hallway he could hear voices and laughter coming from the parlor. He instinctively slowed his pace and softened his footfalls as he neared the room. He leaned closer to the door to hear what was being said. His wife laughed heartily. Malcolm frowned. He didn't know that he'd ever heard her laugh like that. He bent forward and tried to hear what was being said. Suddenly there was someone beside him, and he jerked to attention nearly hitting Carrie the maid and causing her to drop the tray of sweet breads she was carrying.

"Oh! I'm terribly sorry, Mr. Douglas. I thought you heard me coming."

"No . . . no I, uh . . . didn't. Do be more careful!" Malcolm quickly composed himself and followed the maid into the parlor. Christine and McQue were seated on a love seat with their backs to him. They immediately rose when he entered. Carrie set the tray down on a low table, bowed, and left, but gave Douglas a puzzled look as she departed.

Christine demurely walked to her husband's side. "Darling," she bubbled, "Stryker . . . Mr. McQue . . . has just been telling me some of the most amusing stories of his adventures in Africa and Asia."

"I dare say," replied Malcolm. "Well, I think we are keeping McQue up far too late, and myself for that matter." Nodding toward Stryker, he said, "We'll be needing to arise well before dawn to take advantage of as much daylight as possible tomorrow . . . don't you agree Stryker?"

"I do indeed. Please convey my thanks to the general and his wife for a lovely evening. I'll collect my hat and coat from the maid and be off." He leaned toward Christine, and she offered him her hand and hurried off. Malcolm escorted his employee to the door where they wished each other good night.

Later, Malcolm lay on his back in bed listening to his wife's deep breathing and staring into the dim, flickering lamp flame, until well past the hallway clock chiming twelve. The old general's admonitions about the Irishman echoed in his head. He knew he could fire Stryker at any time and find another overseer easily enough, but he also knew he wouldn't do it. No, when the time came the two of them would have to go toe-to-toe, winner take all.

Chapter 10

The fuming black locomotive of the Denver and Rio Grande Railroad cleaved through the humid summer air of the eastern slopes of the Colorado Rockies, belching swirling clouds of black smoke and scalding white steam which wilted the orange Indian paint brush and blue wild iris along the tracks. Male passengers fingered their sweat-stained collars and stuck their dripping faces into the sooty breeze of the car's open windows. The women stole away from the flying cinders to the far dark corners of the car and fanned themselves furiously like butterflies with tiny wings. They all gazed longingly to the west, to the snowfields of Pikes Peak which sparkled and glistened in the sun.

A swarthy man with thick black hair and mustache grew tired of their complaining. These same people in a few short months would be complaining of the cold and praying for this heat and humidity. But then it was not in his nature to complain about anything. Complaining of the weather seemed to him especially futile. He contrasted the warm mountain air to that of Kansas and Texas in the summer and thought it sparkling and refreshing. He remembered vividly his stiff, frozen limbs in a plains blizzard. He settled back in his seat behind the window post to hide his face from the sun.

The woman in the seat opposite him was small, compact, perhaps even spare by some standards. She slept and dreamed. Her eyelids flickered and her cheeks twitched as her face passed from shadow to sun with the curving of the train. Her cheekbones were high and aristocratic looking, her mouth, small and delicate and firm. She had pulled back her hair, bleached blond by weeks of travel in the sun, tightly from her face. The tiny loose curls at her temples glistened with sweat. He wondered how she could sleep so soundly, undisturbed by the heat and noise and smoke. Looking at her he felt contentment and happiness which he had never expected from marriage, or life for that matter. I hope, he thought, she dreams of green mountain meadows, shady streams and cool breezes from fields of melting snow.

Gradually, as they traveled farther south, Pikes Peak dominated the western horizon. To his left, out the east windows of the car, the brown and tan prairie sand hills flowed to the horizon beneath puffy white clouds. The passengers crowded away from it toward the mountains on the right side. The man tried to sleep, but being accustomed to the silence of the plains and woods, the chugging, screeching, and rocking of the train allowed him only to close his eyes and daydream.

Wrenched from his reverie by the screech of the train's brakes, the man sat bolt upright and looked out the window. He looked down onto the dusty streets of Pueblo, Colorado, cooling beneath lengthening mountain shadows. He looked to the woman. She rubbed the sleep from her eyes. Passengers, their backs and armpits darkened with sweat and soot, bolted from the torment of the train only to step out into ankle-deep adobe powder. The man and woman scuffed up a buff-colored cloud on their way to the station platform. The man pivoted his head until he glimpsed a familiar figure slumped on the seat of a buckboard, his chin resting on his chest. Beside the figure sat a panting black and white dog with a white patch over one eye. The man guided the woman toward the wagon. The dog stood as they approached, its ears pricked, stubby tail flying. He snapped his fingers. The dog catapulted itself onto the back of the slumped form and off the wagon toward the man and woman. The person on the wagon jerked up abruptly, swearing, arms waving. He looked to where the man and woman were petting the dog and broke into a toothless grin.

"Moots," said the man on the ground, "it's a good thing we left you with a reliable dog."

"Doc, while you been on a holiday train ride, I been workin' my fingers to the bone gettin' things ready here. Would have done a darn sight better 'cept for takin' care o' that mutt of yours. Howdy, Mrs. Shores."

"Catfish, it's good to see you again," Agnes said bending down and taking the dog's head in her hands. She looked up and winked at the old codger, "and you too, Benton."

"How about wrapping your bony fingers around those reins and getting us to a hotel?" asked Shores. As Doc helped Agnes onto the seat beside Moots he saw another familiar shape. "Good God," he exclaimed, "you still have my old Thunderbolt?"

"I do. Can hit somethin' almost every tenth shot, if it ain't too far away or movin' too fast, which is better than I can do with anything else, and that's good 'nuf for me. Ammunition is hard to find though. I musta reloaded some of those old copper cases near twenty times."

"You best be careful of this thing," said Doc, picking up the weapon and examining its cracked stock which had been repaired with a wrap of crudely sewn rawhide. "They became notorious for exploding in people's faces."

Moots laughed. "Can't hurt this one any morn's already been done."

Moots drove Doc and Agnes to the Columbine Hotel where they acquired a south-facing room, upon Moots advice, to take advantage of the evening breezes. They immediately changed from their salt-stained clothing, while Benton and Catfish retired to a notorious local hangout called the Buck Snort Saloon. By the time the three of them were reunited for dinner in the hotel's restaurant, Moots was in high spirits, challenging the headwaiter to a fight for prohibiting the suspiciously staggering Catfish from entering the dining room. Doc intervened and ordered the dog outside where she collapsed at the edge of the open front door and snapped at moths dropping from the hot globe of the lantern on the door frame.

When they ordered dinner, Doc and Agnes chose small meals of trout. Moots ordered an entire brisket of beef and ate so voraciously that Doc wondered, observing his nearly skeletal frame, if he'd had anything to eat since leaving Hays.

"Like I wrote you, I fig'rd on goin' southwest into New Mexico Territory but an old coot I met up with said that they's still Injun trouble down there and not much to offer in the way of prospectin' and minin'. He tol' me 'bout a place up northwest called the Gunnison that looked promisin'." As Benton described mountains laden with silver and gold, valleys knee-deep in grass and clover, forests thick with game, Doc noticed the story had apparently captured the interest of a large, handsome man at a nearby table pouring himself shots of whiskey. The man had a smooth clean-shaven face except for a neatly trimmed dark brown mustache, the ends of which dropped low, along his jaw. His hair was also a dark brown: thin, short, and straight. He wore the high-topped, mule-eared boots of a range rider. But it was his weapons that most attracted Doc's attention. His gun belt held two revolvers. His rifle, an unusual weapon, lay across the arms of the chair nearest him. Doc recognized it as a single shot rolling-block rifle with an unusually long half-round and half-octagonal barrel. A shrouded front sight was balanced by a vernier tang sight in the rear. Its ornately checkered stock was polished to a high sheen. He had seen only one other like it, a Remington Creedmor .45-70, an unusual rifle, heavy and cumbersome, seldom used except by professional hunters, since lever action repeaters were more sturdy and reliable. It's a rifle, Doc thought, only for a man with deadly intentions. On the table next to a whiskey bottle lay a coil of horsehair rope and another of thin rawhide strips which the man had been carefully braiding into a bosel and reins for a hackamore. The man's experienced fingers deftly plaited each hair, each strand, perfectly. Doc had seen many a cowboy along the Pecos trail practicing this, one of their favorite arts. But he had seen none better than this man.

When Moots mentioned the name Gunnison again, Doc thought it caused the man to turn his head more in their direction, but without looking at them. At length the man rose, glanced in their direction, donned a dusty black sombrero, picked up his braiding and departed. The drinks and dinner lay heavily in Doc's stomach. He felt very tired from their long journey. He interrupted Benton, suggesting that they continue their discussion at breakfast the following morning. Shores and Agnes left for their room leaving Moots trying to find the bottom of a whiskey bottle. Catfish slunk in and curled up beneath his chair.

"Did you notice that fella sittin' at the table behind Bent?" Doc asked Agnes when they got to their room.

"No, why?"

"He seemed to be takin' an uncommon interest in what Moots had to say about the Gunnison Valley. Had a long range huntin' rifle, but he's no hunter. Too many six-guns. There was also somethin' about the way he looked."

"Like what?"

"Well, I haven't seen a colder look to a man's eyes since Bill Hickok."

"Lawman?"

"More likely other side of the law — man." Doc joked.

Doc and Agnes sat again in the hotel dining room enjoying the cool early morning breeze blowing through the restaurant's white lace curtains. Moots careened through the swinging doors with another, equally disreputable-looking man in tow. Some years later a line from a poem by Robert Service reminded Doc of the man: " . . . he looked like a man with one foot in the grave and scarcely the strength of a louse." As they approached, Doc and Agnes quickly maneuvered their chairs toward the window to be upwind of both Moots and the stranger.

"Doc, Mrs. Shores, I want ya to meet the man I was telling you about last night." Doc and Agnes regarded him blankly. " . . . the man who'd been in the Gunnison. This here's Lee Edward Chaney."

"Lee's jus' fine," hissed the man through a tobacco and food-stained mustache that merged with an equally dirty beard. He thrust forward a hand so thin and greasy that it nearly slipped from Doc's grasp. Doc thought he made the gaunt Benton Moots look almost chubby in comparison. His bowed back evidenced years of hard labor and injury. His clothes, little more than rags, hung in folds from his skeletal frame. Frayed-rope braces drew his baggy canvas pants nearly to his chest.

Doc and Agnes nodded a greeting. Doc scooted back a chair with his boot for Chaney. Lee ordered half the menu and consumed plates of food like a pack of starving dogs. He combed drops of coffee, bits of eggs and biscuits from the long hairs of his mustache into his mouth with his grimy fingers. Breakfast tightened the man's pants and loosened his tongue. Lee launched into his life's story and that of the Gunnison country. Doc remarked later to Agnes that Chaney had been far too long without human companionship.

"Begin' your pardon ma'm," he began by addressing Agnes, "I couldn't help noticin' the merest hint of an accent, Virginia or Carolina?"

"Virginia," replied Agnes from behind a hanky she was holding to her nose, "but I attended school in South Carolina."

He nodded. "I was born and raised on a plantation outside Atlanta. Oh, we didn't own it. My father was the 'superintendent'. He was the slave overseer. It was truly a place of beauty, especially in the spring with the smell of lilacs and oleander." He paused and sampled the tainted air around him for a faint smell of the past. "Then came the war. I rode north to Richmond and served as a cavalry officer with Hampton and Stuart.

We were a dashin' lot . . . then came that day in April of '65 when we warn't nothin'. Grant said I could keep my sidearm and my horse and the clothes on my back. The Yanks gave me one solid meal and pointed me in the direction of Georgia. Sherman had been there before me and left me only a pile of bricks and bones and charcoal, so I headed west."

Chaney looked to Agnes. She nodded, understanding. He then took them on a rambling journey through Arkansas, Texas, Indian territories, and Kansas with wagon trains of homesteaders, cattle drives, freighters, buffalo hunters, prospectors, and miners.

"Then I met up with a gent named Bert Smith, a Mormon feller, in Denver one spring. He and another feller were fixin' to settle and farm the Gunnison Valley with a whole lotta followers from back in Iowa and Illinois. They's gonna build 'em a town, a town like Salt Lake City, and colonize and farm all the way from the Gunnison west into eastern Utah and make one great Mormon nation of it. None of us had any idea what we was gettin' into. That first winter the snow was hip deep on the level and so cold the branches at night cracked like rifle fire and fell off the trees. There warn't enough shelter, and the food we'd hauled up in the fall was gone by Christmas. The game had pretty much moved downhill to the west. By the end of January people were breaking off their own frozen fingers and toes and eatin' them. By March they were eatin' the dead and by April they were killin' each other for food. The pass didn't thaw out enough until the end of May for those who was left to walk back to Denver. I was lucky, I was one of 'em.

"One feller stayed, Smith's partner, a man named Douglas, John Malcolm Douglas. You could say he was one of those that turned durn ever' thing he touched to gold, least ways to start with. Well, he struck it rich that summer. He stayed on up there, and then he came back to Denver and got some others to buy into it with him. I heard he was hirin' so I joined on for the next season, that's how desperate a man can get sometimes. We did well next couple seasons; built a town, a mill and smelter, dammed a creek, opened a mine, built a red stone castle for Douglas, and started a cattle company. His house is a wonder, a castle. He had it moved all the way from Scotland stone by stone.

"My God! The gold was thick as the grass. The farther back we mined the thicker and richer the vein got. There was times it was assayed near to a thousand dollars a ton. Everybody was gettin' rich. Well, least ways Douglas and the stockholders were, but none of the workers complained neither. Douglas saw to it that every man was paid morn' fair for his work. He could afford to, he had things pretty well locked up in that valley. The MaxDouglas — General Maxwell Russell was his partner and father-in-law — Minin' and Transfer Company owned the valley, the town of Gunnison, the mine, mill, smelter, all the land, most of the businesses, the cattle, the freighting company, the toll roads . . . and the laws. Douglas hired an Irishman named Stryker McQue to command his own little army of cowboys and desperadoes. Their job was to keep the workers in line, keep the peace . . . most of all, to keep out any interferin' business interests, nesters, and the like. McQue also owned the saloons, gamblin' parlors, and whorehouses. A nice gentlemanly fella, if you're on his side. If not, I seen him near beat men to death with his fists, carve 'em with a sharp knife and shoot 'em down in the blink of an eye. One night we were stnadin' around outside the Columbine Saloon when this whore walks up to McQue with her old dog. 'Mr. McQue,' she says, 'Buck here's gettin' awful old and poorly. Some day would you take him down to the creek where it's nice and still and pleasant and end it quickly for him?' Well, faster'n I could flinch, McQue drew a long-barreled Colt .45 and shot the dog in the head. Ever'body near jumped out of their skins I reckon. That ol' whore commenced to screamin' and hollerin' and ran over and picked up the dog, all blood and brains and ran off into the night. McQue just looked at her and said somethin' like, 'I guess she didn't really want me to kill that dog.' Shit, even J.M. Douglas was scared of him, and Douglas warn't scared o' much o' nothin'.

"But Douglas, he also built houses for widows whose husbands had been killed in the mine or mill and he gave the money to build an orphanage and school in Denver for the children. Didn't have children of his own."

Lee stopped and drew a greasy leather poke on a thong from where it hung down the inside of his shirt and extracted a moldy lump of chewing tobacco. He sawed at it with the butter knife from the table. He cut two pieces, one for himself and one for Moots. He held up the vile-looking plug and motioned to Doc and Agnes, who both vigorously shook their heads.

"Well," he continued, "Douglas couldn't part the sea or hold the mountains on his shoulders forever. The linchpin of the whole minin' operation was the water . . . or rather disposin' of the water. That first year we dammed up the creek above the mine and scooted it off through a hole in the wall. It went underground and most of us thought it probably just went down valley and emptied out into the Gunnison River somewhere — but no one ever knew exactly where it ended up . . . that is until about three years ago.

"I was lucky . . . in a sense. I'd got out of the mine before it happened. I near broke my back when a timber splintered and a ceiling beam fell on me. They near gave up on me several times and could well have left me for dead. It's why I'm as crooked as a piece of bad road to this day. But Mrs.

Douglas and McQue took pity on me. They fixed me a place for me in the hayloft above the stalls in the barn and carriage house back of Douglas' house. I had a real lumber bedstead and a feather mattress and blankets and quilts and a china warsh basin and pitcher on a real dresser . . . first I'd seen since I'd left Georgia. Well sir, it was real cozy in that room, even with no fire — later they put in a stove — for another reason I'll tell you about. The barn was well built with thick red stone walls and heavy timber roof, like the castle, so that little cold air could get in and the heat from the animals down below came right up through the floorin', so there was mornin's, even in winter, when the water in the pitcher and basin didn't freeze.

"Mrs. Douglas'd come over three or four times a day with food and coffee and change my bandages and the bed linen, and when she found out I could read she'd bring me books aplenty. McQue saw to it that there was a shelf put on the wall near to the bed so's they could put a lamp on it and I could read at night. Well, wasn't long 'fore I'd regained my health and could get up and about, and Mrs. Douglas had one of the men go out and buy me some new clothes, and she gave me the job tendin' the Douglas's own horses and stalls so's I could go on makin' a livin' but not have to go back into the mine. Now Douglas himself never came over. Oh, he's a good enough feller I think. But I was told, when given to bouts of melancholy, he took to the bottle and the whorehouses. His wife was the very picture of kindness. But she hated Gunnison and the mountains and the cold and isolation. A tall, beautiful, gentle, woman with bright green eyes, she never smiled the whole time I knew her. She was always bustlin' off teachin' school or Sunday school or tendin' to somebody. Never saw her with Douglas neither.

"Well, I was pretty much doin' all right, kept to myself and tended to business. But then Mr. Douglas up and decides he wants to play polo, because that's what the landed gentry back in Britain do. He's a duke or somethin'. So's he goes out and gets a damn stable of polo horses and puts them in with the herd I got there already, and I can't keep up and I tell Mrs. Douglas so. Well, you can't get no self-respectin' cowhand or miner to come be a stable boy for no amount of money. So she hired a nigger boy to help me out. He belonged . . . well, he didn't, but his daddy once belonged to the kin of a woman whose family owned a bakery and brewery down the river a piece. The father was too old and feeble to really work for a livin' after the war so the part of the family up north in Colorado jus' kept him on and took care of him, sort of like an old dog. Well this nigger boy surprised me, real fine lad, hard worker and smart too. He was big 'n' strong. That boy could fork hay and clean stalls all day long and not stop to take a breath. They let him sleep up in the hayloft t'other side of me. He and I started takin' some meals together. I didn' cotton to it much at first, but he's a nice, polite nigger what knew his place and took orders jus' fine, and I didn' want to be amakin' trouble for myself anyway so I jus' kept my mouth shut.

"Well, it was about that time that I noticed somethin' goin' on. Mrs. Douglas kept bringin' food over real reglar-like. Oddly enough it got to be 'bout that same time that McQue would come by to look in on me. I seen the way they looked at each other when they's in the room together, so I'd mosey back on down to the horses and jus' leave the tray by the door for her to take back. You know, it got to be they'd spend mor'n an hour up there together, sometimes a couple times a day. That's when the two of 'em took a real special interest in my good health, like I's kin or a long, lost friend. They thought I needed a stove to warm the place up a bit. I 'spect it was to keep on my good side so's I wouldn't ev'r say anything to Douglas should I ever see him. Not much chance of that. He ne'r came around for even a minute and spent more and more time up at the mine . . . which is how I got started off in this direction in the first place."

Chaney's words had become little more than blubber. He sat up in his chair and looked about the room. Moots spied what he was searching for near the door. He got up and retrieved the stained, brass cuspidor for Chaney who then bent over it and disgorged such a volume of nearly black liquid that even Doc's stomach turned slightly.

"Well sir," Chaney continued, wiping globs of tobacco juice from his mustache and beard with the back of his hand, "we found out where all that water was goin' . . . it was agoin' into a well of sorts alongside that big vein. One day in the late spring when the snowmelt was at its peak, they blasted right into it and an ocean of water ripped through the mine. They's forty or so bodies washed out in the flood and at least that many what didn't make it out at all. Couldn't nobody get back to the diggings afore autumn, and when they did they found all the shoring timbers had been washed out and the shaft pretty much totally collapsed. Douglas brought in a crew of engineers who looked things over, and they told him that there was almost no way of opening up again 'cause there weren't no way to dam or divert the stream above where it went back in that fissure. By that time too, the vein had narrowed back down and petered out to the point where it wasn't gonna pay to open again. Didn't really matter to Douglas though, 'cause he'd taken his share and what his wife had inherited from her father and bought up the rest of the Gunnison drainage and the railroad right-of-way up from Denver."

"There's a railroad?" asked Doc.

"No. Not when I left, but I hear they's gonna be soon. Oh I reckon they's still plenty of freight haulin' to be done to the outlyin' mining towns and such if that's what you're interested in."

"What happened with Mrs. Douglas and Stryker McQue?" asked Agnes.

"Can't say precisely. When I got well enough, Douglas sent me out with the herds, made me a foreman though and raised my pay. I went back to livin' in the bunkhouse . . . sure got to like that room above the stables. Didn't actually see much of either of them after that." Chaney bent across the table and lowered his voice. "Rumor was, she'd had a baby. Don't know for sure 'cause there was another rumor that she was barren. I also heard she'd died. Jus' don't know for certain. They's a lot more rumors floatin' around. I heard tell that Douglas and McQue had words and came near to a real gun battle.

"Well, I left a few months later and went up into the San Juans — Ouray, Silverton, and Telluride, prospectin' and minin'. On my way I passed through the Los Pinos Agency and won a Ute woman, one of the Uncompahgre band, in a poker game. Never did know her name, so's I jus' called her Kate from someone I knew before. She couldn' speak English hardly t'all and I didn't speak Ute, but we both spoke some Mexican and got along. She were a good woman and could gut, skin, and butcher a deer or elk faster'n you could say 'scat', but she broke her ankle one winter checkin' the traps and froze to death. I did'n find what was left 'til spring. Bears had pret' near carried off most of her. I been alone ever since. Don't have much to show for a lifetime of hard work and misery 'cept for a lot of memories — good and bad." Chaney paused as though sorting through his catalog of memories. "Well, you folks still thinkin' about headin' up into the Gunnison?"

Doc looked at Agnes for a cue but could see none, then to Benton who was studying something on the floor intently. "I reckon so," he said. "We've come this far, I'm not inclined to turn back, nothin' to turn back to, and I don't have anywhere else in mind to go to."

"Gunnison'l treat you good long as you play by the rules."

"Rules?"

"Well, the rules according to Douglas and McQue. They really ain't no law 'cept for the occasional toady sheriff that Douglas puts in office. The law is whatever the two of them say it is and can back up. Like I say though, you stay on their good side and you'll get along jus' fine."

"You goin' back?" asked Moots.

"Nope, I fig'er I can pan me jus' enough gold to keep me alive a while longer, then I'm gonna find a place to hunker down and die, and the coyotes and crows can pick my bones clean."

Doc bought Chaney a bottle of good Kentucky whiskey and gave him another five dollars for a few nights' lodging and food. As they were preparing to depart, Chaney motioned Doc back to the table. "If you do go to Gunnison and need help there's a woman named Stevens who can help if you need it. Jus' tell her you know me." Chaney winked and nodded. Doc thanked him and rejoined the other two.

"What was that all about?" asked Agnes

"Drunk talk, just drunk talk."

None of the three had much to say after that. Doc was wondering if he and Moots had a similar end in store for them someday. He could only guess that his friend was wondering the same thing when Moots excused himself to go look after the stock and wagons. Doc noticed that he headed more in the direction of the Buck Snort Saloon, with Catfish in tow.

Agnes, as if reading his thoughts, said, "That was so sad. That man is living only a little better than an animal. Doc, promise me that no matter how bad things get, you won't end up like that."

Doc stopped and looked directly into his wife's eyes. "I promise you I'll never get beat. I may go down fightin' but not whuped."

They languished the remainder of the day in the hot shade on the hotel's porch swing watching the dust devils nip at the heels of nervous horses and catch playfully at women's skirt hems. They spent the evening in the long shadows of the cottonwood trees along the sluggish Arkansas River. The cicadas clicked and whistled all around them. Trout lurking in the eddies rose to a new hatch of winged insects. They walked hand-in-hand along the riverbank through the golden evening light sprinkled with galaxies of the tiny fluttering insects.

Doc reached out and snatched one of them in mid-air. "They've just hatched," he said. "Do you know that some flies like this hatch, breed and live out their lives within the span of one day? Not much time to have a life."

"Maybe, if you're a bug."

"Well, we're born, live and die same as them. You can bet that when your time comes it will have all seemed like a day. The difference is we know it, and this little guy doesn't, so we can do something with the time given us."

"Doc, why not just stay here and start up our own freighting business?"

He nodded. "Could just as easily I guess."

After a long pause she finished his thought, "but you don't want to, do you?"

"I reckon there's a part of me that does. I'm hankerin' real hard to settle down. I been pretty much on the move since I left Michigan . . . Lord! that seems like a thousand years ago. I'd like to make life a bit easier to live — for both of us. But this doesn't feel quite right. I can't explain it exactly, but I have this feeling that we're headin' in the right direction, and that we will find the right place and be there for a long time. I hope you'll bear with me on this."

Agnes nodded and took his hand in hers and squeezed it reassuringly. "I will, as long as you've got some kind of a plan for us. When I think you're just out there bouncing around for the heck of it, that may change quickly."

"Fair enough."

❂ ❂ ❂

The morning sun had not yet crested the rolling prairie hills to the east when two large, heavily laden freight wagons, each drawn by teams of six sturdy mules, rolled west through Pueblo's dusty streets. Doc and Agnes sat atop the first, Moots and Catfish the second.

The days remained hot and dry, but the nights became colder. White-tipped Blanca Peak to the north towered over sand dunes, scrub brush, and alkali salt pans. The pans were death traps for the unwary and inexperienced. Their thin, hot crust belied treacherously quicksand-like soft mud beneath. A team and wagon breaking through this crust anywhere but its outermost edge was doomed.

"Moots," Doc chided his partner one day, "you'd better get a shovel and collect a barrel or so of that desert mud so you can make half-way decent coffee later." It drew a dark look from the old cook and Doc immediately regretted the suggestion. He'd be checking his cup more closely from now on. Mostly the air hung in curtains of shimmering heat waves draped beneath sparse fluffy white clouds. Suddenly a sirocco would roar up the broad valley south from New Mexico carrying stinging, suffocating alkali dust, or monstrous tumbleweeds and even dead tree branches, panicking the mules. Just as suddenly, so suddenly they would still be yelling at each other, the sirocco having passed through the desert became hot and calm again. Doc recalled the Staked Plains.

They camped briefly outside old Fort Garland. Agnes bathed and washed clothes in the nearby Trinchera River. She did the same again at Alamosa on the Rio Grande. Their red clothes were now a dull rust; the yellows, buff and whites were brown. She yearned openly for clear, clean water. The blue and white mountains remained only a cool, distant promise. Agnes told of reading an incident written by Zebulon Pike. He'd seen a mountain from his camp on the eastern plains and it had appeared so close and so small that when he set out to climb it, he planned to be back within a day. Several days later his party returned, having not even reached the mountain, later known as Pikes Peak.

Doc and his companions turned right, to the north and headed toward the town of Saguache and the blue ridge of ten-thousand-foot Buffalo Pass. Saguache, although a county seat, was little more than a few adobe buildings clustered around a courthouse, but Saguache Creek did offer the luxury of relatively clean water. The heat rising from the valley sucked cool air from the pass down over them. They now felt closer to their goal.

Moots, after turning the mules out onto the clover along Saguache Creek, jubilantly began panning for gold while Agnes basked in the shade of some towering old poplars and Doc explored the village streets. A well-traveled wagon rut ran out of town and wound its way up through the sage and scrub oak disappearing into the cedars, pine, and spruce of the pass. Just beyond the outskirts of the town a rather small clapboard shack stood alone next to an aspen pole fence with a draw-bar gate. As he drew nearer Doc could see a man leaning back in a chair in the shade of the shanty's porch. A large, hand-painted sign was nailed to the side of the shack. At the top of the sign in large, white letters read:

> **Toll Road — Property of the MaxDouglas Mining and Transfer Company Trespassers will be apprehended, fined, and jailed.**

Below that read:

> **Schedule of Charges**
> Livestock other than cattle 50 Cents per head
> Cattle 10 Cents per head
> People One Dollar per person
> Wagons Five Dollars per wagon
> Commercial Carriers 1 Cent per pound

Doc read the sign and sauntered up to the man dozing on the porch. The man teetered precariously on the rear legs of the chair, his back resting against the boards of the cabin. Doc noticed, leaning against the wall of the cabin on either side of the man, a Winchester rifle and a shotgun.

"Howdy, name's C.W. Shores." Startled, the man dropped the front legs back to the porch with a loud thump and came half-up out of the seat. "Howdy," he said, straightening his sweat-stained straw sombrero to the top of his head. He didn't offer a name.

"Toll road, huh?"

"From here to Gunnison. Don't get many customers on foot or hoof, 'cause they can go over the pass otherwise and still get there. Most of our business comes from herds and freighters and settlers."

"Prices are a bit steep."

"Don't have nothin' to do with that. I jus' make sure that them that wants to use it pays accordingly. You want to talk prices you got to see Mr. J.M. Douglas."

"Heard of 'im. Where is he?"

"In Gunnison."

As they spoke, a large wagon loaded to the brim with crates, boxes, and machinery clanked up and squealed to a halt at the cross-arm of the gate. The man on the porch waved a greeting and shuffled out to unlock the gate and raise the crossbar. He exchanged conversation with the driver of the wagon and after locking the gate arm returned to his port on the porch.

"He didn't pay you," Doc said nodding in the direction of the departing wagon.

"Didn't have to. He's drivin' a MaxDouglas wagon."

"So Douglas owns the freighting company as well as the road?"

"Owns one of them, and it wouldn't make much sense to make him pay for the use of his own road, now would it?"

"S'pose not."

"Where you from?"

"Kansas."

"Where you headed."

"Gunnison area."

"Mine's closed down."

"So I heard. Doesn't matter, I'm not a miner."

"What you do?"

"Freighter maybe."

"Maybe's right. You want to haul freight in and out of Douglas and the Gunnison you got to get J.M.'s permission and buy a license to operate, then you got to pay the toll road fees, then J.M. only lets you haul what he wants to let you haul and probably gets part of that."

"Sounds like he's cuttin' a real fat hog."

"That he is, and he's got his own little army to help him butcher."

"Much obliged for the information," Doc said as he descended the porch. "Reckon I'll be seein' you again in the next few days."

The news depressed him. Had they traveled all the way from Hays to become servants to some "petty prince?" He returned to camp and relayed the news to Agnes and Moots.

"We're here," said Agnes firmly. "We'll make the best of it for the time being and see what fate brings us."

Moots nodded in agreement. "We both been through a helluva lot Doc. Can't be no worse'n some of the things we already faced."

Doc delayed their departure a few days to rest up and enjoy the cool weather and the water. Moots proudly maintained that he'd not bathed since accidentally falling into the Pecos years ago, whereupon Doc and Agnes lured him to the edge of a shallow eddy in the stream to look at some fish and pushed him in. He shot to the surface screaming and swearing. Doc then jumped in himself and handed Moots a bar of soap. He wouldn't let the old man out of the cold water until he'd thoroughly scrubbed both body and clothes. Moots spent the rest of the afternoon sulking and drying on a sunny slab of sandstone.

Agnes, on the day before their departure, commanded the two men to dig the copper bathtub and a large iron kettle from one of the wagons. She heated water while the men discretely journeyed upriver. On their way back they crossed a set of hoofprints pointing in the direction of their camp. Doc broke into a trot with Moots shuffling along as best he could. Neither was armed. Doc panicked. The bathtub lay on its side in the mud. "Agnes!" he yelled.

"Here!" came her voice from one of the wagons. Doc looked toward the sound of her voice as her head, hair still long and wet from the bath, rose above the sideboards of the wagon, along with the muzzle of Moots' old Thunderbolt rifle.

"Good God!" he exclaimed. "Are you all right?"

"Yes, just scared. " Agnes absent-mindedly climbed down from the wagon in only a thigh length shift. Moots cleared his throat and went for a blanket.

"We came across some hoofprints and hurried back. What happened?"

"Actually, not much, but he surely did scare me. I was in the tub splashing about, singing, talking to myself. That's probably why I didn't hear him come up. Well, I heard a horse snort right behind me, and I thought it was you until I remembered that both of you were afoot. I think I even said something and when there was no answer I looked over my shoulder and there was a man on horseback just standing there watching me. Then he drew up alongside the tub and just stared while I asked him what he wanted and who he was. He never said a word. I told him the two of you were only a short way away and would come running if I called out. He didn't say a thing, just tipped his hat and trotted off in the direction of the road. Well, I didn't waste any time getting dressed and armed." She looked down at her wet shift and tried to hide the more transparent areas as Moots came up with a blanket and averted his eyes as he handed it to her.

"Did you see what he looked like?" asked Doc.

She nodded. "Tall, at least in the saddle, thick dark mustache like yours, well-dressed; striped shirt, vest and waistcoat, black hat. When he tipped his hat I could see that his hair was thin and fine and plastered down and cut short."

"How was he armed?"

"Sidearms, one low on the right hip and one high on the left with the butt pointed for a cross-draw. He had some kind of strange looking long gun in a saddle scabbard.

"What kind of a rig did he have on his horse?"

Agnes's brow furrowed. "Smart, fancy bridle woven out of leather or . . . "

"Horsehair," interrupted Doc.

"Yes. That's it, horsehair. How did you know?"

"I saw him back in Pueblo. I remember the bridle, actually it was a hackamore, no bit."

"That's right."

"Have any idea who he is, Doc?" asked Moots.

"No, but I'd be willing to bet he's well known somewhere. He carries a Creedmor Rifle but he ain't no hunter."

Early the following morning the three packed up and lumbered up the road to the toll shack. Doc paid the agent in greenbacks and asked, "Fella come through here yesterday afternoon?"

"Lotsa fellas come through here."

"This one was a tall man on a chestnut gelding with a black hat and wearin' two pistols."

"Yeah, he came through here. In fact he comes through here ever' once in a while."

"Know who he is?"

"Can't remember the name. Works for J.M., calls himself a 'stock detective'."

"Pinkerton man?"

"Maybe, don't really know. Don't really look or act the type. I think he's on his own . . . a pistolero."

Doc returned to Moots' wagon. "That fella who came by camp yesterday is somewhere up ahead of us, so keep your eyes peeled."

"Road agent you reckon?"

"I don't think so. Gatekeeper said he was a 'stock detective,' whatever that is. Hired gun, I'd guess. But we may look like a good opportunity to him."

"If he was gonna do something wouldn't he have done it yesterday when Agnes was alone?"

"Good point. He may not have because he couldn't be sure that we wouldn't come upon him unexpected and get the drop on him. If he can pick us off with that rifle long distance, he'll know that we're out of the way for sure." He climbed onto the seat next to Agnes and clucked to the team but didn't tell her of the conversation with the toll agent. For a long time they didn't speak as the wagon rumbled up the ruts.

Finally Agnes inhaled deeply and looked at her husband. "Doc, what have we gotten ourselves into?"

He heard a note of fear that hadn't been there before. "Nothin' we can't handle," he said, smiling reassuringly. "A new place always takes some gettin' used to. In a year or two, once we get settled in, have a home and make friends, it'll be like we lived here all our lives."

"It's not us, not you and me that I'm worried about."

"Moots is no fool. He can take care of himself, been doin' it all his life."

"No. Not him."

"Who?"

She sighed and took a long time to answer. "Doc, I think I'm pregnant."

He turned in the seat, his mouth open, unable to speak. Her eyes filled. He felt a surge of love and affection for her stronger than he had imagined even on the loneliest nights along the Pecos. He wanted to say something, but nothing he thought of seemed strong enough. He took the reins in one hand and put his right arm around her and drew her to him and kissed her.

Chapter 11

Frank Shores gasped his first breaths of thin mountain air on a drizzly, early spring day in his parents' log cabin on the banks of an unnamed Gunnison River tributary. Moots remarked to Doc that he could hear the baby's caterwauling in his own cabin nearly fifty yards away.

The two cabins lay nestled in a clearing between a stand of blue spruce on one side and aspen on the other. Moots called them "quakies" because of the distinctive clatter of their leaves in the breeze. Doc had chosen the spot, in what Agnes termed a "fit of nostalgia," and he admitted that the setting reminded him of his boyhood home in Michigan. From the bedroom window one could see the town of Gunnison to the northeast, blue smoke from its shops and frame houses merging into the morning's gray overcast. The cloud ceiling hid the massive surrounding snowcapped peaks, so welcome in summer and so daunting in winter. At the onset of labor Agnes had insisted Doc leave the cabin. He busied himself splitting firewood. Even if she had not insisted, the heat would have driven him out. She wanted no doctor nor midwife, relying instead on her nurse's training and years of assisting her father.

After their arrival in the Gunnison Valley, they had enjoyed a brief autumn when they labored mightily to build substantial log cabins for what they knew would be a fierce winter. To their surprise and dismay, they unearthed a conglomeration of decaying timbers, children's toys, axes, shovels, picks, and household items. Then, worst of all, bones. Whether game, livestock, or human they didn't know. Later in town Doc learned they had built in the same area once occupied by the ill-fated Smith party. He remembered Chaney's story. Upon his return he told neither Agnes nor Moots. This reminder of Gunnison's savage winters unnerved him.

Winter never just arrived in the Gunnison Valley, it charged in like the Four Horsemen of the Apocalypse, thundering down from the peaks in great swirling clouds, the spindrift slicing painfully through wool and fur. It changed the land. Valleys, gulches, and draws drifted into hills, bunkers, and hummocks, and hilltops became valleys. Meadows of saplings were actually the tips of forests of mature trees. Men became lost and perished because they could no longer distinguish landmarks. Metal shattered like glass. A man's occupation could be guessed by how much of his nose and ears had been cropped by frostbite. Few cowboys, cattlemen, or lumbermen could honestly lay claim to full sets of fingers and toes. Some said there were only three seasons in the Gunnison — winter, summer, and mud — to which the stock reply was, "Not so. We had a lovely spring last year. As I recall, it was on a Thursday."

Thanks to Ed Taylor's legacy and the sale of the Hays property, the trio had plenty of money to last the winter. This was lucky, because in winter no jobs were available and there was no chance of hauling freight by wagon over roads and trails clogged with twenty-foot snowdrifts. Besides, they were occupied building homes, corrals, and outhouse shelters. Indefatigable and ever faithful, Moots took on all jobs the other two avoided. The game had gone, but they found beef readily available from the Douglas Cattle Company's slaughterhouse and canned goods through the Douglas General Store — at prices which stunned them. Doc noted that there were precious few businesses in the town or the surrounding area whose name wasn't preceded by the name "Douglas." Being sequestered for the winter had made Doc restless and within a few days of Frank's birth he rode to town looking for work.

The toll keeper's warning echoed in his ears. The MaxDouglas Mining and Transfer Company either owned or controlled all the freighting companies in the valleys. And to further sew things up, it owned or controlled the merchants and businesses which provided work for the freighters. J.M. Douglas ruthlessly ruled from his red sandstone castle on the crest of Douglas Hill. He could have, Doc thought, saved himself a day's time if he'd stopped with the advice proffered by the proprietor of the first establishment he entered, a sawmill and lumberyard. He'd introduced himself and only begun to offer his services when the lumberman gruffly interrupted him.

"Got a license?"

"For what?"

"Haulin'."

"No."

"Can't do business with ya. Take my advice, don't try to do freighting business in this town or this valley without first goin' over to the Mad Doug offices and clearin' it with them or just turn around and fergit it."

"Mad Doug?"

"MaxDouglas Minin' and Transfer."

Doc did not take kindly to the advice and continued to slog back and forth to one business after another across the river of muck called Main Street. At day's end he had only soggy boots and socks, frozen feet, and bitter disappointment to show for his trouble. He reluctantly mounted his horse and headed home.

"Don't worry Doc," Agnes consoled him that evening over dinner. "We're all right for the time being and something will turn up. Maybe you'll have to get the license. How much is it?"

"Thousand a year and ten percent of the gross, and then there's the toll fees on top of that. Hell, I'd buy the license tomorrow, but I don't like the thought of bein' robbed"

"It's a lovely bit of business all right."

"Well, maybe I can get on as a driver with one of the other outfits."

Doc and Agnes were awakened the following morning by drumming on the cabin door. "Better come look at this," said Moots, hurrying off toward the stream. When they arrived, Benton pointed toward the ominously rising water. "Snowmelt and rain. We best be buildin' a levy."

Doc agreed. The two men set to work felling trees and moving dirt and rock. They broke at midday to refresh themselves. As Doc neared the cabin he saw a wagon approaching. He waited. The driver wore a large sunbonnet which obscured most of the face. As the wagon drew closer he could see that the face evinced no particular age or gender. Ruddy skin appeared unwrinkled except for the corners of the eyes and mouth. He assumed, because of the bonnet, it was a woman, but a soldier's wool greatcoat buried the rest of the body except for a pair of well-worn Brogans on the feet and gnarly, red little hands. The wagon pulled up to him and stopped.

"You Shores?" the driver asked in a high-pitched woman's voice.

"I am."

"Name's Kate . . . Kate Davis Knight. I heard in town you're looking for work."

"Yes."

"Come see me tomorrow. I live just down the river, got a mill, brewery, and bakery down there. I got a proposition for you." With that she wheeled her team and reversed direction.

Doc cocked his hat back on his head and watched as she turned from the lane to his cabin back onto the main road on the bluff heading west downstream above the Gunnison River. He hadn't heard Agnes come up behind him.

"Who was that, Doc?"

"Our new boss. I think."

As he returned to work on the levy something nagged at him about the name. He'd heard the name before but couldn't remember from whom or where.

They piled the levy higher the next day. The water pushed back even harder. Doc told Agnes to pack the essentials and be prepared to move. On the third day cold, dry air cleared the skies and again dropped temperatures in the mountains below freezing. By night the water level in the stream had dropped by more than half. He rose early and, saddling his buckskin, Skip, followed the river road west.

The buildings of the Knight Milling, Baking, and Brewing Company occupied a large shelf of rock and earth, located three or four miles west and downstream from the Shores' homestead. The shelf had been left hanging eons ago when the river cut downward another twenty feet or so. An upstream diversion canal supplied waterpower to the mill and irrigation to a small acreage of pasture and garden land. A shallow artesian spring supplied water to the brewery.

But all the buildings were hidden from sight by intervening sagebrush hogbacks, even to those passing within a few hundred yards on the main road. The only thing marking the lane which intersected the road and meandered off toward the river was a large, heavy post from which hung a thick wooden shield. Emblazoned upon the shield, varnished to a high gloss, a medieval knight in plate armor, painted in brilliant red and yellow on a chestnut charger, leveled his lance in the direction of the descending lane. On the guidon waving at the tip of the lance were carved the letters KDK. Now, Doc could see smoke rising above and behind the ridge.

A gristmill dominated the cluster of buildings and silos. A full two stories tall and constructed of heavy timber and thick lumber, it looked every bit a medieval castle. An enormous paddle wheel groaned in the canal traversing toward the river. Two other buildings modeled the mill, except instead of a mill wheel their smoke and steam evinced the ovens and cauldrons of the bakery and brewery. A large granite manor was set back a few hundred feet away, somewhat demurely separated from the other buildings, in a clump of cottonwood and spruce. Outlying the house were barns, stables, and workers' apartments. Doc drew rein at the house. The hitching post was yet another knight whose lance served as the rail.

An immaculately dressed, elderly black man with snow-white hair and a scarred upper lip answered the door. Doc introduced himself and explained the purpose of his visit. The man, who Doc decided was a butler, motioned him in and seated him on a silk upholstered chair in an ornately decorated parlor and asked him to wait. Doc scanned the room's crenelated walnut paneling and ceiling-high book shelves packed with leather-bound volumes. His muddy bootprints stood out painfully on the first wall-to-wall carpeting he'd ever seen.

A low, round table in the cove of a bay window caught his attention. On it lay some piece of knitting. Curious, Doc crossed the room and picked it up. It was a simple small square of some drab coarse yarn which had been knotted at frequent regular intervals. A woman's voice from behind made him jump. "It's a dishrag. I crochet them from flour sack strings." He turned to see the small-faced woman of two days ago.

"It's . . . uh, very nice." He offered.

"It's very miserly, is what it is. I come by it honestly, but I stop at weaving stockings from them as my mother and grandmother did. Mine is a very frugal, if outlandishly wealthy, family." Her tightly wound gray hair pulled the skin of her face back from large, dark eyes. She walked directly to him extending a hand which he found surprisingly small but strong. "Kate Knight."

"Doc Shores, thanks for the invitation."

She nodded in the direction of the knitting. "Old habits die hard, Doc. My grandmother baked the bread in her kitchen oven and my grandfather delivered it. They were so broke they wore the sacks for underwear and crocheted the strings. The crocheting isn't so bad, it's washing and tying all the strings together. But you couldn't care less about that. You're interested in the job. Come back into my study where we can be more assured of privacy. I think," she said, lowering her voice to a whisper, "that the workers sometimes come around and listen at the windows when I have visitors. The valley is a veritable nest of spies."

"Ben," she yelled back through the house, "bring us some coffee in the office." The old black man materialized ghost-like from a dark hallway. He acknowledged her order then faded again into the shadows. Kate led Doc through a dark labyrinth of halls to another baroque room festooned with a collection of figurines, busts, small statues, paintings, and plants. But, in contrast to what he'd seen of the house otherwise, the room virtually blazed with midday sunshine from several bay windows and a very large skylight. She invited him to sit and seated herself behind a brightly polished oak desk. While they exchanged small talk about the weather and his newborn son, the butler entered with a silver coffee service and delicate porcelain cups. Without speaking he exited the room and closed the heavy oak doors behind him.

"I understand from some of my customers in town that you're interested in starting a new freighting business."

"I was until I came up against Mad Doug's rules. Guess I'm just looking for a job right now."

"I have a proposition." Kate stopped and chewed thoughtfully on her lower lip. "I pride myself on bein' able to quickly size up a man. Shores, you strike me as someone who can think, a rarity in this valley. What do you know about the politics hereabouts?"

"Only that MaxDouglas owns or controls just about every business here."

"That's about it. Do you know who MaxDouglas is?"

"J.M. Douglas."

"Now, what do you know about me?"

"Absolutely nothing," Doc lied. He still couldn't remember how he'd come to know her name.

"Then allow me to summarize. My father, Charles Davis, came to Colorado Territory from Wales and began a milling business in Denver long before J.M. Douglas. He was blessed, if that may be the applicable term, with only a daughter, Kate. He tried marrying me off to some of the more eligible bachelors in Denver, but I had my own ideas and married a surprisingly clever Englishman named Steven J. Knight who expanded the mills into baking and brewing. He thought that each of the isolated major Colorado mining towns would provide a ready market for the bread and beer made from grain grown and more easily transported from the mountain valleys. He was right for the most part, but didn't reckon with the mines playing out as fast as they did. The Gunnison was spared that fate by the fortunes of the Douglas Cattle Company. Steven died a couple of years ago. At my age I had no further use for the highfalutin' Denver society, so I moved up here. My sons, Steven Jr. and Roger, look after things in Denver."

"How come Douglas doesn't own this as well?"

"Wasn't worth going up against the Knight power in Denver. Steven is a senator and Roger a congressman. But he did force us to locate out here rather than within the city limits. Besides, we're practically a captive enclave. Since he nearly owns the county he can tax the property to the limits of our existence and squeeze every penny out of what comes in and goes out — as you're discovering. He planned originally, to bring a narrow gauge railroad spur in from Denver through the passes, but he's found it more profitable for right now to control the wagon freighting. The other mines and towns up and down the valleys are fighting him tooth and claw to get the railroad in, because they have to pay exorbitant costs to either ship their ore out or for his mill and smelter to process it and then again to ship out the bullion. He's preoccupied with another battle as well — sod busters and sheep. So far he's been able to stave off those fighting to get into the valleys. He brought up a small army years ago."

"Commanded by one Stryker McQue," interrupted Shores.

"Used to be," Kate corrected. "He and McQue been at each other for years now. He pretty much removed the killers from McQue's control by parceling out land to them — just like a feudal lord. Still maintains an allegiance though. Oh, Stryker too has a following of stalwarts but neither he nor J.M. can tip the scales one way or the other. How did you know?"

Doc just shrugged and said, "Ran into an old prospector with a hurt back who used to work for Stryker."

"Fella named Chaney?"

"That's him."

"Lord! I wouldn't have guessed that Lee was still alive. Where'd you see him."

"Pueblo. Doesn't look well, frankly. Talks like a man with one foot in the grave."

"What else?"

"Not much. That if I needed help to come to you."

Kate seemed to ponder this. "Anyway, as you may be aware from talking to Chaney, McQue has become a bit of thorn in the Douglas side. Mr. Shores, that brings me to you and whether or not you're willing to take a bit of a risk."

"Maybe, what is it?"

"A good forty percent of my overhead is devoted to hauling costs, MaxDouglas companies, of course. I estimate that I can cut that figure by fifty percent by bringing in my own man, my own company. I haven't tried this before, because there hasn't been a person in town with the spine to go up with me against J.M."

"What makes you think I would?"

"You're a newcomer and more desperate. Like I say, I'm a good judge of men."

"We still have to pay the licensing."

"Not if you're my employee and hauling exclusively for me."

Doc nodded. "I'm not afraid for myself, but I do have a wife, a son, and an old friend to think about."

"I'll hire your friend as well. As for the safety of your wife and son, well, let's just say that I have an ace in the hole to play if things look like they are getting a bit too rough. J.M. suspects I'm holding a card, and that's another reason that he hasn't really bothered me, but he doesn't really know how high the card is. But if I'm to play it, it'll have to be for all the stakes, because once it's played it's gone for good and if it doesn't work he'll have the whole pot, meanin' you and me both. The other side of the coin is he's gonna have to weigh that against the possibility of an all-out rebellion from the businesses that he's been bleeding dry for years, if they see us winning. We'll need to let him save some face. And we make it easy for him to overlook us by you being my employee."

"What about the law?"

"You mean what passes for law in these parts. McQue has appointed himself town marshal and pretty much runs the town outright. As such he maintains an uneasy peace with Douglas, provided that J.M gets his fair share of the theft and extortion. McQue's smarter'n Douglas, and he'll ignore what he knows he can't control or what'll get him into deep trouble. Don't misunderstand me though. He's dangerous, real dangerous, and as good with his fists as with a pistol or a knife.

"Gunnison County has a sheriff who's J.M.'s lapdog. He collects protection money, called "taxes" everywhere else in the county, but pretty much stays out of McQue's way. He's reelected every two years by plebiscite. J.M. stuffs the ballot boxes and gets a handful of people to vote against his candidates to make it look good. He'd be voted out of office in a minute in a fair election."

"Who else?"

"Judges, commissioners, coroner and, of course, the county treasurer."

" Damn!" exclaimed Doc, shaking his head. "The dice ain't just loaded here, they're heavily armed."

"Yep. Back to the job. Don't give me an answer now. Go home and talk it over with your wife and friend. Remember if we win, we win big, . . . if we lose . . . "

"Much obliged," Doc said, rising from his chair and taking her hand again. He was ushered to the front door by old Ben who opened the door for him and then followed him outside.

"Mister Shores," he said quietly, "may I have a word with you?"

"Of course."

"Mister Shores, I been with Miz Kate since I come up from Mississippi after the war." He reached out a hand gnarled with arthritis and drew Doc in closer. "She be a strong woman, but she gettin' old, like me. She need your hep, she need someone she can depend on. What she know can get her in all kind trouble, can get her kilt. Me too, if Mr. Stryker or Mr. Douglas ever learn of it. She can hep you, and you can hep her, but the two of you has to be mighty careful."

"What does she know?"

"Not time yet Mr. Shores, not time yet. She'll let you know if'n the time come. Mistah Chaney know too, that's really why he snuck out. " He patted Doc on the shoulder and guided him down the steps. "There'll come a day of reckonin', even for an ol' slave man. But we all have to be patient."

On the way home through another late spring snow squall, Doc pulled the collar of his slicker up around his neck and the brim of his hat low on his head and pondered what he had heard this day as he instinctively kept sight on the disappearing trail between his horse's ears. He looked at the broken ice and tree limbs drifting swiftly along with the spring runoff on the Gunnison and thought how much he felt right now like that debris, being carried inexorably along on a swift current. It was, he thought, not a man's place in life to drift helplessly with the current.

By the time Doc reached the warmth of the cabin his slicker had long since been soaked and seeped icy water into his shirt and pants. He shivered violently as he fed his horse. Agnes met him at the door and immediately gave him a cup of coffee strongly laced with whiskey while Moots took his sodden coat and clothes and hung them on the old hall tree next to the fireplace. He warmed himself at the stove and told them of his meeting with Kate. They listened attentively and then as they sat down to a dinner of a turkey that Moots had shot that afternoon, Agnes asked, "What do you think you'll do?"

Doc sighed. "I reckon if we're to make this our home for some time to come we got to either bend to their will or fight 'em. I've got mor'n myself to look out after these days. Easier and less dangerous to bend to their will and do as they say. It probably makes life a whole lot easier to live if you just keep movin' away from trouble. We could stay here, and I could get a job punchin' cows for Douglas and we'd probably do fine."

Doc paused and looked at the other two and his son asleep in the cradle. Lord, he thought, I just want to go on livin' peaceably.

Agnes spoke first. "But you have to live with yourself. When are you going to tell Mrs. Knight?"

"Tomorrow," he sighed. "Bent, you in or out?

"I plan on dyin' right here — one way or t'other."

Agnes nodded. "I pretty much gave up on being afraid when Father and I moved from Virginia. If I'm afraid at all, it's for Frank, but he might as well get used to standing up at an early age. It's a useful skill in life."

The next day dawned bright and clear, and by midmorning the crocuses, buttercups, and tulips that Agnes had planted in the autumn on the south side of the cabin were basking in the warmth of the sun. Doc awoke late feeling refreshed and with only a mild remnant of a cold he thought might be returning. He stood in the doorway in his underwear soaking up the brilliant sunlight and drinking sweetened coffee while watching Agnes contentedly clear brush from a garden plot. Catfish dozed on her back with all four paws in the air next to Frank's wooden cradle. Doc felt as certain as he could that he was doing the right thing, and "the devil take the consequences." He dressed and by noon trotted Skip downriver to Kate Knight's, Moots bouncing along behind on a mule. By evening they returned employees of Knight Milling, Baking and Brewing. Before week's end the skirmishing had begun.

"Vermin!" sputtered Kate when she heard Doc's account of the incident. "Douglas and McQue have a web of spies all up and down the valley, men that'd sell their mothers down the river for a new nickel. They been watchin' you boys makin' deliveries. Well, I knew this was gonna happen, just hoped it'd be later rather than sooner. Either you boys get hurt?"

Doc shook his head. "Naw, they just stopped us and asked to see our licenses. I told them we was workin' for you and didn't have licenses."

"That do the trick?"

"Seemed to. They let us go on our way."

"Good. Well, they'll be reporting back to someone. I guess that I can be expecting visitors pretty quick. Like I said though, might as well get into it and get it out of the way. You boys let me know soon as you have any more trouble. Help yourselves to a drink on the way out if you feel like it."

Moots asked Doc on the way out, "A widow you said? I'm here to tell you, 'ats a spunky woman."

Doc shot him a surprised glance. "First time I ever heard you say anything about a woman, good or bad . . . and she said a drink not a bottle."

"I may be an ol' man. I'm not a dead man," he said, returning a crystal decanter to the bar in the atrium, gulping all the way.

Spring finally wedged its way into the mountains, a full month later than in Denver. The waxy buds which had just appeared on the aspen branches, overnight became leaves.

"Frank Shores," yelled his mother as she plucked him from a furrow in her newly finished garden, "God did not put worms on this green earth for children to eat."

Doc and Moots, who had just walked up, laughed at the sight of Agnes dangling Frank like a suitcase from his diaper while he squawked and grabbed for Catfish's ear. The dog raised an eyebrow and backed away.

"Nothin's coming up," she said.

"No. Kate says that she made the same mistake when she first got here. Growin' season's too short, only a couple months. Says you have to stick to plants that grow real quick."

"Like what?"

"Can't remember. Doesn't matter 'cause the deer eat 'em anyway."

"Well . . . ask."

"All right. Be seein' her in a bit. We got some deliveries to make."

Returning from a delivery north to the small mining community of Crested Butte they could see a group of riders a few hundred yards away heading up toward them as they descended the lane to the brewery. "Trouble you think?" asked Moots.

"Could be," replied Doc. "I don't think they come all this way for a loaf of bread and a bottle of beer."

The riders approached in single file. The lead rider reined in as he drew abreast of their wagon. Doc counted eight riders, all armed with rifles in saddle scabbards and revolvers strapped to their waists by cartridge belts laden with ammunition. The leader was a strikingly handsome man with a well-trimmed blond beard and reddish-blond hair flowing from beneath a wide-brimmed black hat. He rode straight and tall. His horse, a tall, black thoroughbred, pranced restlessly beneath tack heavily encrusted with hand-engraved silver. Although both Shores and Moots were armed with revolvers, Doc could readily see they wouldn't stand a chance in an open gunfight with these men.

The leader touched the brim of his hat. "Gentlemen, allow me to introduce myself. My name is Douglas, John Malcolm Douglas. I am the owner and President of MaxDouglas Mining and Transfer and also the Douglas Cattle Company, Gunnison County Administrator, Chief Prosecutor and Judge and at various times — various other things. If I may be immodest . . . I own just about everything and everyone in the Gunnison drainage, and then some. I hear some enterprising fellas were lookin' to start up a freighting business without benefit of license. That wouldn't be you would it?" Douglas grinned, revealing a mouthful of the most even and beautifully white teeth Doc had ever seen.

"We couldn't afford a license so we took jobs with Kate Knight, but I'm sure you know that, since you've obviously been down there to visit her."

"So she says. I'd say it's a pretty convenient way of avoiding the law." Douglas grinned broadly.

"Maybe," Moots interjected, "but say what you please, we're not breakin' any laws."

Douglas's teeth disappeared. He ignored Moots. "Kate and I reached an understanding, but if you boys so much as step over the line, so much as fart in the street in Gunnison, you'll be answerin' to this man." Douglas jabbed a thumb over his shoulder toward the rider directly behind him, an obese man with tobacco-stained stubble and a dirty plug hat. A metal star adorned the left side of his ragged vest. The man said nothing. "This here's Sheriff Vernon Patterson, duly elected minion of the law, tough as woodpecker lips and lightnin' fast with that Colt strapped to his hip. But his one true love is hangin' lawbreakers . . . after a fair trial that is." Some of the other men smirked.

"Back where I come from," said Doc, "we had judges and juries decidin' such things."

"Again . . . that'd be me," said Douglas tipping his hat. "We like to keep things simple and quick in this county. Well, I got business to tend to in town. You boys keep your noses real clean, and I'm sure we'll get along fine. Please extend my greetings and good wishes to Mrs. Shores and your son Frank." Douglas spurred the thoroughbred into a quick canter. Each of the file of men passing by glared at Doc and Benton as though having suffered some personal affront.

"Like I said," Kate wagged a finger at Doc and Moots, half the county works for Douglas, and the other half spies for him. Didn't take him long to know who you are and who you're workin' for. He probably knows what you had for breakfast. If he doesn't, Stryker does. He won't trouble us any more for now, but understand, he'll be watching every minute for an opportunity to do the two of you in, legally if he can, otherwise if he can't."

Kate poured three cups of strong coffee from the silver service, swept Benton's forlorn hat from his head and placed it in his lap without missing a word. "I don't think your family is in any immediate danger — but that bunch is not above anything either. You folks pretty settled in where you are?"

"Pretty," replied Doc, "Why?"

"I got this old carriage house out back that isn't being used these days. You can have it rent free. It's good and solid, safe and secure, but it'll take some fixin' up. Plenty of room for all of you. It's got a tack room off to one side that Benton could use. It'd be nice to have a family around here. Save you trips back and forth as well."

"I'll bring it up with Agnes and let you know here in the next few days. Whatever we decide, I do thank you for the offer."

Agnes was overjoyed at the thought of more civilized surroundings and almost immediately began packing. Much to Moot's displeasure, Doc left him to help Agnes during the move while he continued making deliveries.

Agnes excitedly confided to Doc that she'd found in Kate both a mother she'd missed for years and a close woman friend. Doc said he thought Kate was similarly starved for female companionship. The two spent the succeeding days together cleaning and decorating the carriage house and playing in the thick clover with Frank while Moots hauled trash, repaired wagons and tack, and cared for the horses and mules. He escaped with Doc whenever he could or hid out in the springhouse with Ben and consumed crocks of beer secreted from the brewery. Doc happily settled into the rhythm of their new life and his new job and luxuriated in a contentment he'd never before known. His memoirs recorded later that that alone should have put him more on guard.

To the west of Gunnison lay the Valley where the dry summer heat seemed like a great blanket on the ripening barley and wheat, turning them to crackling gold. This golden harvest flowed in great wagon trains from the railhead at Cimarron to Kate Knight's silos.

But the heat ripened the grain so quickly that Doc was forced to add men, wagons, and draft animals to haul the bountiful harvest. He, himself, often worked eighteen hour days seven days a week. All this, Doc noticed, came under the watchful eyes of Douglas's outriders who reconnoitered from the ridge lines up and down the drainage. They didn't interfere. They didn't harass. They didn't fire their weapons or threaten. But Doc had to pay off more than one man leaving his employment for fear of reprisals from Douglas' toughs. Though unintimidated himself, he also was not totally without concern. He intended to play it straight and narrow hoping that Douglas and McQue would eventually tire of the game. But fate is beyond any man's control or comprehension.

Chapter 12

"Men's lives," Doc would later record, "can be completely changed in the split second it takes to pull a trigger and a gun muzzle to flash orange or a man to move an inch or two."

On such a fateful late summer's day Agnes asked Doc to ride into town for some medicine for Frank who was suffering from what appeared to her to be a bout of colic. Doc shook his head.

"Have to get Bent to do it. I got a train to meet in Cimarron."

"Tried already. He's laid up with a case of the gout. He won't be moving from his rocker for at least the rest of the day, probably the week."

Doc grumbled but set out to saddle Skip, secretly relieved for an excuse to take the day off, leaving his reliable and experienced superintendent, Jack Keady, in charge of organizing and managing the wagon trains. Doc looked forward to the soft, easy gait of the horse beneath him rather than the bucking, jarring hard seat of the wagon. As he departed the compound onto the lane, a meadowlark trilled in the branches of the cottonwood overhead. It made him feel light and happy. He stopped to watch the bird, but a yell sent it into flight.

"Doc!" Moots shouted as he hobbled across from the old tack shed with a rifle in one hand and a gun belt in the other, "you forgot these."

Doc waved him back. "Won't be needin' them, jus' be gone this morning."

"I know," puffed Moots as he limped up, "but Douglas's boys would dearly like to see you in town unarmed. I'll feel a heap better for you takin' these."

"Benton's right," called Agnes from the iron fence in front of the carriage house. "I don't think you can be too careful. Maybe you should even take some of the boys into town with you."

"Nah, I'll be all right," said Doc taking the weapons from Moots. "Jack's gonna need all of them on today's trip." He slid the Winchester 73 into its scabbard and slung the gun belt over the saddle horn. With a wave over his shoulder, he continued his journey up the lane noticing dark clouds gathering among the nearby mountain peaks. Damn! he thought, forgot my slicker too. Looks like it might not be my day after all.

The bell atop city hall at the end of Gunnison's Main Street pealed noon as Doc warily passed the open door of the Gunnison County Sheriff's Office. Two things caught his eye. Hitched to the rail in front of the office were three tall, pure-blooded horses of the same breed as he'd seen Douglas riding, animals seldom seen in the mountains, and the silhouettes of several men were visible just inside the door. As he passed, Vern Patterson appeared in the doorway, his eyes sliding up the street with Shores. Doc glanced over his shoulder every few seconds until he stopped at the mercantile store. He just looped Skip's reins over the rail once in case he needed to make a quick getaway. He scanned the street. People wandered in and out of the stores and shops or gathered in small clusters to exchange gossip. Carriages and wagons clanked and squeaked by each other in the street. The smell of distant rain clotted the air. Doc's eye briefly caught sight of an ominously familiar figure entering the Columbine Saloon at the end of the block of buildings across the street from him, a tall man wearing a broad-brimmed black hat. Shores paused, but the man disappeared almost instantly.

Doc explained to the clerk at the counter what he needed, and the man withdrew into a back room. Bottles clanked and pestle ground against mortar. He wandered about the store picking out a book of poetry for Agnes, candy and a ball for Frank, and a can of Qboid granulated plug tobacco for Moots. It took a disappointingly short time to make his purchases, finishing well before one o'clock. He'd not eaten since early morning, so Doc decided to treat himself to a hot roast beef lunch at the cafe across the street. As he stored his purchases in his saddlebags he saw the three horses that had been hitched outside Vern Patterson's office being ridden up the street toward him.

The riders contrasted sharply in appearance to their sleek mounts. All three looked rough and unkempt. Doc instinctively tensed and quickly eyed his weapons, now grateful that Moots and Agnes had talked him into bringing them. Before reaching Doc, the riders veered off and disappeared down a cross street. He relaxed, feeling foolish at his apprehension. He felt even more foolish when he noticed that one of Skip's loose reins had slipped from the rail to the ground and the horse had stepped on it snapping it off near the shank of the bit. He took out his pocketknife and began repairing the rein. A muffled shout from somewhere across the street interrupted his work. Doc glanced up, but seeing no one he returned to his task. Two quick explosions caused him to drop both the rein and knife and reach for the empty spot on his right hip. Cursing his own carelessness he quickly retrieved the gun belt from the saddle horn and crouching down, buckled it in place. He slid the Winchester from its scabbard. Heedless of any danger, Shores raced across the street toward the building, the Gunnison National Bank, from which the shots had been fired. He levered a round into the chamber of the Winchester as he ran. Upon reaching the bank's front door he quickly peeped through the decorated glass and saw a man lying on the floor in a pool of blood, while another upon seeing Doc's face, pointed toward the sunlight streaming in through a back door and shouted. Doc raced up the boardwalk and around the same corner where the riders had earlier disappeared. There he nearly collided with Sheriff Vern Patterson going the opposite way. Their eyes met and Doc dashed on to where an alley intersected with the street. He heard Patterson puffing along behind him. Cautiously stepping into the open intersection he saw the three men mounted on their thoroughbred horses break hard for the far end of the alley. One man fired point-blank into the face of a man on the ground. Doc raised his rifle and took aim at one of the fleeing riders.

"Don't shoot!" came a call from behind him. "You'll hit someone else."

Doc hesitated. Someone at the far end of the alley stepped out into the paths of the charging horsemen. Whoever it was raised a rifle. The three robbers fired shots wildly at the man and reversed direction. Again Doc raised his rifle, but before he even took aim there was a distant explosion and one outlaw's hat flew from his head, along with a sizable portion of hair, skull, and brain. Doc froze in astonishment as the nearly headless rider galloped toward him for a few more strides, and then pitched backward off his horse leaving a lingering fountain of greenbacks and coin which erupted from inside his shirt and vest. Another of the riders stopped and looked back at his fallen comrade. Before he could again spur his horse to flight another shot boomed out and his head, too, nearly disappeared from his shoulders. Two empty and panicked horses followed the third outlaw, who by this time had so quickly closed the distance between himself and Doc that it was all Shores could do to flatten himself against the wall of a building as the man thundered by. A third time Doc raised his rifle and took aim. The outlaw turned in the saddle and fired from a distance of fifty or sixty feet. The shot went wild, whistled passed Doc's ear, and thunked into the boards of the building. Before he could squeeze the Winchester's trigger, from the corner of his eye Doc saw Vern Patterson step out from his hiding place in the shadow of that same building and level his Colt revolver at Doc's chest. Doc froze with surprise. I'm dead, he thought.

Shores didn't even hear the bullet that whipped by him and buried itself nearly a foot deep in Vern Patterson's chest, causing his grossly fat body to convulse violently, even lifting him from his feet, before slamming him into the dust of the street. The sheriff's filthy bowler hat went spinning with the wind. Doc instantly fired at the receding figure causing the last bank robber to jerk momentarily to a halt but then spur his horse back to a dead run and vanish quickly down a side street. Shores wheeled, expecting to take a bullet himself from the man at the other end of the alley, but he saw no one until curious citizens began to congregate and gape at the bodies.

Doc gazed down at the massive lump of lifeless flesh which had once been Vern Patterson, wondering beyond comprehension why the sheriff had been about to kill him.

"Well laddy," came a voice from beside him, "if t'was you that killed him, you've done the town a service and should be rewarded. If t'was them, I think the one left must hang for it."

Doc looked up to see a finely dressed man, the finest he'd seen since Bill Hickok. Even through his finery the man stood tall and slender and taut like a cable. He wore no hat to conceal his long black hair which neatly swept back from a finely shaven face with tawny, hawklike features. His well-formed mouth broke into a broad grin beneath a carefully trimmed, jet black mustache revealing two rows of nearly perfect white teeth. He wore a gold shield emblazoned with the words "Town Marshal" on his black velvet lapel.

"Nope," replied Doc. "Neither one. All I can lay claim to is maybe wingin' that fella who rode off. You dig the bullet out of Patterson and you'll find it's a rifle bullet considerably larger than this Winchester and the same that brought those other two fellas down. It was someone down at the end of the alley. I think it was a man that I saw earlier going into the Columbine Saloon. Only shots the robbers got off were inside the bank and at me."

"What about the fourth?" asked the man in black.

Doc had forgotten about the man the robber had killed in the alley. "Shot in the face by the one that got away," he said.

"It was Ed Coulter," offered someone in the gathering crowd. "Musta been in his office in the back of the bank when the robbery happened."

The man in black turned back to Doc and shrugged. "Local lawyer. Be a small funeral." He held out a hand weighed down by an enormous diamond ring. My name's McQue, Stryker McQue, businessman and Town Magistrate."

Doc grasped his offered hand, amazed at the strength of the finely manicured fingers. "Doc Shores."

"I've heard of you. You a doctor?"

"No. It's a long story."

"We all have at least one," laughed McQue. It seemed to Doc that McQue was taking the bank robbery lightly, and he didn't seem particularly interested in the man with the rifle. McQue turned to a man also wearing a badge standing next to him. "Collect the bodies and take them over to Lilly's Lumber to get them outfitted for pine boxes. Then come on back to the office and we'll round up a posse for the one that got away. Doc, had lunch?"

"I was on my way when the ruckus broke out. I got to hitch up my horse."

"When you get finished come on up to my office. It's over the saloon at the end of the street."

As Doc finished repairing Skip's rein he watched McQue walk up the street and disappear into the same saloon where the man in the black hat had gone earlier, the same man that was at the end of the alley with the rifle. Perhaps, he thought, it was no coincidence that McQue had not questioned him further about the marksman. When he finished repairing the rein, he crossed to the saloon. Doc looked through the crowd of men for a tall man in a black hat but abandoned his search when he found himself surrounded by a throng of well-wishers who wanted to fill him with whiskey and beer and talk of the day's excitement. Doc was relieved when the crowd parted, and Stryker McQue ushered him upstairs to a dining table set with linen, crystal, porcelain, and silver. The poached trout, he thought, was much different than the fare he'd been looking forward to at the cafe.

"The sharpshooter who laid out those two robbers came from your saloon. I saw him walk in here earlier."

"Quite possible," remarked McQue as he poured Doc a glass of wine. "Many men frequent this saloon and almost all of them armed in some way. Probably some hunter passing through who thought he needed practice."

"Maybe. You're not interested in who it was?"

"No, not really. It's done. Two men were killed — a cashier inside the bank and the lawyer — and they didn't get away with any money, to mention. We'll catch up to the third man eventually. Anyway, I believe you deserve a modest reward for your efforts." Stryker slid a stack of twenty dollar double eagles across to Doc.

"I appreciate your kindness, but I can't accept it. I really didn't do anything 'cept wing that one.

"Nonsense! you risked your life to stop the robbery. A man should be rewarded for his good citizenship. I insist that you take it. I've sent a posse under the direction of one of my deputies. You understand, I have to stay in Gunnison. I can't leave the town unprotected."

Doc nodded in agreement as the waiter served him his trout and tender young potatoes. As discretely as possible Doc slid the coins from the table into his vest pocket without any further protest.

As if on cue, Stryker sipped from his wine glass and said, "I have a proposition for you, a career change if you will."

Doc looked out the window behind Stryker. It provided an unobstructed view of the Douglas castle. It'd also begun to rain.

"You're what?" cried Agnes, releasing her grip on Frank whom she'd been assisting in his toddling across the floor. The child swayed back and forth momentarily and then sat down with a thunk and a surprised look.

Doc bent over and picked up his son. "Acting sheriff," he replied as blandly as he could. "I think that fall jarred something loose; he needs changin'."

"If you don't beat all . . . I send you into town on a simple errand and you get involved in a bank robbery, four killings and . . . and . . . sheriff?"

"Acting sheriff. It ain't official until Douglas puts his stamp of approval on it. And I didn't get involved in a bank robbery. I only tried to help stop one." Shores attempted to change the subject. "Anyhow, I bought you all some presents in town," Doc said, opening his saddlebags. "And a small advance on my salary," he lied as he produced the stack of gold coins that glistened brightly in the late afternoon sun streaming through the window onto the table.

Agnes gasped when she beheld the amount. "Graft! Doc you take that back right now . . . no, first thing tomorrow morning."

"It's not graft." He corrected himself. "It's a . . . uh, reward for helpin' stop the robbery. It's a common practice for lawmen to collect rewards."

"You're not a lawman and you have to consider the source."

Moots, who had been sitting with slack-jawed amazement throughout the conversation finally spoke. "Agnes is right Doc. You're gettin' yourself in between two plenty mean fellas, neither of whom would give a second thought to makin' flower food out of you. You wouldn't even have to take sides; all you'd have to do is get in the way a little bit."

"Maybe," came a voice from the open door to the carriage house. The three turned to see the outline of Kate Knight standing in the doorway. "Sorry," said Kate entering the sunlit room, "I heard what happened in town today and thought you'd be talking it over. News travels fast here, especially if Old Ben happens to be in town at the same time. They may both be right Doc, you may get caught in their grist mill. But if you're smart, you stand a good chance of playing McQue and Douglas off against each other and comin' out on top. This town, this county, isn't the fiefdom it was a few years ago. Neither McQue nor Douglas has the hold on it they once did, especially now that they're working against each other. Most of the townfolk were damned ready to see that toady Patterson laid to rest and are about ready to back someone against the Douglas machine. The trick here is to let each of them think you're their boy without being either's. I don't know if that tightrope can be walked, but if it can, you're the man to do it. The next trick will be to pick up support enough in the county to run on your own in the next election . . . and win."

"We still got your ace in the hole?" asked Doc.

"We do, but like I said before, it'll only go so far, the trouble bein' that we won't know for certain how far until we've passed the point."

The four stood silently contemplating each other for long seconds. Agnes looked close to tears. Moots was shaking his head. Doc handed his wet son to his wife. Kate stood rigid, her mouth a thin line of resolve.

Doc looked into his wife's filling eyes. He wanted so badly at that moment to take her into his arms with his son and say that it was all right, and that he was not going to venture forth into this journey of darkness and danger. He wanted to comfort them and tell them that he would, God willing, be a good, responsible husband and father and would provide them safety and security in a land as near to paradise as was possible on earth. But he also felt the tug of destiny. He remembered the day his father came home with the star on his chest and the Colt on his hip and knew that someday he too would wear a star or shield of a lawman whatever the cost. Instead, he put his free arm around her shoulders, kissed her gently on the forehead and said, "This is our home. This is where we make a stand."

The following day Doc returned to Stryker's office. He stopped on his way through the saloon to exchange pleasantries with the patrons who he recognized from the previous day and was pleased to find that many at the bar were already calling him "Doc" or "Sheriff." He ascended the stairs and waved to an acquaintance at one of the poker tables, when a shadow crossed over him, and he looked up to see the silhouette of a tall man standing at the top of the stairs. He excused himself and maneuvered to avoid a collision. As they came abreast of each other on the landing, he saw it was the man in the black hat. The man unblinkingly returned Doc's gaze. "Finally we meet," Doc said, extending his right hand. "Name's Doc Shores."

The man's handsome, even features produced no hint of a smile, and his eyes remained gray-cold, but he nodded and replied simply in a pleasant voice, "Howdy." He did not immediately offer an introduction.

"I'm grateful for you saving my life yesterday," Doc offered pleasantly. "You're an excellent shot with that Creedmor."

"Yes, I am."

Finally, the man extended his hand. "Tom Horn. Shores, I'm pleased to meet you." Doc took the hand but continued to look the man directly in the eyes. Horn continued, "Please extend my apology to your wife for riding up on her and causing fright. I meant no harm."

"I will. No harm done."

They regarded each other in an uneasy silence like two wolves circling, not provoked, but not willing to be the first to give ground. At that moment McQue stepped from his office and approached the two. Horn cast a quick glance toward him, brushed quickly past Doc, descended the stairs, and walked out the door of the saloon.

"What was that all about?" inquired Stryker.

"Oh, Mr. Horn and my wife Agnes crossed paths a while back at an embarrassing moment."

Stryker put his hand on Doc's shoulder and ushered him to the sitting room where they had lunch the day before. "There's someone you need to meet."

Doc was not terribly surprised when he walked into the room and looked directly into the face of John Malcolm Douglas. He sat with legs crossed, deep in a massive leather overstuffed chair. He held a long, black cigar in the crook of the index finger of his right hand. It sprinkled him and the chair with ashes as he rose to greet Doc.

“Well, you seem to have accomplished a lot in the short time you’ve been here. Stryker tells me you’re quite the long-gun eye. The town owes you a debt of gratitude. He also tells me that he’s . . . uh, persuaded you to change jobs?”

Doc cast a glance at McQue who gave no hint of what he’d told Douglas. “I really can’t take any credit for anything. The only one of the bunch I clipped got away. And, yes Mr. McQue has offered me the position of acting sheriff, with your approval.”

“The third one only made it up the road a bit to Ohio City,” said McQue. “My posse caught up with him there. Your shot hit him in the leg, then hit his horse. We found ‘em both bled to death.”

Doc was stunned that he’d actually killed a man. Perhaps, he thought, if it’d happened yesterday in the heat of battle with so little time to think about it he would have felt differently, but now, in the cool quiet of the office it seemed enormous. He’d never killed a man before, even as an accident, and his stomach tightened. He struggled to smile. “Probably just luck.”

“Not a bit of it.” said Douglas in a cloud of smoke. “Quick thinking and a good aim is what it was. Yes, I agree with the disagreeable Mr. McQue’s choice for Vern’s replacement. We need a smart man in the office, and he told me that you provide evidence of being a smart man.”

“I appreciate the vote of confidence, and I’ll accept the job if offered, but I do have to return the reward money. I just didn’t earn it . . . ” He was interrupted by a wave of Stryker’s hand as he placed the gold coins on a table.

“My, my,” Douglas’s words directed toward McQue dripped condescension and sarcasm. “Looks as though you’ve even picked an honest man. Too much honesty in Gunnison is not necessarily a virtue, Mr. Shores.”

“Doc Shores is much too modest,” said McQue as he scooped up the coins, “too modest for his own good.”

Douglas made no immediate reply but drew heavily on his cigar and exhaled a plume of blue smoke toward the Irishman. “Perhaps, perhaps,” he mumbled eventually. “Well, then let us proceed with the swearing in.”

At precisely 1:47 p.m. on the afternoon of August 7, 1882, C.W. Shores was officially sworn into office as Acting Sheriff of Gunnison County by J.M. Douglas, Chairman of the Gunnison County Board of County Commissioners and County Administrator and witnessed by the Gunnison Town Magistrate, Stryker McQue.

Chapter 13

The mountains and fierce winters of the Colorado Rockies which had once damned the flow of settlers into the verdant valley meadows no longer remained a substantial impediment by the last quarter of the nineteenth century. Myriad railroads, roads, and trails into western Colorado obliterated the tracks of deer, elk, grizzly bear, and moccasin-clad feet. The siren's song of the mountain breezes through the grass on the banks of the Yampa, Eagle, Uncompahgre, Grand, and Gunnison rivers beckoned to the poor, the landless — the dreamers. Few claimed the dream. More often, their blood, flesh and bone fed the predators and nourished the soil. The green spruce and pine were crucified upon the crossbars of the telegraph poles. The long silver tentacles of the Denver and Rio Grande Western and the South Park railroads probed into every habitable nook and cranny. The open ranges became neat squares of corn, wheat, oats, and rye. Like the guardian mountains, John Malcolm Douglas, though resolute, could no longer stem the tide into the valleys of the Gunnison.

Doc enjoyed two years of relative peace after his election which encouraged him enough to buy a house in town and move his small family. Moots remained in his converted tack room at the mill until he and Kate surprised everyone with a small wedding.

Doc's apprenticeship as sheriff had been uneventful, mainly because no issues arose which involved either Douglas or McQue. He intervened in drunken brawls, gunfights over property and water, a miners' strike in Crested Butte. When the election did roll around Doc had no trouble winning support from both men. The remainder of the county always followed their lead. The sheriff had not yet been tested.

In the mountain meadows and coulees of the Gunnison Valley cattle reigned supreme; but to the west, in the Uncompahgre, lurked an unlikely menace — soft, white and bleating. Their legions were directed not by Satan's minions but by brown-skinned herders speaking the soft, melodic Castilian and Basque dialects of the Iberian Peninsula. They were armed only with shepherds' crooks and obedient dogs. Grazing pressures grew with their numbers. In the spring and summer they moved farther and farther into the high mountain pastures. The sheep and goats, claimed the cattlemen, killed the grass by grazing too closely. But more significantly, the rules by which the landed aristocracy conducted business have always held that men who are armed and strong shall instinctively hate to death those who are not. And that was the real reason for the range wars.

J.M.'s petty empire had indeed changed. He remained lord of the realm over several fiefdom cattle companies commanded by the aging condottieri of the cowboy army he had chosen to elevate to wealth and power. He imposed on them an organization called the Gunnison Valley Cattlemen's Association. J.M. dictated association policy, which in Gunnison County, others revered as law. Otherwise these semi-autonomous cowboy nobles fought almost continuous, small, internecine wars which were put aside only during the Annual Cattlemen's Association conclave at the La Veta Hotel. These rendezvous were but excuses for ranchers to leave their remote ranches for a week of debauchery and random gunplay.

The years had taken a heavy toll upon John Malcolm Douglas. His once lithe, taut body had become bloated with disease and drink. Most of his servants had abandoned him. The red stone castle had become a dungeon of horrors. Almost nightly he drank himself into towering rages, ranting for hours and swearing vengeance against both real and imagined enemies. Rumors circulated that his drunken harangues resulted from bouts of the "pox" — the result of regular visits to McQue's brothels, which increased after Christine's death. He frequently bought large amounts of quicksilver from the apothecary at the mercantile. The remaining servants securely locked themselves behind the castle's sturdy oak doors for fear of being attacked.

Stryker patiently watched Malcolm's deterioration with cold deliberation. He could wait, he thought, until the Scotsman destroyed himself. Yes, he wanted Malcolm dead. McQue's town remained an island surrounded by Douglas's county. Douglas still had too many loyal followers to risk an all-out war. McQue ruled the saloons, gambling houses, and brothels. He hated being the petty prince, paying tribute each month to the monarch of the Gunnison. He prided himself on being a rational businessman. Douglas and his lawless rabble generated a disruption that was bad for business. Stryker cared nothing about the color of his customers, their clothing, their language nor their professions, rancher or farmer, cowboy or nester. As long as they lost money at his crooked tables and spent the remainder on whores and drink, he prospered. Sheep and cow manure smelled the same to him. Both smelled like money. Shores kept the peace; and peace was good for business. In return McQue made certain, as certain as he could, that the idealistic sheriff was not faced with any ethical dilemmas. It'd been a fine day when Vern Patterson had confided the planned bank robbery to him and dropped a thousand in gold coin into the drawer on his desk. But, it'd been a finer day when Horn put a .45 caliber bullet right through Vern's heart. He was certain that J.M. in his continually befuddled state, didn't have an inkling that Horn was playing both sides of the fence. Five hundred of Patterson's bribe to McQue was a small price to pay for that ace in the hole. Douglas, even when he could think at all, wasn't nearly as smart as he once had been. The Scotsman's insufferable ego would eventually demand more of the moralistic Shores than it was possible for the sheriff to give. McQue knew his time would come. It was just a matter of patience. Odd that most people thought drink and bravado were the downfall of only the Irish.

The joker in the deck was Kate Davis Knight. The old woman kept Douglas at bay with something other than her family influence. Probably the same thing he, McQue, feared. That certain something had to do with Christine's mysterious death, painful for him to dredge up even now. But what did Kate know? How? Ed Chaney? Old Ben's boy? McQue desperately wished that things could have gone differently. He had been genuinely fond of the woman — but they'd have all been destroyed, Douglas too, had the truth been discovered, and certainly now that much of their previously combined power had dissipated. Stryker chuckled mirthlessly.The termites of popular opinion and democracy were replacing the time-honored dry rot of autocratic power. Survival meant less in the way of "bare knuckle" tactics and more in the way of thought which he calculated Douglas was now incapable of. He needed not only to dispose of Douglas but also Kate, discretely. No hurry though, he reminded himself once again, the time will come.

McQue backed away from the eyepiece of his telescope where he'd been intently viewing Douglas watching him through another telescope in the castle window. Disgusting snoop, he thought, reaching for a dead cigar resting in a Waterford crystal ashtray. He lit the cigar and blew a cloud of smoke toward the window. Then he proceeded to the front window of his office which looked out onto Gunnison's main street. A delivery boy dashed from the telegraph office and ran down the street. McQue opened the curtains and watched the boy disappear beneath the awning of the butcher shop and wondered what news could be so urgent for a butcher.

Had McQue been able to see the other side of the awning he would have observed that the boy didn't enter the butcher shop at all but rather the sheriff's office. And, if he'd stayed at the window, he'd also have seen Doc Shores jog with the boy back across the street to the telegraph office. But Stryker McQue by that time had turned from the window and was headed downstairs into the saloon for a drink and a few hands of poker.

Doc tore a leaf from the telegrapher's pad and grabbed the stub of a pencil from the counter. He wrote:

Marshal Jim Clark, Cimarron Colorado stop
Message received stop
Will proceed immediately to area you directed North Rim of Black Canyon stop
Meet me there tomorrow stop
Cyrus Wells Shores

Doc hurried back to his office where Moots was just serving up coffee. "Bent, you're going to have to hold down the fort here for a couple of days.

Looks like there's been some killin over 'round the canyon, some sheepherders. Killers ran the herd over the canyon rim. I'm meeting up with Clark on the North Rim." Doc gave him the details as he collected his revolvers, rifle, and ammunition.

Moots opened his mouth to speak. His lips parted but his teeth didn't, and he clapped his hand to his mouth. He turned aside and replaced his false teeth. "Dad blamed things," he said sheepishly. "Kate says I'll get used to them but it's been over a year and they're still tryin' to get away from me."

Doc laughed. "Dad blamed?" Kate had cleaned up Moots's mouth in more ways than one since they got married. Moots's wool suit (complete with deputy's badge), clean-shaven face and a new hat along with the teeth rendered him almost unrecognizable from that first fateful meeting on the road to Hays.

"You figure J.M's behind this?" asked Moots.

"Wouldn't doubt it — somehow. If not in person, you can bet J.M. and the Cattlemen's Association knew about it."

"That'd have to be one god awful mess at the bottom of the canyon wouldn't it?"

"Yeah, I'm not overly fond of either sheep or Mexicans, but this is enough to turn my stomach. I'll stop by the house and tell Agnes."

As Doc expected, Agnes heaved a great sigh but began helping him get his bedroll, food, and canteen together. "Is Benton going with you?"

"No, someone has to be here to look after things."

"You need another deputy."

"The office can't afford one; 'sides Jim Clark's comin' up from Cimarron to meet me."

"He's worse than nothing. You watch him. He isn't any better than Douglas or McQue."

"What! You'd say that about a fine southern boy, good confederate soldier, and a duly appointed minion of the law?"

"He was neither southern nor confederate. He was a murdering, pillaging, renegade who rode with those murdering brigands, Quantrill and Anderson. Is Douglas in on this?"

"I reckon."

"Don't underestimate him. Even a sick snake can still bite."

"Not if you grab 'im like this and hold 'im real tight." He playfully reached out and took Agnes by the neck. She screeched and tried to turn around to swing at him, but he held her out at his long arm's length. They whirled around in circles finally collapsing on the bed laughing.

They stopped and jumped to their feet when a small boy with smudged hands and muddy face entered the bedroom. His thick, tousled black hair was a tangle of twigs and mud. Frank reminded Doc of himself at that age. The venerable Catfish trailed the boy. One of the braces on the boy's overalls had broken so he'd fastened the other across his chest to the opposite clasp. The overalls bagged open on one side.

"Whatcha doin'?" he asked.

Doc reached down and stroked the dog's head. "Packin' up for a huntin' trip."

"Can I go?"

Doc hoisted the boy into his arms and sat down on the bed. "I don't think you're quite ready for this kind of a huntin' trip yet. You have to stay home and take care of Mommy." Doc could only manage a weak smile as the boy dropped his eyes and tucked his dirty hair under his father's chin. "Tell you what, Frank, I'll take you fishin' down on the Gunnison when I get back. We'll take a picnic lunch and spend all day together and bring back lots of big fish for Mommy to clean and cook."

"Oh boy!" said Agnes. "Sounds like heaps of fun for everyone."

"Can Catfish go?" asked Frank.

"Humm. Can Catfish fish? Sure." Doc laughed.

"Well," said Agnes, "Frank'll watch Catfish, you'll watch Frank, but who's going to watch you? You're not leaving me at home."

Doc laughed. "All right, everyone goes." He set the boy back on the floor. "Now take Catfish and run outside and see how many flowers you can dig up in an hour."

"Frank! Don't you or that dog touch those flowers." Agnes yelled as the boy, trailed by the dog, ran out the front door of the house.

Doc took his wife in his arms and hugged her. "Ag," he asked, "are you happy?"

"Blissfully so . . . except . . . "

"Except for my job?"

"Yeah." she nodded.

He gave her a little squeeze. "I'll be all right. Justice always prevails."

"Justice goes to the strong," she said simply.

Only a small, brilliant dome of sun had cleared the eastern mountain peaks and the dew lay heavily upon the sage as Doc cantered from the house and down the lane the next morning. The cold breeze snapped at his ears and nose and made his eyes water. Old Skip, normally slow and sluggish these days, arched his neck high, champed at the bit, broke from a walk to a trot, then to a rhythmic canter. When Doc reined in at Jim Clark's campfire the sun had descended behind Black Canyon's rim at least on hour earlier. He'd been in the saddle for nearly sixteen hours. Skip's chin was almost dragging the ground. Doc dismounted. He almost collapsed when his feet hit the ground and he had to steady himself with the saddle horn.

"Doc", said Clark, bringing him a tin cup of black coffee, "I was beginnin' to wonder if you'd make it tonight."

"I sure 'nuf was about played out and ready to camp when I saw your fire from that last ridge. It was a sight for sore eyes."

"Go on over by the fire. I'll take care of your horse, hobble him over on that patch of grass with mine. There's no water but the grass is lush. I'll heat up some beans and bacon."

"Thanks, Jim, I could sure use a bite to eat. It's been a long day. Reminds me of my days as a Pecos cowboy, eatin' and sleepin' in the saddle."

Before dinner Clark brought out the bottle and afterward cigars which they lit with piñon tapers from the fire. Doc unbuttoned the top of his pants and leaned back on his saddle. He poked at the fire with the twig. "What happened here?"

"The short of it is that some cowboys, reckon they were from up around your stompin' ground, shot up a herd of sheep and drove the rest off the edge into the canyon. You can take a look tomorrow. Not much to see, way too far down. That'd probably be the end of it 'cept they also killed a couple of herders."

"How'd you find out about it?"

"One of the herders, son of one of the killed men, had gone to relieve himself when the others got bushwhacked. He hid out and watched the whole thing and then made his way back to Cimarron. Caused quite a commotion at Mrs. Ember's boardin' house. She's got a couple of Mesi-cans workin' in her kitchen who could understand 'im enough — he don't speak reg'lar Mesi-can — to head 'im in my direction. I got no use for them folks but a killin's a killin', even in Gunnison County, so I telegraphed you."

Doc nodded. He neither liked nor trusted Clark who had come west after the war to escape his past. He thought Clark a ruthless opportunist who played both sides of the law as it profited him. If he wasn't on Douglas's payroll he sure knew who was in charge in the county. "He get a good look at any of 'em?"

"Yeah, nearly as I can tell. He thinks he can recognize some of 'em again."

"Where is he now?"

"Got 'im in a cell in Cimarron."

"Under arrest?"

"Naw, just to make sure he don't run off."

"We'll go into town tomorrow and have a talk with him."

Early the following morning the two men walked to the edge of the canyon. An area of trampled sagebrush and scrub oak led toward the edge of the canyon. Doc followed Clark out onto some slickrock which had been thoroughly scratched white by hundreds of panicked hooves. He strolled up beside the marshal and lurched backward at the sight. "Aaah!" he yelled. Just inches beyond the tips of his boots the earth fell away for more than two thousand feet to the river. He landed on his butt and scrambled backward over the crushed sage on his hands and heels. Clark watched him scuttle like a crab and laughed. "Watch that first step, Doc."

"Oh thanks!" Doc said, regaining his feet.

"Come on, don't you want to see this fine piece of scenery?"

Doc crept to the edge of the canyon. He stretched his torso forward keeping the soles of his boots firmly planted on the shelf of rock. Never had he looked so far down. Never would he have thought he would ever gaze down several hundred feet to the back of a soaring eagle. Nothing about the thin green ribbon below recalled to him the broad, surging Gunnison River which flowed past his home. The view began to rotate, and he immediately stepped back and fixed his eyes on the opposite rim.

"See them white dots down there?" asked Clark.

"Yep," Doc lied.

"Woolies."

"Yep." Doc edged further back until he felt his dizziness dissipate. "Well," he said as bravely as he could, "reckon I've seen enough here. What say we mosey on back to Cimarron and talk to that young fella?" Clark agreed and walked from the edge. Doc stifled a sigh of relief.

"I planted them two Mesi-can fellas what got killed over there by that cedar. You wanta see?"

Doc just waved his hand and wobbled toward camp. The land still moved under him, and the horizon revolved slowly when he could bring himself to look at it. He had no appetite for another meal of pork and beans so he nibbled on jerky and hardtack washed down with sips of water from his canteen. By the time the sun had cleared the horizon he felt more like riding. The two men saddled and backtracked east until they found a place where the canyon flattened out enough so they could ford the river. From there they wound their way west through and around ravines and cliffs. It took them another full day to reach Cimarron.

They checked in on the Mexican herder, a boy Doc guessed from the absence of whiskers, of no more than his early teens. The boy sat forlornly on a metal bunk attached to the flat iron bars of his cell. He wore only a thin, berry-dyed cotton shirt, a pair of crude homespun wool trousers, and a sheepskin vest. A dirty old mattress and blanket covered the cell bunk. At his feet lay an untouched tin plate of bacon and beans and a cup of coffee. Doc felt a twinge of pity for the boy.

"Well," said Clark. "I'm bushed. Let's turn in. You're welcome to the empty cell next to the boy or you can spend the county's money for the Black Canyon Hotel.

Doc opted for the hotel room. He thought the Gunnison County taxpayers wouldn't mind.

The next morning as Doc luxuriated over a large plate of ham and eggs, Clark pulled up a chair and sat down. He unfurled a newspaper and said, "Take a gander at this." The headline read: "SHEEPHERDERS KILLED, SHERIFF INVESTIGATES." "How the hell'd the newspaper find out?" Clark asked.

Doc thought for a moment. "The telegrapher or his messenger. I think they were the only ones to see your telegram and my answer."

"Guess I should have been more particular about what I said in my telegram."

"Well," Doc shrugged, "can't be helped now. Let's eat up and go talk to the boy."

"Oh, this also came for you." Clark handed Doc a telegram. Doc read it and scratched his chin. "Problem?" asked Clark.

"Could be. It's from Douglas. Says he wants me to contact him soon's I find out something. I guess I'm just the suspicious type, but it almost sounded like he knew I was onto something."

After almost two hours of laborious interrogation with one of the boarding house cooks interpreting, they'd learned four things: The boy's name was Santiago. He was Spanish, not Mesi-can. He had no relatives in the United States other than his father and brother, the two dead men, and he could identify the men who had killed them.

"What do wc do now, Doc?"

"I'm going to take him back to Gunnison, but first I'm going to let Douglas know that's what I'm doing. Instead of following the river back I'm going to go the long way, out toward Lake City across the Lake Fork just in case there's a greetin' committee."

"Good plan. While you're finishin' your breakfast I'll mosey on over and telegraph Douglas for you. Save you some time."

"Thanks," said Doc. "I appreciate that." He's a real sidewinder Doc thought as he watched Clark exit the dining room. Looked me straight in the eye and didn't even blink when he said that.

Doc prepared for his and the young Spaniard's return to Gunnison. Through the interpreter he let the boy know what he was going to do and not to be afraid. The boy smiled weakly and nodded. Doc noticed that at least he had eaten a meal.

Doc and his charge left Cimarron after exchanging farewells with Clark and headed east over Blue Mesa and the Little Blue on the south side of the river. But after backtracking several times to be sure they weren't being followed they laboriously recrossed it and climbed up the palisades to a ridge between eastern Black Mesa and western Soap Mesa. That night around the campfire he and Santiago shared jerky and beans and laughed at each other's attempts to speak the other's language. It crossed Doc's mind to shackle the boy before going to sleep, but he thought the better of it and hoped, as he closed his eyes, he hadn't misjudged him. The next morning the sound of breaking wood startled him awake. He opened his eyes and saw that Santiago was already up boiling coffee. The dewy sage smelled particularly good that morning.

They rode east; Doc taking care that they were hidden by the ridgeline which ran parallel to their right just above the river. Occasionally Doc would peek over the ridge just enough to see down into the river valley and across it to the rolling sage hills on the south bank. He saw no one until about midday, when his eye caught the glint of sunlight reflected off something. He focused on the glint. The light flickered. He thought he could also see the hint of a dust cloud moving with the reflections. Enough. He dropped back down below the ridgeline and continued upstream toward Gunnison until, hidden by an aspen grove, he looked down to the lane which led from the main road to Kate's. He waited several minutes but could see no movement throughout his range of vision. Deciding it safe, he led the way down to the lane. But instead of taking the lane home he cut across the intervening low hills staying just out of sight of the buildings. From behind the last ridge, he dismounted, removed his hat and slithered to where he could just barely peek over. No strange saddle horses to be seen. As he watched, Doc saw Moots shuffle around the yard and return to the house. Satisfied, he mounted and led Santiago down the hill to the houses.

Moots's teeth fell out again when he discovered Doc and the boy sitting in the kitchen after having sneaked through the back door. "Jesus, Doc!" He glanced over his shoulder to make certain that Kate hadn't heard him swearing. "What the hell are you doin' here and who's this?"

Doc quickly explained what he'd found on his trip. "Santiago can identify the men who killed his father and brother but we're only an eyelash away from being shot ourselves. That's why we're here instead of the office or my house. Clark sent a message to Douglas supposedly telling him that I'd found something, had a man who could identify the shooters, and that I'd be headed back. I told Clark that just in case of an ambush I was going to take the route out toward Lake City, but I changed routes on the way. Well, about noon today I caught sight of what I suspect were some bushwhackers out there on the south side."

"You reckon there's anyone we can trust around here?"

"Yeah. You, me, Agnes and Kate — and Frank only because he doesn't know who Douglas and McQue are and hasn't learned the value of a dollar yet."

"What's the plan now?"

"I haven't gotten beyond a square meal and good night's rest for the two of us. I'm hopin' that I can think more clearly in the mornin'. Douglas and his boys will be lookin' for me to show up in town with

Santiago. I need you to sneak into town after dark and let Agnes know that I'm all right."

Moots took Doc and Santiago to the parlor where Kate sat in a rocking chair in the bay window crocheting dish rags. "I got some boys in the mill that speak Mexican," she said. "I'll get one of them to translate."

"No," said Doc. "We can't take a chance on anyone, and I mean anyone, knowing we're here for right now. We'll just have to make do with sign language for a while."

"I'm fluent in Spanish," said Kate. "That'll help out." She stopped and added, "Don't look so surprised; you should know by now that women have at least the brain of a man."

Doc and Santiago feasted on chicken and dumplings and fresh bread that evening after Moots left for town and almost immediately retired to the guest bedrooms where Doc drifted into blackness. He awoke late. The sun poured in through the curtains. He picked up his watch from the night table. My God! almost twelve hours of sleep. He stumbled from bed and dressed. In the kitchen he found Santiago and Kate practicing their respective languages over coffee. Santiago had discarded his homespun woolens and fleece vest for clothes from Benton's closet.

"Amazing coincidence isn't it," exclaimed Kate, "that a sixty year old man and a thirteen year old boy can be nearly the same size."

"That it is," smiled Doc.

Moots had returned from town in the early morning hours before sunrise and slept until almost midday. Later he reported to Doc that Agnes and Frank were fine, and Agnes was relieved to learn of Doc's safe return. He also had heard a rumor that Douglas and some of his men had ridden out of town yesterday morning. Doc expressed no surprise but was inwardly dismayed and chagrined that his standing with Douglas had proven so temporary and fragile, and that Douglas himself had probably led the ambush party.

He'd drawn out the suspected murderers but now he was in a quandary. He couldn't stay here and expose his friends to danger nor could he go home and risk the same. He might as well paint a bullseye on the boy's back and set him out on Gunnison's main street as put him in jail. Kate came to the rescue.

"For the time being," she suggested, "just leave Santiago here and go on back into town. Tell Douglas and McQue that you didn't find anything more'n the graves and . . . "

"You're forgetting Clark's telegraph."

"You're right. Tell them that the boy tried to get away and that you shot him crossing the river. By the way, why do you suppose Clark didn't just dump the father and brother in the canyon when he found them?"

"Beats me. He probably did and just piled up some rocks for appearances. Or maybe he was in on it from the beginning and wanted to try and keep himself in the clear with me. Come to think about it, he probably did just that. Anyway, your idea has some merit, but I think they know me well enough that if I tell them I just out-and-out plugged the kid, they'd smell a rat. I need to think of something else, that he got killed trying to get away. Anyway, if they do buy the story I'll sneak the boy into town later. They still don't know what he looks like. We'll see if he can identify some of the men."

"Just be real careful. If they catch the scent of a trap you'll both be coyote bait for sure."

Doc waited for Moots to get dressed, and the two of them departed for town in the early afternoon heat. They went directly to the sheriff's office where they were surprised to find the door open and J. M. Douglas seated with his boots resting on Doc's desk. After exchanging insincerities, Doc told him that his "prisoner" had panicked, made a run for it, and drowned while trying to swim the Gunnison. As he told the story, Doc could feel his mouth turning to cotton. He wasn't a good liar. Douglas, he thought, eyed him suspiciously. He hated the man for forcing him to compromise his honesty as much as anything else Malcolm had done. Douglas seemed to buy the story and left the office with a wave of his hand and a "good riddance." Doc and Moots heaved a collective sigh of relief.

Doc wanted to attack head-on, have Santiago point out the men, and arrest them. "No," advised Kate. "Let the dust settle and let 'em forget about this for a while. My guess is that they're a bit on edge right now and expectin' you to make a move if you have somethin'. Go on about your business as usual and make a plan. It'll also give Santiago some time to learn some English, and that could be a help. If the boy points out the killers and you just wade in and try to arrest them, likely as not you'll just end up pushin' up daisies."

Doc decided to bide his time.

Chapter 14

"Here's the plan," said Doc. Everyone stopped eating and looked to the head of the table. "The Cattlemen's Association is having its yearly brawl at Louden Mullin's La Veta Hotel second week in November. Sooner or later during the week everyone — cattlemen, cowboys, and gunmen — turn up there. Mullin will have to hire extra help for that week, doesn't matter to him who it is as long as they're cheap and can speak a word or two of English. Kate, you know Louden pretty well. I need you to take Santiago over to Mullin and feed him some story in order to get Santiago a job as a waiter. He'll be able to take a look at almost everyone that comes through the hotel."

Kate thought for a moment. "I have to lay people off in the fall anyway, so I'll just tell Louden that he's a good worker and I'm tryin' to help him find another job."

"That's the easy part, Doc," said Moots. "What'll you do once you get 'em pointed out?"

"Arrest 'em."

"Well you know you can count on me to help. I can still shoot straight. I'm just not as quick as I once was. You can be sure that they won't go peacefully and more'n likely there'll be a pack of 'em. You got anybody else in mind that'll give us a hand?"

"Nope. I'd say that everyone else in town is either on the payroll or too damn scared."

"All right, Sheriff," asked Agnes. "How do you plan to jail these people?"

"Take 'em by surprise. Surprise 'em one at a time."

"That should work fine . . . with the first one."

❁❁❁

Stryker McQue, much to Douglas's chagrin (and the other cattlemen's and cowboys' frustration), strictly enforced his own code that none other than sworn lawmen wore guns in town the week of the Cattlemen's Association meeting. In years past, men had forfeited their lives breaking his unwritten law, but only the insanely drunk or foolish did so anymore. Squads of men were stopped on Main Street upon their arrival in town by McQue's town "deputies" and relieved of all openly carried weapons. Doc told McQue about his days on the Concho, and how he and other cowboys had secreted pocket pistols in their chaps and shirts. Now, suspects were forced to nearly strip in the streets of Gunnison. McQue, armed with a Winchester, watched such proceedings from a balcony on the Red Lion Inn, the town's most famous and expensive brothel. From across the street, Doc watched McQue from the porch of the sheriff's office. It was, he thought, a very fragile peace which was based on their mutual concern that Douglas, with enough men, weapons, and alcohol, might decide to reassert himself.

Louden Mullin, at Kate's insistence, unwittingly cooperated with Doc's scheme by hiring the young Spaniard. Kate had drilled Santiago for days in English and table service. He surprised everyone, including himself, by garnering as much as ten dollars a day in tips.

Doc stood watch at the La Veta bar and dining room under the pretext of swapping cattle drive yarns with the older of the crowd, some of whom had known Ed Taylor or ridden the Concho and Pecos themselves. Doc and Moots met secretively each night by candlelight with Santiago in an abandoned mine shaft and discussed who the boy had observed during the day. What the boy told him both delighted and dismayed Shores. Yes, he was happy that Santiago could identify the three men. Two of them, the Miller brothers, Clell and Tom, Doc recognized by their reputation as being among the worst of Douglas's mercenaries. More than one killing and robbery in western Colorado had their names associated with it. But, he was dismayed when the boy identified Douglas himself as one of the killers, something which Doc had feared.

"Now we've got the devil t' pay for sure," sighed Moots after Santiago had left for the hotel. The vapor from his breath nearly blew out the candle.

"Yeah," agreed Doc. He regarded his old friend's face in the yellow glow of the candle. The shadows in the dim light highlighted his lines and wrinkles and reminded Doc of Bent's age. He felt a sudden surge of guilt. "Sure would be a lot simpler to just walk away from this wouldn't it?"

"Sure would . . . but I s'pose we're not goin' to. Are we?"

"No . . . I'm not, but I came into this with my eyes wide open. I got elected knowing that something like this would happen some day. But why would you want to?"

"Coupla reasons. Doc, do you have many friends?"

"Oh, a few I reckon."

"Well, I got one — his name is Doc Shores. That's the first reason. The other is that this may be the single most important thing I've ev'r done in my life — providin' we get it done."

"You also got a wife to think about now."

"Yeah, and we both know what she'd say. I guess you and me better start plannin' our next move."

"Like I said before, 'bout the only thing we got goin' for us is surprise. We really need to get the drop on all three of 'em at once. I doubt if that's possible because Douglas almost never hangs out with any of his men. If we wait too long to make our move, it increases the chance they'll get wind of what we're doin'. I think that we're gonna have to be on our toes for the right opportunity to get the jump on the Millers and get 'em jailed, and then we quickly nab Douglas before he hears about it.

"O.K., we got that part perfected," chided Moots. "Whatta we do then? We got a jail with one cell that won't stand up to a good strong wind and a herd of cattlemen and cowboys who outnumber us about fifty to one."

"We've gotta get the Millers out of town."

"Where? Sure as hell not Cimarron. Montrose?"

"The state prison in Cañon City. I'll contact the prison warden and get his permission. Soon's we get 'em rounded up I'll ask for a change of venue. Judge Gilpin won't be any more anxious to face his boss in a Gunnison County courtroom than we will be to have him tried here — which is also why we won't be goin' to the judge for warrants. My guess is he'll jump at the chance to get 'em down to Fremont County."

"How? It ain't safe to telegraph out of Gunnison."

"No. You're sneakin' down on the train."

"Oh."

"O.K. Let's get back and put on our best act. It's business as usual."

Doc had been wondering for days how to break the news to Agnes. "Ag," he suggested one night at dinner, "why don't you and Frank visit your relatives in Denver for a few weeks?"

"What're you talking about? I don't have any relatives in Denver. I don't even have any relatives."

"We'll say you do."

"All right. Let's have it. What's up?"

Doc told her of the plan. "I don't know that there's any danger, but it could get rough, and I wouldn't put anything past Douglas if he gets desperate enough. I need to know that you and Frank are out of the line of fire."

Agnes argued, but she knew Doc had his mind set. "All right," she sighed. "When do we go, and where do we stay?"

"As soon as you can get packed. You'll stay at Kate's house. She'll already be there 'visiting her sons.' It won't be for long."

Agnes nodded and walked silently to the bedroom without looking at Doc. When he'd accepted the job, and later after being elected to it, they both knew there would come a day when he would regret it. But Doc hadn't thought it would be so soon, nor the occasion so serious. The conversation was sparse and forced as Doc helped her pack. He was relieved when Frank, chased by Catfish, ran through the bedroom and distracted them. He caught his son and hoisted him above his head while the dog clawed at Doc's pant legs.

"Guess what?"

"What?"

"You get to take a train ride all the way to Denver with Mommy and visit Grandma Kate, and she'll take you downtown to see the tall buildings and ride on a steam elevator."

"Oh boy! Can Catfish go too?"

"Sure."

"Are you goin'?"

"Not right now. Probably later at Christmas."

"Oh."

"But when I do, we'll go out to City Park and build snow forts and throw snowballs and go for sleigh rides . . . ."

"Oh boy!"

Doc from the corner of his eye could see his wife's face softening, and he reached out with his free arm and caught her around her tiny waist and pulled her to them. Frank reached out and put his arm around his mother's neck, and the three stood tangled in one embrace.

Doc and Agnes made love that night for the first time in months. It was awkward and strained and made Doc realize how his job had distanced him from his wife. He felt remorse and vowed to himself that he would somehow make it up to her when this business with Douglas was over, provided he was still alive. Afterward she wrapped as much of her small body around his as she could and clung tightly to him. "Ag," he whispered in her ear, "I hate to admit it, but I'm scared to death. If there was any way to get out of this gracefully, I would."

"No you wouldn't. It's not in you to do anything easily or gracefully, and you don't own an ounce of give-up. Sure, there's times when I wish you were satisfied with just being a cowboy or teamster or shopkeeper, but then if you were, you wouldn't be the man I fell in love with and married."

"But you didn't exactly bargain for this."

"That's what you say. When you get married you bargain for whatever comes along. In fact, that's just life in general. But I would prefer that you don't get yourself killed."

"I'm proud of you. I'm proud to be with you. You're the best thing that ever happened to me."

"You can bet I'll remind you of that from time to time — for the rest of our lives."

He lay awake listening to her breathing deepen as he tickled the small of her back with his fingernails. He listened to her and inhaled as much of the lilac scent of her hair as he could. It would be a while before he would be doing so again. Doc hoped that he would be doing so again.

Doc made sure the Gunnison Criterion reported in its Monday edition that Agnes Shores would be leaving town to visit relatives in Denver. It did not mention where she would be staying. On the day of their departure they said good-bye twice, the tearful one at home, the other one, a cheerful "see-you-in-a-few-days," on the station platform. As Agnes boarded the train Doc whispered, "Thank you" in his wife's ear. She quickly grasped his arm and squeezed it.

Doc and Moots casually watched the faces on the platform and in the station for a hint of suspicion. Doc remembered Kate's comments about the valley being a nest of spies. But they saw only red-cheeked passengers and well-wishers embracing in the early morning vapor and then scurrying off to the train or station to escape the cold. He waved a final farewell as the train lurched and chugged its way from the platform in a cloud of black smoke.

The two men returned to Doc's house for breakfast.

"Bent, you stay here in town with me. Jack Keady can take care of things out at the mill. We'll ride every other day or so to check on things there. Santiago can go back out there and help Ben around the house. We'll bide our time until we can find an opportunity to catch all three of 'em by surprise."

The two found it difficult to watch the comings and goings of Douglas and the brothers without attracting attention to themselves. Douglas might not leave his castle for days and nights on end. Then he might depart suddenly in the middle of the night for the saloons, casinos, and brothels, and be gone for days. More than once Doc and Moots were nearly caught by Douglas returning to his house.

The Millers proved to be almost as elusive. Working cowhands spend most of their time in the company of other cowboys at the line shacks or bunkhouses, or in the snows of the mountain meadows where a person approaching could be seen more than a mile away.

"I fairly don't know when we'll get an opportunity," complained Moots one night after sharing the same pot of venison stew with Doc for the third night in a row.

"I know," agreed Doc. "I think that manhuntin' is one of the most frustratin' and disappointin' things you can do. Just when you think you're on their trail or you've got 'em whipped, you come to a dead end and have to start all over again."

Christmas passed in a flurry of clouds, wind, and snow, and still the opportunity to act did not present itself. The wait had become nearly unbearable when fate suddenly took matters in hand.

Late in February, three men robbed the Denver and Rio Grande Western train in the canyon between Cimarron and Gunnison. When they couldn't open the safe in the baggage car they robbed the engineer, fireman, and passengers of about forty dollars in cash and valuables and rode upstream toward Gunnison. The engineer telegraphed Marshal Jim Clark in Cimarron from the halfway house. Clark telegraphed Doc in Gunnison that the train robbers appeared to be headed his way. Clark didn't wait for a reply but saddled up and proceeded toward Gunnison.

Doc told Moots to be on the lookout and to inform McQue that the outlaws might be on their way. He collected Skip and rode out to make a wide sweep to the west of town to see if he could pick up any fresh tracks in the snow which had fallen during the night. Instead of following the road directly out of town he started out to the north then swung wide to his left where he intercepted the road, then he continued circling toward the south.

As he passed over the road, he observed wagon tracks but gave them little consideration. By midafternoon the sun had turned the wet snow into a sea of muck. When he arrived at the gravel bank of the river he turned and headed east toward town. As he was hitching Skip to the rail in front of his office, Jim Clark walked through the door. "Sheriff," he said touching the brim of his hat, "have any luck?"

"Not a bit. I covered about three miles either side of the road and didn't pick up any tracks 'cept for a wagon. They might have swung out farther away from town so's not to be seen or they came through early enough that the snow covered up their tracks." He thought for a moment. "You don't suppose they could have backtracked toward Cimarron?"

"Possible I 'spose. Well, I ain't headin' back this afternoon. I'm gonna get me a room at the La Veta and relax and have a good steak dinner." Clark stopped to look at something he'd seen.

Doc turned and looked into the street to see what had interrupted Clark but saw only a wagon heading out of town. Then in a panic, he saw Santiago driving the wagon. Doc's heart stopped. He couldn't breathe. Mind blank, mouth dry, he turned back around and faced Clark.

"Hey!" yelped Clark, "isn't that the Mesi-can boy?"

"What Mexican boy?" Doc asked, struggling to regain his composure.

"You know . . . the one I had down in . . . the one you let get away and drown in the river."

Doc jumped forward and snatched Clark by the lapels, jerking the man's face so close their noses were practically touching. "I didn't let anyone get away. The boy broke and ran and was in the river before I could do anything about it — and I sure as hell wasn't going to jump in to save some no-count Mexican." Clark reached up and grabbed Shores wrists, and the two men wrestled back and forth for a few moments.

"All right! All right!" yelled Clark finally. "He just got away. You're sure a might touchy about it, Shores."

Doc relaxed his grip. He could see over the top of Clark's hat the wagon heading out of town at a trot. "Yeah, well, I take my job seriously and get a mite riled up when someone says I let a prisoner slip away. You'd probably feel the same way if I'd said that to you."

"I reckon," said Clark straightening his jacket. He started to turn around.

Doc caught him by the shoulder to prevent him from turning around and in his best conciliatory tone said, "Sorry. Just to show you there's no hard feelings, let me buy you a drink and that steak dinner."

"All right," smiled Clark. "I'll take you up on that."

Shores breathed a sigh of relief. Apparently he'd been able to distract Clark. The two men separated. Doc took Skip to the livery stable, promising to catch up with Clark at the La Veta. As soon as the marshal was out of sight he caught up with the stable boy. "You know what my deputy, Benton Moots looks like?" The boy nodded. "Here's a silver cartwheel. You keep an eye out for him, and if he ain't got back to town by the time you finish up here this evenin' you head out to Knight's Mill and catch hold of him and tell him to get to my house and stay there and wait for me." Doc went back to the office and pulled his gun and belt from the drawer. He drew the hammer back to half-cock, opened the loading gate, and twirled the cylinder on his shirt sleeve. He checked the cartridge belt and filled the few empty loops with .45 caliber cartridges from a box in the drawer and then strapped on the belt. It felt good and snug and secure around his waist. He loosened the buckle a notch and dropped the holster an inch or so lower on his right hip. Doc relocked his office door and headed toward the La Veta.

"What's up?" asked Moots. The clock in the hallway was just striking eight when Doc walked in the door of his house.

"We've got to make our move — soon! In fact, it may be too late right now."

"Why! What happened?"

"Clark's in town chasin' some train robbers and saw Santiago drivin' a wagon out of town."

"Jesus! I clean forgot that the men have been takin' turns drivin' into town once a week for supplies now that Kate's gone. Usually she did it. It must have been Santiago's turn. Did Clark recognize him?"

"I think so. I picked a fight real quick to distract him, but I'm not sure it worked. Then I kept my eye on him at the hotel for as long as I could. But I had to get back here and let you know what's happening."

"My guess is that he made a beeline to J.M. as soon as you left him at the La Veta. The next question is, even if he knows the boy's still alive, does he know where to find him?"

"Yeah, the company name was on the side of the wagon. They'll sure 'nuf sniff him out sooner or later. The other thing is, now they know I lied about Santiago. I'd say, as of tonight, we're marked men. From now on we don't go out alone, and we don't go out unless we're fully armed."

"I got a suggestion," said Moots. "We make our move tonight while we still got surprise on our side. The Miller brothers are in the line shack up in the Almont area and don't know what's goin' on. Douglas is alone down here. Even if Clark got to him tonight, which he might not, it'll take a while for Douglas to plan his next move. He won't be expecting us to act quickly."

"Bent, my hat's off to ya. But we've got to move fast and get them all rounded up tonight, because the word'll be out tomorrow and they'll be ready for us."

From the office they collected rifles, another revolver apiece which they stuck in their belts, and a shotgun each. Moots insisted, over Doc's protest, that he carry the old single-shot "Thunderbolt."

They exited the back door of the office into a moonlit alley which they followed to the back of the stable. The men saddled their horses and were soon cantering on the road north toward Almont.

The line shack, a remnant of the early days of the Douglas empire, had been a remote outpost accessible only by foot or horse. In the depths of winter the snowdrifts still prevented resupply by wagon. But now, in early spring, Doc and Moots cantered steadily along on the frozen road leading to Crested Butte until they came to a trail leading off to their right through the spruce, fir, and aspen. They slowed to a trot, and after a couple of miles upon spying a light in the distance, to a walk. They dismounted and removed their jingling spurs and buried them inside their coats. Even then, they stopped a good quarter-mile from the shack and tied their horses. Doc led the way trying to step in already frozen foot prints rather than the crusty snow.

He stationed Moots behind a tree and crept to the window in the rear of the cabin from which they'd seen the light in the distance. He removed his hat and peeked one eye over the windowsill. Two bearded men sat in dirty long johns playing cards in the glow of a smoking lantern. Doc recognized them as the Miller brothers. In the center of the room a small pot-bellied stove glowed a light orange. The card players passed a half-full bottle of whiskey back and forth. No firearms could be seen. He motioned Moots forward. "I'm going to try the door," he whispered. "Let's not tip our hand and let them know there's two of us just yet. You stay here and cover me. If they get the drop on me, break out the window and shoot 'em." Moots nodded

Doc gingerly tiptoed around the corner of the cabin toward the door. Every breath echoed through the night air like a Chinese gong. Every footstep was a cannon shot. Light from the lantern inside leaked through the top and bottom of the door where it was warped away from its frame. A cord attached to a small antler handle ran through the left side of the door. Doc figured the other end went to a draw bar on the inside. He could see no evidence of another latch or a lock. Inside the men argued and laughed loudly. Shores cocked and very gently rested his sawed-off shotgun against the door frame. With his left hand he pulled down gently on the wooden handle. It didn't budge. He pulled down harder and still it didn't move. Dizzy from holding his breath, he backed away from the door and inhaled deeply. Probably, he thought, the door is so warped that the bar is caught against its latch. He tried again, pushing ever so slightly on the door at the same time. This time the cord moved slightly. He drew downward harder and could feel the drawbar lift from its latch. The door moved an inch or two inward. Doc pushed the door open with the shotgun muzzle. Startled, the two men jumped to their feet.

"Stay where you are!" Doc shouted. "Keep your arms at your sides."

"What the hell is this? Who are you?"

"Sheriff Doc Shores. You're under arrest for murder. Get your clothes on and saddle-up, I'm takin' you into town." They hesitated. Doc's eyes followed theirs around the room. He saw rifles and six-gun holsters hanging from wall pegs. "Hold it! Stand where you are and put your hands on top of your heads. Now circle slowly around to your left one step at a time. As they circled Doc also circled to his left and positioned himself between them and their guns. Keeping them covered with the shotgun, he began tossing their clothing across the room to them. They regarded him with fierce eyes and menacing frowns.

"You must be crazy, Shores," said one of them. "You know who we work for?"

"Yeah, I know. In fact the three of you are goin' to be sharin' the same cell right soon." They stopped dressing and looked at him with surprised expressions. "Come on, hurry up, I haven't got all night." As they dressed Doc called to Moots. The Millers looked at Moots with utter hatred when he entered the door. "Bent, light up a couple more lanterns, these boys are gonna need some light to saddle their horses."

After the Millers had saddled their horses under the muzzle of Doc's shotgun Moots brought his and Doc's horses up to the cabin and all four mounted. "Boys," said Doc, "I want you to start off for town at a walk and stay at a walk until we get there, even if it takes us the rest of the night. We're gonna be right behind you, and the first man so much as breaks into even a trot will get at least two barrels of buckshot in the middle of his back. Now! head out."

Morning's pale light was just beginning to silhouette the eastern peaks when Doc finished shackling both his prisoners, arm and leg, inside their cell. He further secured the locked cell door with a log chain and padlock. Benton built a fire in the stove and tossed the shivering men a couple of blankets.

"What about breakfast?" groused one of the brothers. "We ain't et since last evenin'."

"Sure," said Doc, winking at Moots, "here's some jerky and coffee'll be ready soon." He handed each of the surly men a slab of dried meat and a biscuit.

"Uh!" said one of the brothers after tearing off a shred of the meat and chewing on it, "this is awful. What is it?"

"Mutton," replied Doc. "Should serve to remind you of those two sheepherders you killed."

"Don't worry none," added Moots. "The coffee'll make up for it." He winked at Doc.

After they had fed for their prisoners, Doc and Moots discussed their plan to arrest Douglas.

"We can't jus' march up to the front door can we?" asked Moots.

"I am, but first we're gonna sneak around back and find you a way inside just in case he gets the drop on me or tries to bolt out the back. If that happens, give him one chance to stop and disarm himself and then shoot 'im real quick."

The sheriff and his deputy crept through Gunnison's semi-dark, empty streets and alleys until they reached the edge of town where they sprinted from shadow to shadow as they approached the castle on the hill. The rear of the house did indeed have a door, but it was locked, as were all of the first floor windows. Doc stepped back and examined the stone wall above them. He whispered. "I think I can see a window up there on the second floor that's cracked open just a mite. Now we got to figure how to get you up there."

"Up there?" Moots rasped. "I got to tell you Doc. I ain't no friend to high places, and I sure ain't no mountain goat."

"I think we can do it if you get on my shoulders," said Doc, ignoring his companion's concerns. "I'll at least get you up as far as I can and then you should be able to catch hold of the window frame and scramble up the rest of the way." Doc squatted down and Moots climbed onto his shoulders. Doc could hear his friend clawing at the stone and came close to toppling over backward. "Lean into the wall," he hissed. "Lean into the wall." That seemed to help; they stopped rocking backward.

"Doc," rasped Moots. "I still can't quite reach it."

"Hold on . . . O.K. lift up your left boot and step onto my hand." Doc let go of Moots's ankle and formed a platform with the palm of his hand into which Moots gingerly placed his boot. "O.K., now the other one." Doc was surprised at his skinny deputy's weight on his left arm. He nearly collapsed again. Doc leaned into the wall as Moots stepped up onto his right hand. He pressed up with all his shoulder strength. More scratching on the rock. Just when he thought he could no longer hold his arms up, there was a sudden release of pressure and the sound of boot soles scratching against sandstone. He backed away and looked up just in time to see Moots's boots disappearing in the window.

After a few seconds a head popped out.

"Made it," Moots whispered hoarsely.

"Good. Can you see anything?"

"Not a thing."

"O.K. We'll wait until it gets light enough for you to look around."

"Hand me up my long-gun."

Shores picked up the old breechloader by the tip of the barrel, and standing on his tip-toes, lifted it up to his deputy who had to lean halfway out of the window to catch the butt plate with his finger tips.

Doc hunkered down in his coat and sat back against the red stone. Suddenly exhausted, he realized that he hadn't slept in twenty-four hours nor eaten in twelve and he had ridden all night. Though shivering violently, he could barely keep his eyes open. He daydreamed of being curled up around Agnes' warm body, beneath flannel blankets and down quilts. He dozed but awakened with a start when the rising sun touched his face. He looked around quickly but saw no one. He called up to Moots in a loud whisper. Nothing. He called out as loudly as he dared. No response. Did he now wait until Moots woke up and possibly lose the element of surprise or act now and possibly lose their quarry? He crept to the front of the castle.

The massive double door looked as though it had been built to withstand a siege. Oak cross beams and wide iron bands bolstered its tall oak planks. Doc slammed the heavy bronze knocker against its strike plate sending a cannonade echoing through the morning stillness. Nothing happened. Doc banged again, louder. Now he thought he could hear someone inside and the sound of an iron bolt being drawn through a latch. Still the door did not open. Doc drew his revolver. From inside, Douglas's voice called, "Enter." He pushed at the door with his boot, and it creaked open to a dark entryway — save for a shaft of morning sun coming through the open door. He could see the figure of a man standing several paces back from where the sunlight glanced off the flagstone floor. Doc brought his six gun up and cocked it. The figure didn't move but yelled out, "Don't shoot Doc. It's me."

"Bent, where's Douglas?"

"Right here, Shores," came a voice from somewhere in the room. "I got the drop on your deputy. Pesky critter climbed into my bedroom last night, evidently was gonna rob and kill me. Guess I'm gonna have to shoot 'im."

Doc instinctively backed several steps away from the door. "You do and I'll drop you."

"Maybe. Then again I might get both of you."

"Shoot a sheriff and his deputy?"

"Doc, think about where you are. I still own this town, this county. You think Stryker's gonna arrest me for killin' the two of you? Not likely. Hell, sheriffs are easy to come by here. Make you a deal though. You and your sidekick walk away from this. No one gets killed, and you both get your salaries doubled plus a bonus."

"No thanks. I'd still have to live with myself."

Douglas stepped from the shadows behind Moots into the reflected light of the atrium. Doc could see he had a rifle trained on his friend's back. Moots had his thumb hooked into the front of his gun belt and Doc tensed when he saw the deputy wiggling his index finger back and forth. He hoped he was reading it right.

"You're crazy, Shores. You think someone in this town, this county, gives a damn about what happened to some G'damn sheepherders? You want to lose your life over this?" Douglas stepped farther into the sunlight behind Moots. Doc acted instinctively.

"Now Moots!" he shouted and palmed the hammer on his revolver back to full cock. Moots dove to his left away from the muzzle of Douglas's rifle. He didn't have time to aim, so Doc fired from the hip hoping that the shot would hit Douglas somewhere and give him time for a second shot. Through the cloud of blue smoke he could see Douglas still standing. Malcolm too fired from the hip. The old rifle erupted in smoke and flame. Doc braced himself for the bone-crunching impact of the large caliber bullet. Instead, he heard Douglas scream and saw him disappear backward into the darkness. Doc dove to the ground and fired his revolver into the empty doorway. In the calm that followed, nothing moved except clouds of smoke drifting in the morning sun. He heard only a groan. "Bent!" Doc called out, "are you all right?"

"Never better."

"Where's Douglas?"

"He's down. Looks like he's down and out. You musta plugged him for good."

"Careful. I think I missed him."

"If you did, you missed him real close because from here he sure looks like he's bleedin' a heap."

Doc, six-gun ready, got to his feet and crept toward the door. Once inside, his eyes adjusted to the dark. He saw Douglas lying on his back. Angling his gun at the body he inched forward. Out of the corner of his eye he saw Moots stand up. Douglas moaned louder. The rifle lay almost ten feet from his body. Doc slowly dropped the hammer of his revolver with his thumb and returned it to its holster. Moots had called it right. Douglas streamed blood from his head to his waist. Doc first thought his lucky pistol shot had hit a large vein in the man's head or neck, but then he noticed that there was very little blood on the floor. Both men approached the body cautiously.

"What the h . . . ?" Doc began but was interrupted.

"Doc, you were right about missin' him. Looky here." Moots bent over and picked up the remains of the old Thunderbolt, nearly broken in half. The chamber and lock were missing and what metal was left was twisted and stained with powder burn. “I’ll be switched, blew up — just like you always said it would. I knew I was keepin’ that rifle around for some good reason.”

“Bent, go fetch the doctor. I’ll stay here and keep an eye on J.M.”

“Doctor?” exclaimed Moots in surprise, “I say we just let him go nice and peaceful right here and spare ourselves a heap of future trouble. Maybe even plug ‘im again.”

“I reckon I may live to regret, it but I still can’t just stand by and let a man die. Go on now and fetch the doctor like I asked.” Moots sauntered out the door as though headed for a dental appointment. “And don’t stop for breakfast and a nap on the way!” Doc called after him.

Shores pulled a red velvet pillow from a divan and put it under Malcolm’s head. He could see more clearly now that the wounds, although numerous, were superficial and guessed that probably the concussion from the exploding weapon and the fall backward onto the marble floor had knocked him unconscious. This speculation was confirmed by the doctor upon his arrival. Doc was reminded of his own youthful misfortunes with old guns.

“Doc,” said Moots while the doctor examined Douglas, “I think we may have more trouble comin’ up. As I was fetchin’ the doctor, I saw Jim Clark and Tom Horn hightailin’ it west out of town.”

Shores thought for a moment. “Santiago!” he nearly shouted. “I didn’t fool Clark with my act, and he knows where to find the boy from the sign on the side of the wagon. Evidently Douglas thought he could get this taken care of today before we came after him, and that’s why he didn’t try to run. Bent, stay here with the doctor and don’t let Douglas out of your sight until I get back.”

“Right. Oh, Doc . . . sorry I fell asleep and let Douglas get the drop on me.”

“Well we picked the wrong window. ‘Sides I fell asleep myself. Get some rest today if you can. I’ll be needin’ you later for sure.”

Doc checked in on his two surly prisoners before leaving town. “You boys are gonna be havin’ company soon enough.”

Both men reacted with surprise. “You got Douglas?” one of them asked.

“Yep,” Doc replied. “He’s a bit beat up right now, but soon’s he gets well enough the three of you are gonna be roomin’ together for a while — least until I can get you down to Cañyon City.” The brothers sat with their mouths agape.

Shores trotted to the livery stable. “Sorry to make you work so hard old fella,” he said, slapping the saddle blanket on Skip’s back. “You put in a good day of it today, and I’ll try not to bother you again for a while.” The horse burst from the barn at a gallop almost running over Stryker McQue who jumped back and raised his hand. Doc reined in.

"You know about Clark and Horn?"

Surprise. Nothing escaped McQue. "Yep." How much did the Irishman know?

As if to answer Doc's question: "That Spanish lad's going to be crow bait if you don't catch up with them. I heard the shootin'. You kill J.M.?"

"No, but he's not feelin' real perky right now."

"Need any help?"

Again, Doc was surprised. He certainly didn't trust McQue enough to depend on him in a gun battle. "No, thanks, but if you wouldn't mind, I'd appreciate it if you would check in on Moots up at Douglas's sometime today."

"Sure. Watch yourself out there, Shores. Clark's a coward and won't give you any trouble unless he gets a chance to shoot you in the back. Horn's the one. He's fearless, and he's dead on with that Creedmor, would think nothin' of usin' you for target practice."

"Yeah, I've seen him in action. Thanks, I'll keep it in mind."

"Good luck . . . and may you be in heaven an hour 'fore the devil knows you're dead."

"Not the parting words I'd hoped for," grinned Doc.

Doc galloped out of town toward Kate's, mud and ice flying from beneath Skip's hooves. But instead of taking the road south, which curved in and out of the hills and ravines he dropped down to a wide trail that ran along the river. He hoped to get to Santiago first, because he had no idea what he would do if he intercepted the two men. He was certain he could beat Clark in an up-front fight, but Horn was another matter. It was more than seven miles downstream to Kate's. Skip, exhausted from being ridden for most of the past twenty-four hours, stumbled badly after the first mile. Doc couldn't prod him out of a trot after the second mile. His chances of getting to Santiago first were rapidly disappearing. Upon clearing the last bend in the river, his heart sank. A group of Kate's workmen clustered around something in the yard in front of the mill. He rode up to them. They parted to reveal the body of a man with blood-stained clothes lying on the ground. The supervisor, Jack Keady hailed him.

"Doc, they's two of 'em wearin' flour sacks over their heads. They came into the mill with pistols and told me to get all the men together in the yard. When I did, one of the men came over and pointed at the boy. He didn't say nothin' just pointed, and the other one shot him with his pistol."

A wave of exhaustion nearly forced Doc to his knees, and he felt sick to his stomach. Turning away from Jack, he retched but nothing came up. Doc swallowed hard and turned back to the foreman. "Did you see anything unusual about either of the two men? Their weapons? How they were dressed?"

"Not much. One of them, the one that done the shootin', was a big strong-looking man, a good bit bigger and taller than the other, and he wore high-topped boots with mule ear pulls. Now that you mention it, he had a big ol' long-barreled, single shot rifle in a saddle scabbard. Neither one of 'em said much at all. What's this all about Doc?"

"Maybe I shoulda let you boys in on it. This boy here was a witness to two murders a while back. I planned to keep him hidden until we could make our move on the killers. We just didn't move soon enough. Jack, I'd be much obliged to you if you would build a pine box for him and put him in the icehouse for the time bein' until I can get back out here."

Doc looked at his spent horse. "My horse is dead on his feet. I'm gonna trade him out for one of Kate's for the time bein'. Would you look after him?"

"Sure thing, Doc. Put him in one of the stalls, and I'll get one of the boys to hay and grain 'im."

The mud of the lane revealed four sets of recent hoofprints: two horses arriving and two leaving. When he reached the intersection of the lane with the road, one set of outbound prints split off and headed downstream toward the Black Canyon and Cimarron, and the other headed back toward town. When Doc finally reined in at his office the sun stood low in the sky. Several times he'd fallen asleep in the saddle and nearly toppled from his horse. He unlocked the door expecting Moots to be inside, but he wasn't. Doc stabled the horse and wearily staggered back to the office where he collapsed into his desk chair, put his boots on the desk and was almost instantly asleep.

He didn't know how long he slept. He opened his eyes to someone standing in lantern light and clanging the lids on the stove. "Bent?" he asked.

"Yeah, sorry to wake you. What happened out at the mill?"

"Clark and Horn got there before me. Santiago's as dead as our case against the Millers and Douglas. Clark identified 'im and Horn shot 'im."

"Anybody see it?"

"Yeah, damn near the whole crew, but the killers were wearin' hoods, and even if they weren't, you're not goin' to get anybody in this county to testify against those two."

"Reckon you're right there. What'll we do now, turn 'em all loose?"

"I don't know. As of right now none of the three of 'em know that Santiago's been killed. Let me think on it. Maybe there's a way we can still make some chicken salad out of chickenshit. How's Douglas?"

"Doctor says he'll be all right 'cept he'll probably lose one eye and have a face that looks like a shotgun target. McQue wandered by, said he'd talked to you. The three of us took Douglas over to the Doc's office. He's got a bed there, and we got him handcuffed to the bedstead. Now we can charge him with tryin' to kill you."

Doc nodded his head. "Maybe we're makin' progress here. I'm hopin' that the Millers will also implicate him in the murder of the Spaniards."

"Well, at least we don't have to worry about keepin' things a secret anymore. What's goin' on with McQue?"

"He's just hedgin' his bet in the remote possibility we come out on top."

"What about Clark?"

"I doubt if we'll be seein' him up this way for a good long time. My guess is that he'll just want to lay low from now on, or until he gets a chance to backshoot us."

"Somethin' else," added Moots. "McQue said that nosey critter what owns the newspaper came around askin' about the shots at the castle. I'm sure more'n one person heard 'em."

"Yeah." Doc washed the sleep from his eyes in a basin of cold water. "O.K. Here's what we'll do. First you take the horse I brought to town and go back out to the mill and get Skip. Tell Jack Keady that I want the loan of one of his Mexicans, a young one and fresh out of Mexico. Make sure he hasn't been here long. Tell 'im we're repairin' the house and need extra help. Tell 'im anything you want, but bring 'im straight to the office early as you can tomorrow mornin'. I'll be waitin' here for you." Doc quickly outlined the rest of his plan.

"Right," agreed Moots when he finished. "I'm beginnin' to catch your drift. See you early tomorrow."

Doc staggered back to his cold, dark house and lit a fire in the fireplace. He found a bottle of Milt's good Kentucky whiskey that he'd been saving in a cabinet on the fireplace mantle and pulled a big swallow of the fiery liquid. It made his eyes water and his lungs suck air. He didn't do that often, but above all right now, he needed something to help him sleep. He searched for something to eat and found a jar of home-canned pork and beans. Before finishing the jar, he pulled off his boots and was fast asleep on the sofa in front of the fire.

Doc awoke to a clatter of horses' hooves on the stone walk in front of the house. He rolled off the sofa onto the floor and sat there rubbing his eyes. Moots burst through the door with another man, or rather a boy. The boy, brown skinned and wide-eyed, followed at a respectful distance. His eyes showed apprehension. Doc regained his feet and looked more closely at the boy that Moots urged forward and lay a comforting hand on his shoulder. "Do you speak English?"

"Si . . . yes."

"Just enough," replied Moots for the boy. "He understands what we want. I explained it to him on the way, but he's pretty scared after what happened to Santiago."

"Don't worry, amigo," reassured Doc. "We'll make sure that you're safe. Let's get us all some coffee and find some breakfast and get on with it. First Bent, we get everybody together in the same room, then we'll try to start a fight." The boy's eyes got even wider.

After a quick breakfast the two men hurried the boy toward the sheriff's office. "Leave him at the office; get the two prisoners from the jail and bring 'em over to the doctor's office, but don't let 'em see or talk to Douglas. I'll meet you there."

"Where you goin'?"

"I've got a couple of things to do."

Doc had already arrived at the doctor's office and sat a few feet from Douglas's bed when Moots arrived with his two prisoners. Malcolm's eyebrows shot up when the Miller brothers, shackled hand and foot, clanked into the room.

"Gentlemen," he nodded, "I'm glad to see you looking so well. I hope you'll excuse me if I don't rise to greet you." The brothers just nodded. Doc motioned to Moots with his head and Moots left the room. "What the hell are you doin', Shores?" asked Clell Miller.

"You'll see soon enough."

Moots returned with the boy. Doc smiled at Douglas's look of surprise and bewilderment. The brothers regarded the boy suspiciously but uncomprehendingly. The boy's eyes were wide and wild. He shivered.

"Now," said Doc to the boy. "Do you know, do you recognize, any of these men?"

The boy hesitated, then nodded. "Who?" asked Shores. The boy pointed first at Douglas and then at the Miller Brothers. "Are these the men that killed your father and brother and ran your sheep into the canyon?" Again the boy nodded.

"This is bullshit!" exploded Douglas, straining at the handcuffs which tethered him to the bed frame. Everyone else, including Doc stepped back from the man's wrath. "He can't identify anybody," said Douglas.

"Why's that?" asked Doc. "Because you had Horn kill him? Apparently he missed, or maybe he shot the wrong boy, or maybe he took your money and lit out." Doc let this sink in for a few seconds. "Looks like you boys are all screwed for sure. I'm arrestin' the three of you for the murders of the sheepherders, Torrio and Cesar Escalante." He turned to Douglas, "I'm also chargin' you with conspiracy to murder Santiago Escalante. You'll all hang."

The brothers stood sliently, their expressions turning fearful. Douglas remained defiant. "Bullshit! This beaner ain't never gonna make it inside a courthouse."

"Yes he will," replied Shores, "because this time we're takin' him away for protective custody and puttin' a twenty-four hour guard on him until the trial." Doc turned to leave the room but stopped and pretended to think for a few seconds. "Tell you boys what I'm gonna do; I'm gonna give you the chance to save your necks and the good people of Gunnison County the cost of a trial. Any of you decides to confess right now and give the state evidence on conviction of the others, I'll see to it at least you won't hang. But you'll do it now and here, because the minute I leave this room the deal's off." No one spoke. "O.K." he said, once again turning to leave the room, "you had your chance fair and square. Bent, take 'em back to the jail." He turned to leave the room, and Moots motioned toward the door with his shotgun.

"Hold on," mumbled Clell Miller. "I'm not gonna hang for somethin' I didn't do."

"Shut up, Miller," hissed Douglas. "He's shootin' in the dark. That kid'll never make it to trial, and if he does, it won't do 'em any good because I still own the town and any jury."

"Not any more, J.M." Doc interuppted. "That might have been true once, but the people of this town and this county put you on notice when they elected me sheriff that they wanted new management. As far as the boy not makin' it to trial, this time it's gonna be real different." He turned to Clell Miller. "You got somethin' to say to me, you better do it right now."

"O.K . . . O.K. Tom and I stampeded the sheep into the canyon. Douglas was gonna tear up their camp and chase the herders around a bit while we were doin' that. We all did a lot of shootin'. Tom and I could see from the rim of the canyon that Douglas sure 'nuf set the place on fire, but when we got there we found two bodies. He told us to pile up some rocks and put crosses over 'em, but to take the bodies and dump 'em off the cliff with the sheep."

"Clark wasn't in on this?"

"He'd told us where to find 'em and rode out later. Both he and Douglas agreed that it would look better if it appeared that he just came upon the scene by accident."

"You son-of-a-bitch! You whinin' coward! yelled Douglas. "I'll have your asses too. This is still my county, my town. I built this place from nothing. None of you would be here, and this place wouldn't exist if it wasn't for me. I'm the person who makes it all work. No one gives a shit that I killed a couple of sheepherders. As long as we stick together no one's going to do time and no one's going to hang. I'm the king here."

"So," asked Doc. "You admit that you killed them?"

"For all the good it's going to do you, sure, I killed 'em. Anyone else would have done the same thing to protect their property, and this valley is my property. You and your deputy and the Millers gettin' up in court are not gonna amount to a hill of shit anywhere in this county, not in Gilpin's court."

"Well, two things," said Doc, rubbing his chin. "The first is that I told Gilpin what was goin' on before coming up here this morning. He gladly signed a resignation — after he'd agreed to a change of venue. Second thing, it's not going to be just Moots and me testifying against you. Oh, you can forget about the boy. He's dead. Horn killed him just like you ordered. This one," he nodded toward the boy standing next to Moots, "is just someone who we picked up last night to go fishing with us. Worked too, bagged a nice catch. No, not the boy." Doc turned and pulled open a door to the adjoining doctor's office to reveal Stryker McQue.

Malcolm's mouth fell open in surprise, then contorted with rage. "You miserable back stabbin' son-of-a-bitch . . . " he began, but Stryker brought up his hand.

"Steady, old hypocrite. I'm not doing anything that you wouldn't have done first to me if you'd gotten the chance." Stryker produced his trademark, a long, thin cigar, and lit it with a match from his ornate silver matchbox. "And I'm not the one to have shot two escaping men in the back. Doc Shores is right; the county is overdue for new management. You and that worn-out bunch of thugs you hired me to beat up are bad for business, which endangers my rather splendid livelihood. You've had your time in the sun John, most of us do, and God knows you've enjoyed it, but it's time for a change now."

"I'm not finished just yet," snarled Douglas. "This is the second time you've betrayed me McQue, and I guarantee you my day'll come to set things straight."

"Now, now, let's not air our personal dirty laundry in front of strangers. Should you, by some inconceivable piece of luck, escape the hangman's noose, you know where to find me. Now, Sheriff, if you have no further need for me, I have business to attend to."

"I reckon not, McQue. Thanks for your help." Stryker exited the room in a plume of blue cigar smoke.

"Shores," sneered Douglas, "You're gonna get yours too, if not from me, from Stryker. He can't take a chance on having an honest sheriff in the county watchin' over him."

True enough, thought Doc.

Chapter 15

Doc leaped from the stairs of the train and ran down the platform of the Denver Union Station before the train had stopped. He'd seen Agnes and Frank and timed his jump to almost land on top of them. Agnes shrieked with surprise, and Frank yelped and stumbled over backward. Doc laughed and scooped up his son with one arm and wrapped the other around his wife. He held them close to his face to smell their freshness. He kissed Agnes long and hard like when they were first married. They each backed away and looked at each other and embraced again while young Frank pulled at his father's lapel for attention.

"My Dear! It's so good to see you again," said Agnes. "I was worried I wouldn't . . . ever. Is it over?"

"Mostly," said Doc reassuringly. "We got J.M. and his boys trussed up pretty good and safe, and we're gettin' ready to take them to Cañon City for trial." As they collected his bag and walked from the station to a carriage, he told her details of Santiago's death, ambushing the Millers in the middle of the night, and the gunfight with Douglas. "Who'd ever thought when I bought that old rifle in Detroit mor'n twenty years ago that it'd end up saving my life in Colorado? Life does take some strange twists and turns."

"How's the old man?" asked Kate after embracing Doc.

"Still alive and kickin' the last time I saw him. Left 'im in charge. But he was probably in need of a square meal or two."

"And a bath I'll wager," added Kate. "Looks like you could probably do with some of the same yourself. I'll have one of the boys draw up a bath, and we'll get some pot roast and fried chicken into you." Kate rang for one of the servants and hurried back to Doc. "You reckon it's all right to get on back to Gunnison? I miss it. I guess I'm not much of a city girl socialite any more."

Doc laughed. "Hard to imagine you ever were, Kate. No, I'm sure it's okay to go on back . . . you sure that it's Gunnison that you miss?" kidded Doc.

"You go on to your bath, Shores. I'm going to my room and pack for the trip home."

"Doc," Agnes pleaded, "let's stay for a few days, maybe a week. You can take Frank to the park like you promised, and we can have breakfast in bed and go out to dinner and the theater — and go shopping. Please!"

Doc smiled. "I reckon I could do with a few days off."

❁ ❁ ❁

Doc, Frank, and Agnes saw Kate off at Union Station the next morning. They spent the remainder of the day shopping and sight-seeing. That evening they left Frank in the care of the servants and went to dinner at the Brown Palace Hotel. The grandfather clock in the hallway chimed one o'clock when they returned. Doc checked his watch.

"Decadent," he exclaimed drunkenly.

"Let's do something else decadent," said Agnes leaning against him.

"Like what?"

"Sleeping past sunrise for one thing."

When the maid knocked at their bedroom door, the strong spring sun had already driven the night's chill from the room. Doc sat up in surprise as the girl entered the room, discretely averting her eyes from the bed. She set a loaded breakfast tray on the table near the window. She paused. The open shades seemed to confuse her.

"Good morning," she said. "Hope you had a pleasant night's rest. A telegram came for Mr. Shores. It's on the tray." She turned and left the room, her eyes never having touched upon the bed.

Doc climbed out of bed and donned the robe the butler had left out for him the night before. He poured two cups of coffee and delivered one to Agnes who was sitting bleary-eyed against a stack of pillows. He picked up the envelope, tore it open, and read. "Damn!" he said and handed the telegram to Agnes.

❂ ❂ ❂

"Well, that didn't take long, did it?" Agnes complained as they watched the black cloud of smoke approach the station as the shrill scream of the locomotive's whistle split the morning air and scattered the pigeons along the platform. "Seems like you just got here a couple of days ago . . . wait a minute! You did only get here a couple of days ago."

Doc smiled weakly. "I'm sorry, but we sure 'nuf got trouble this time."

"It'll be different this time Doc," she warned. "The cat's out of the bag. He's the hunter. Douglas could well be waiting for you when the train pulls into the station. And you'll be alone."

"Yeah, I reckon . . . but he's only got one eye."

"That, and a dozen killers. What about McQue? Where will he stand now?"

"Damned if I know, with whoever he thinks is gonna win this round, I reckon."

"Doc, let me go with you," she pleaded. "You know I can handle a gun as well as a lot of men."

"Not a chance. We've got Frank to consider." She didn't agree, but nothing more was said. "Ag, I'm sorry. There's lots of times, like right now, that I wish I'd never let myself in for any of this. When I was back on the

Pecos, I put myself to sleep every night by dreamin' of havin' you, a cattle ranch, and a litter of kids. I'm not really cut out for all this."

"No Doc, you're wrong. You are. You always were, and it's a good thing. You're honest and courageous and have a good sense of what's right and wrong and you're willing to go to war over it. Those are rare qualities in a man. You believe in the oath of office, and everyone who comes into contact with you, and some that don't and never will, are the better for it. And I believe in you. I'd rather have you as a lawman than someone else as a farmer or rancher or shopkeeper. We're in this together, like it or not, for as long as we both shall live. When you get ready to meet your maker and take inventory of your life there are only a few things you have to answer for: whether you truly made good use of the talents you were born with, whether you were honest and brave when those things really counted, whether you struck a blow for justice during your life, and whether you were faithful to your friends and family. That is all we can ask of ourselves and others can ask of us. Now the conductor says it's time for you to go, and all I can say is be as careful as you can."

Doc felt tears burning his eyes. He held her close and whispered in her ear, "You're the best thing that ever happened to me."

When Doc stepped from the train in Gunnison he was weighted down by newly purchased guns and ammunition, shotgun in one hand, Winchester rifle in the other and two holstered revolvers, a Colt and a Smith and Wesson Schofield. Neither friend nor foe greeted nor confronted him. He trotted to the livery stable and saddled his faithful old buckskin. He slid the Winchester into a saddle scabbard and placed the shotgun at the ready in the crook of his left arm. Many curious eyes followed him down the street, but he noticed one pair missing — Stryker McQue's from his usual perch on the Red Lion's balcony.

Doc pushed the old horse at a slow but relentless canter the seven miles to Kate's house. Skip seemed to sense his rider's urgency and responded by leaving a trail of lather flecks in the dust of the road but never slackening his pace. Doc drew in at the rail in front of the house just as Jack crossed the yard and caught the bridle reins. Doc asked, "Have you seen Moots?"

"Yeah. He's not real good. Gut shot. He's been askin' for you. Kate's with him upstairs in the master bedroom."

Doc slipped the rifle from the scabbard and strode up the walk to the door. The sheriff who once took pride in walking Gunnison's streets unarmed now carried over twenty pounds of weaponry and ammunition wherever he went. Ben met him at the door. Doc laid a hand on the old black man's shoulder as he stepped past him . Their eyes met, but neither spoke. Doc took the stairs two at a time.

Kate sat in her rocker close to the bed and crocheted. Doc first thought his friend dead. Moots' skeletal, toothless head lay nearly indistinguishable from the snow-white pillow upon which it rested.

Kate looked up and held a finger to her lips. "He's sleeping," she whispered.

"Am not," came a reply from the bed. "Come on close over here, Doc. I can't see real good and my voice don't carry."

Doc approached the bed and placed his hand on the old man's bony shoulder.

"Glad you got here," Moots rasped, barely audible. "I think I'm about to the end of the trail, but it's been a helluva ride hasn't it?"

"It sure has. Can you tell me what happened, Bent?"

"I was watchin' Douglas real good, and he was behavin' hisself jus' fine. We even played a few hands of cards together from time to time. Then I let my guard down. I usually arranged for somebody from the cafe to bring meals over to us. Things were goin' too good. I went over to the cafe the day 'fore yesterday to pick up lunch. Someone must have been watchin' and slipped him a gun while I was gone. Next thing I knew I was lookin' down the barrel of a hogleg the size of a cannon. I turned 'im lose, shoulda saved myself the trouble, shoulda knowed that he was gonna shoot me anyway. Gut shot me . . . you should've listened to me that mornin' at the castle when I wanted 'im to die real slow."

Doc nodded his head solemnly. "Yeah. I'll do everything I can to see to it you get your wish the next time. He coulda laid me out the minute I stepped off the train. Why didn't he?"

"Wanted both of you to suffer is my guess," put in Kate.

"Bent, I'm real sorry about this . . . " Doc's voice broke. Moots raised a bony hand from under the covers.

"No!" he croaked, "don't be sorry. I had one helluva ride with the best man I've ever knowed. You remember, we both were afraid we were gonna end up under a pile of rocks somewhere? Well, I'm thankful as hell that I'm gonna die in bed between clean sheets with my two best friends right here with me when I cross over. I ain't really scared, but I could use some help gettin' across."

"It'll be all right, Benton, the old skipper knows 'bout such things. He's a good one to cross rivers with."

"Kate," Moots reached out his other hand to his wife. "Thanks for the best years of my life. I'm just sorry I couldn't have stayed longer."

"Me too, Bent. Meet you on the other side." She grasped his hand in both of hers.

Moots gasped sharply, his eyelids fluttered, he exhaled, and Doc felt the hand he held go limp. His old friend had moved on, but at least not beneath an anonymous pile of rocks on the bank of some muddy desert river. His eyes burned, and he choked back a sob as Kate rested her head on the sheets covering the old man's chest. Finally Kate raised her head off the bed, and daubed at her eyes with a corner of the sheet. Doc gently rolled Moots' eyelids closed with the tips of his fingers and pulled the sheet over the nearly transparent face.

"Well," he said calmly to Kate, "I guess it's time to settle scores. I'll be headin' back into Gunnison. You know where he is?"

Kate shook her head. "Don't do it Doc. You're out-manned and out-gunned."

"Got to, you know that. I guess I knew that it would come to this the day I took this job, so I got no complaints now. Where is he?"

She sighed and shook her head. "I don't know. Ask Jack. The boys comin' from town'll know."

Doc embraced Kate and kissed her on the cheek and promised a quick return. He knew that neither of them believed that to be true. The setting sun silhouetted the low palisades to the west with orange and pink and crimson when Doc finally caught up with Jack and asked to borrow a horse. The foreman pointed out the best of the stock, a young rangy thoroughbred. Doc exchanged his soaking-wet saddle blanket for a dry one and began saddling the horse.

"Douglas holed up in the castle?" he asked Jack.

"Word is at least one of the Miller brothers lit out of town and that Douglas and some of his boys from the Cattlemen's Association moved into the La Veta, waitin' for you I reckon."

"I reckon," Doc said mounting his horse. "Jack, if I don't make it back, would you see to Skip in his old age? He's done me good over the years, and I like to go thinkin' that he's headed for an easy retirement."

"Sure, Doc. Uh . . . Doc, I'd like to go along with you, but I ain't much with a gun and I'm a bit of a coward."

Doc smiled, "Just offerin' to go shows you're no coward. Thanks for the offer, but no, I don't need any more of my friends getting killed. If I had to watch out for you it'd take my mind off business." Doc trotted out of the stable and up the lane to where the dim road led into town.

When, he wondered as he rode, would be a good time to try to get the drop on Douglas? In the early morning when he would be still hung over, blurry-eyed and slow-fingered? At night when he would be wide awake but drunk? Would the darkness help or hinder either of them? The exact time and how he would strike were the few things he had left in his favor. In order to survive he would have to choose wisely.

He entered the empty, moonlit streets of the town shortly after midnight and considered going to his house and lying low until morning but decided against it. He wasn't sure but what they hadn't planted someone in the house to ambush him. Now even in late spring, he shivered under his wool vest and coat. He thought of the one building where they might not expect him to show up.

Doc pushed gently at the jailhouse door. It creaked open. The lock had been either broken or shot off. He peeked around the edge of the door. In the dim light he could see the cell door open. He led his lathered horse inside so it wouldn't be seen in the morning. Only a few days ago the Miller brothers occupied this cell. Now Doc swept the foul mattress and blankets from the bunk and tried to bury himself in the poncho from his saddle. He tried to sleep, but his rifle kept falling from his grasp with a clatter. Putting the rifle aside, he unholstered the Colt and snoozed holding it.

He dozed until the first light of dawn crept through the chinks in the jailhouse door. The warm light beckoned him, but he disciplined himself to stay in the cold concealing shadows. What I wouldn't give, he thought, for a cup of Moots's coffee.

Doc prepared to make his move to the La Veta but realized that he didn't know Douglas's room number and cursed his short-sightedness. Certainly, he thought, even Douglas had breakfast sometime. Doc would position himself in the hotel so that he could see people coming and going, but remain hidden himself until he spotted Douglas. But it'd be a real trick getting into the hotel without running into someone who knew him and could warn Douglas. The horse was released to graze on a grassy field on the edge of town. Doc knelt to hobble the horse so he could more easily catch it later but caught himself and chuckled mirthlessly. Odds were, he wouldn't even be alive then. His coat would be a hindrance to drawing and firing quickly. Shivering, he removed it and put it with the poncho on the bunk. From his saddlebags he took two bandoleers of ammunition, 12 gauge for the shotgun and .44-.40 for the rifle and slung them over his shoulders and across his chest. A final check of his weapons and he was off toward the hotel.

Doc sneaked low through the dewy grass of the hillside between the jailhouse and the south-facing backs of the town's buildings at the east end of Main Street. There he paused, breathless and sweating. His heart pounded in his head and his tongue stuck to the roof of his mouth. He took off his hat and peeked from behind the saloon out on the end of the street. It was empty except for an occasional shopkeeper sweeping the boardwalk.

The La Veta blocked the end of Main Street. Its front door faced down the street and was about two hundred feet from Doc's hiding place. People were beginning to exit the hotel, and he knew the risk of being seen and recognized was great. Doc forced his cold and fatigue-numbed mind to work. How could he get in and hide without being noticed? A heavily armed man was almost sure to be spotted by the kitchen crew. He was inspired. He could use the entry to the wine cellar where he used to deliver kegs of beer from the brewery. The cellar door was nearly hidden by a grove of aspen trees and evergreen shrubs and was usually locked only with a large clip though a tongue and hasp. From there he would have access to the staircase and hallways leading to the dining room where all the hotel guests ended up eventually. He waited until he could see no one between his hiding place and the hotel. But instead of running and attracting attention, he pulled his hat low over his eyes and walked straight for the hotel like a cowboy off the range. Doc slipped into the grove of aspen surrounding the cellar door. Quickly, he glanced over his shoulder. It appeared no one had seen him. He heaved a sigh of relief that the flimsy door was still held shut with no more than a rusty clip. He opened the door and slipped inside to the top step of a dank, musty, stone stairwell leading down to the cellar. Reaching his index finger back through a crack between the double doors, he flipped the tongue back over the hasp and sat down briefly on the damp stone steps to let his eyes get accustomed to the darkness.

The odor of musty, vinegary wood filled his nostrils. Now, somewhere on a ledge was a corked bottle of matches. There! From the match light he easily found the lantern and made his way down the aisle between the casks and barrels, rats scuttling before him. At the end of the aisle was a large oak door. Cautiously, he lifted the latch and pulled gently on an iron ring nailed to the door. It creaked open. He peered through the crack, but there was only darkness. He held the lantern up to the crack of the door. Stairs led to a landing and another door. His heart skipped a beat with each creak of the stairs. At the top, he set aside the lamp and cracked open the door into a hallway between the kitchen and dining room.

Another hallway from the lobby intersected across from where he stood. An empty cloakroom occupied the corner of the intersection. Heavy, red velvet curtains were drawn across its counters. The counters offered an almost unrestricted view into the dining room. He blew out the lantern flame and made a final check of the hallways before sprinting across to the cloakroom. Locked! He heard voices in the hall leading to the lobby, so he tried to slip back behind the wine cellar door. No. It'd locked behind him! The voices came closer, so he ran back to the room, slid the velvet curtains aside and jumped over the top of the counter just before a group of men passed by. He could scarcely believe it! Over the pounding of his heart in his ears he heard the all too familiar, raucous voice and laughter of John Malcolm Douglas. Paralyzed by surprise he berated himself as the voices disappeared toward the dining room, for not having acted quickly and gotten the drop on his man right then and there. Taking off his hat he peeked through the opening in the curtain. Four men were being seated by a waiter. John Malcolm, distinguishable by a black patch over one eye, sat facing him. Two of the other three men

Doc recognized as members of the Cattlemen's Association, and the third looked like a clean shaven Tom-Miller.

He slumped down behind the counter. Thoughts raced. Slow down. Need a plan of attack. Walk in and rush the table and surprise them? J.M. would see him coming across the floor and have too much time. Besides, he had to consider innocent bystanders. Confront Douglas as he walked up the hall when he'd finished breakfast? Might work, but almost certainly one and probably all four would draw. He'd be a great target standing alone in the narrow hallway. No, he'd wait until they had passed him and get the drop on them from behind with the shotgun. The first to draw, he'd gun down immediately. Maybe that'd stop anyone else. He reached up and slipped the lock off the cloakroom door and tried the doorknob. It worked and the door opened a crack. He shut it and sat back to wait.

The men were in no hurry. They ate, joked, laughed, and drank coffee and ate some more. The minutes crept by, and Doc, with each peal of laughter or sliding of a chair across the parquet floor, would rise up, heart beating wildly to check on his targets. After more than an hour some of the quartet were beginning to scoot around restlessly. His moment was fast approaching. John Malcolm signaled for the bill. The four slid back their chairs. Doc stood up and shook his numb legs. In the dim light of the cloakroom he again checked the cylinders of both six-guns and opened the breech of the shotgun. His tongue stuck to the roof of his parched mouth. He'd leave the rifle just inside the door where he could retrieve it quickly. The men walked across the dining room and started down the hallway. His hand tightened around the knob. They passed the cloakroom door. Doc sucked in a deep breath, opened the door wide, and stepped out into the hallway. He leveled the shotgun at the back of the nearest man and bellowed, "Stop and raise your hands. Douglas, you're under arrest. Don't turn around." He was surprised and relieved when all four men stopped practically in mid-step and began raising their arms. Two of the men attempted to look over their shoulders, but Doc yelled again, "I said, don't turn around!" The men immediately faced forward.

"I should never underestimate you, Doc," said the man at whom the shotgun was pointing. "You know, it's a shame we couldn't have worked out our differences. We would have made a great combination. I guess we're well beyond that now, aren't we?"

"Damn straight. We were well beyond that a long time before you gut shot old Moots."

"How's the old boy bearing up?"

"Dead."

"Pity that . . . but it did bring you right back. What do you intend doing now? You put me back in jail, and I'll be out before noon and you'll be dead for sure this time."

"Nope, I'm takin' you to Denver on the train. The sheriff down there has a special cell for you and a twenty-four hour guard, and I'm lockin' these other yahoos up until we're at least out of town."

"Yer dreamin' Doc. You'll be full of lead before we ever make it to the station."

"We'll see about that. Now all four of you up 'ginst that wall to your right, and startin' with the man closest to me, one by one, unbuckle your gun belts with one hand and let 'em fall to the floor."

Doc stepped back and bumped into one of several curious men from the dining room who had gathered behind him. Startled, he whirled and buried the muzzle of shotgun in the man's stomach. The bystander fell backward. Doc whirled back, but Douglas and his men had seen their opportunity and were reaching for their holsters. Doc leveled the shotgun at the first man to step back with his gun drawn and let fly with a load of buckshot. The smoke from the blast nearly obliterated the scene, but he could see his target leap from the floor, go nearly horizontal, and crash backward into the others. All landed in a heap on the floor.

Shores struggled to assess the situation through the smoke and tumble of bodies in the dimly-lit hall. One man on the floor aimed a revolver at him. Firing from the hip Doc pulled the second trigger on the shotgun. The blast lifted the man's body off the floor in a convulsive heave. Doc flung the shotgun aside and drew his Colt. Another man knelt, firing wildly as fast as he could thumb the hammer of his six-gun. Doc could see the flashes and hear the bullets buzzing by with a thunk into the wood behind him. In a flash, he remembered Hickok telling him that the man who keeps calm in a gunfight and takes time to aim steady, wins. Doc dropped to one knee and took careful aim at the shadow in the smoke. It fell. Another flash from the gun of the man lying on the floor. His shots too, were going wide. Doc lay down himself and flattened his Colt against the floor and pointing in the general direction of the man's boot soles, he fired. The man screamed in pain, threw his gun aside, and curled up into a ball. Doc fired a quick, poorly-aimed, shot upward at a standing man and rolled for the safety of the cloakroom door. Only then did he become aware of the pandemonium coming from the dining room. Men and women, waiters and busboys, in their haste to escape the wild shots crashed into tables and chairs. Men either rushed to the battle scene in curiosity, or from it in panic.

Doc began to reload but then holstered his six-gun and snatched up his rifle. He jacked a round into the chamber and jumped back outside the coatroom ready to fire from the hip. But no targets offered themselves. Quickly, he examined the three blood-spattered men on the floor of the hallway kicking revolvers from widening pools of blood. The man he thought to be Tom Miller had been hit in the middle of the forehead by a .44 bullet from his Colt. Where the top of his skull had once been the convolutions of his brain now presented the appearance of plastered-down, wavy, gray hair. Doc couldn't identify the other two bullet-riddled men.

He paused only momentarily, then leaped over the bodies and shouldered aside bystanders in his way. Seized by the heat of battle he dashed recklessly down the hallway toward the lobby where people scrambled to hide behind chairs and beneath desks. A tall man struggled furiously to exit a revolving door in which another man had fallen, blocking the door. The tall man stepped back and fired his pistol through the glass door into the face of the hapless, trapped man. Shores shouted, "Douglas!" The man at the door whirled, firing. Doc ducked, but there was no need as the bullets whistled high overhead. He brought the Winchester to bear, but his target moved too quickly among the roomful of tables and chairs. Douglas picked up a ladderback chair from a writing desk and swung it with one hand through the large, frosted window next to the revolving door, showering the hotel's floor and porch with broken glass. Before Doc could get a clear shot, Douglas disappeared through the opening. Doc lowered his rifle and bolted after his man. He skidded to a halt in the shattered glass. Rifle at the ready, he stuck his head through the window and quickly looked right and left and then down the street where he could see people either scattering wildly for the protection of buildings or staring slack-jawed at the hotel. But there was no sign of Douglas.

Doc, finger still on the trigger, slowly lifted a leg over the jagged window frame. Lowering the rifle across his chest, scanning the street, he walked to the edge of the high porch. Suddenly his eyes caught sight of something just over the edge of the porch, and he drew back as fast as he could, but too late. An explosion, a tongue of flame and a cloud of blue smoke were the last things he saw before the bullet ripped through the planks of the porch floor and hit his rifle's receiver with sledge-hammer force slamming it back into his chest, knocking the air from his lungs and hurtling him backward against the hotel wall. Hot lead from the ricocheting bullet spattered his face, neck, and eyes as yet another bullet whistled past his ear and buried itself in the wood siding of the hotel. Despite surprise and his wounds, Doc reacted instantly. Dropping the ruined rifle, he drew his Colt and fired his remaining shots in the direction of the edge of the porch. When the hammer snapped ineffectively on a spent round, he dropped the Colt, drew the Schofield from his other holster and waited. He was too slow. A figure darted from in front of the porch and dashed, zigzagging, toward the Columbine Saloon. He wiped his eyes with his shirtsleeve. The street was a blur. He waited, the Schofield cocked and ready, eyes burning, vision dim. Fear gripped him. If Douglas suspected the extent of his injury he would be back at him in seconds. Rising unsteadily, he jumped from the porch and dashed toward the saloon, hoping it would be empty at this time of the day.

He slammed his back against the front of the saloon and peeked over the bat-wing doors. The saloon was dark and quiet. Eyes ain't gonna last, he thought. Better move now. Doc crashed through the door expecting Douglas to rise up over the bar and fire. Instead there was a great crash from the bottom corner of the bar, and his right leg felt the pickax force of a .45 caliber bullet slamming into it. The shock wrenched a scream from his throat. The leg buckled, and he fell back onto the floor. Leg's broken, he anguished. I'm a gonner for sure.

From his prone position he could see a large dark hole in his right pant leg just above the knee. His vision nearly gone, Doc fired two shots from the Schofield wildly toward the corner of the bar. Silence. A voice echoed through the empty saloon.

"Shores, you're finished. Your leg's shot out from under you. All I have to do is wait and finish you off."

"Go ahead," Doc challenged. "Poke your head out and see how finished I am."

Doc's mind raced. An hour ago he'd thought himself too well armed, but now he had only two, or was it three, shots left in the Schofield. Douglas wouldn't give him time to reload. He tried to edge backward on his elbows toward the door. He heard something in the direction of the bar, then, the crash of a shot and yellow flame. Doc fired twice — but wildly, long after the figure at the bar had disappeared. He fired a third time into the front of the bar hoping it would go through and catch Douglas. In his excitement and anger Doc cocked and dropped the hammer a fourth time. A loud, heart-breaking snap echoed throughout the saloon. Too late he realized his mistake. He hit the cylinder catch release with his thumb and smacked the barrel against the top of his wounded thigh without even noticing the pain. The barrel lever opened and spent cartridges tinkled on the oak flooring. Frantically he fumbled with the cartridges in his belt loops but froze when a dim figure appeared once again above the bar.

"Hold it right there," Douglas snarled. "I've gotta hand it to ya. I didn't think you'd last this long. But I guarantee ya; this is the end of the trail."

Doc instinctively raised his gun hand to ward off the shot. He clenched his teeth and closed his eyes against the pain. The explosion flattened him to the floor. But the sledgehammer force he expected did not come. He felt nothing. I must be dead, he thought. Then he heard a man cry out the name "Stryker" and another explosion.

Opening his eyes, Doc could no longer see the figure standing behind the bar. He heard the creak of footsteps on loose boards, and from the corner of his eye, he saw someone descending the staircase from the second floor. The figure reached the floor and slowly approached Doc. The walk was familiar.

"Doc, I was hoping that you'd give up on this thing and move on. But I can see you're a stubborn, patient man. I'm one myself." Stryker bent down and removed the Schofield from Doc's hand and tossed it across the room. "Excuse me while I check on something." McQue walked to the end of the bar and peeked cautiously around the corner. He bent down for a few moments and then arose. "Dead," he proclaimed. He walked back to Doc, pulled up a chair, and sat down.

"Well, this episode was going to have to end with at least one of the three of us dead . . . him," he said, nodding in the direction of the bar. "I don't really mind. Had a lot of 'sand' in him as you American westerners are fond of saying but also 'rotten to the core', to mix metaphors. Killed his own mother, you know, to finance the mine and ranch . . . No, probably you didn't. Oh, didn't shoot her or push her off a cliff. Poisoned her when she refused to liquidate her trust. I didn't know it either at the time. Christine told me one night. Said he'd confessed to her once in a drunken rage when he wanted to scare her. But then you didn't know Christine either. A lovely girl, deserved far better than the treatment she got from J.M. He thought her barren. I knew that wasn't true . . . thought I'd proved so myself." Stryker paused.

"But the child wasn't yours, was it?" panted Doc.

"So you knew about the child. No . . . it wasn't. Who told you?

"Kate."

"Well, I declare! and the old man, Chaney, told her."

"Nope, although he may have confirmed it."

"I'll think on it a minute. Anyway, I figured that you knew something, and that it was only a matter of time until you felt obliged to arrest me. Am I right?"

Doc shrugged his shoulders. "Maybe, I doubt it. You probably overestimated my devotion to duty this time."

"A tragedy if true. Well anyway, the whole matter was dangerous and embarrassing. She and I talked after she found out she was pregnant. I told her to just claim it was J.M.'s. She said no; he wouldn't believe it. I didn't know why until the baby was born. Then she had the baby that night in Chaney's room. He sent for me. She and I argued about keeping it, and she fell over the rail and broke her neck. That's all there was to it. "

"No," Doc groaned. " Oh, Chaney sent for you all right, but not because he thought it was your child. He sent for you because the baby was black."

Stryker flinched visibly and just nodded.

"It really wasn't your child as you feared. It was the nigger kid's, old Ben's son. You and she fought all right, because you wanted to kill the baby and throw it in the river, and she wasn't going to stand for it. Not that she was going to keep the child herself. She'd asked Kate to take it. But you didn't know that. Yeah, she went over the rail and broke her neck but you pushed her. And then you did take the baby down to the river. Chaney saw the whole thing. You knew that too. You paid him off, put the fear of God into him, and sent him packing. Douglas was crazier than a shithouse rat and didn't really care one way or the other by that time; although I'll bet he suspected Christine wasn't as barren as he thought. Probably that's what led to the falling out between you two. Anyway, he was more than willing to close out the books, and bury the whole matter along with the lynched boy."

"Pretty good, Shores. Apparently, what Kate didn't tell you managed to figure out on your own."

"I had some other help. And that's what you wanted to know earlier. The man who filled in the gaps is right behind you with a shotgun."

"That isn't even a good try, Shores," chuckled McQue. "It ranks right down there with my shoelace being untied." McQue was interrupted with the ominous clicking of the hammer being drawn back. He tensed. Doc could see his grip tighten on his weapon.

"Look out Ben!" Doc shouted just as Stryker rose and whirled to shoot. Two crashes, so close together they almost sounded as one, echoed through the room. McQue left his feet as more than four ounces of lead balls struck him in the chest and sent him crashing into a poker table beside Doc. His body convulsed, arched, and settled back on the floor. The two small, dark, silhouettes, backlit by the morning sun streaming through the saloon door, walked cautiously forward out of the blue smoke from the shotgun blast.

Doc put his hands behind his head and lay back on the floor. "I really didn't expect visitors. But I'm glad you dropped by."

"You hurt bad, Doc?" Kate asked as she knelt down beside him.

"Leg's broke. I'm probably bleedin' to death, and I'm almost blind. Other than that I'm just fine." He looked at the old Negro and held out a hand. "If you don't mind a little blood, Ben, I sure would like to shake your hand and thank you for savin' my life."

"Mistah Shores, it would be my pleasure." The old man grasped the blood-soaked hand in both of his and knelt down beside Kate.

Doc looked at Kate. Both their eyes filled. "You know," said Doc, "You two are really a pair to cross rivers with."

Epilogue

As I was growing up, before my Ivy League education squeezed much of the fun out of life, my father and uncles, in the late spring every year after branding, would combine their herds, and we'd all strike out for the meadows of Hanks Valley on the far side of Horsefly Ridge. They weren't big as far as herds go, and the drive wasn't far as drives go. But for a week or so we all got to be cowboys.

We wore chaps and broad-brimmed hats, ate steak, bacon, and beans tasting of cast iron and wood smoke and slept in bedrolls, not sleeping bags, under a dome of stars. We woke up in the early morning, damp and shivering, to the sound of coffee boiling, eggs and bacon sizzling. But what I remember most fondly, even before opening my eyes in the early dawn, was the smell of the dew on the sage.

When I attained adulthood I no longer cared for such things, even at times, disdaining and depreciating them. Then I became old enough and sophisticated enough to enjoy them again.

Cyrus Wells Shores did what few men can do. He lived twice. Once on the frontier and then day-to-day with me for decades. I think there was not a day when either he or his manuscripts did not cross my mind at least once. Doc and I grew old together. We became constant companions. We confided secret fears, hopes, and longings. We didn't always agree. He shunned my computer, as I did his pen and ink. But he appreciated its efficiency and I appreciated the art of the handwritten word. We did, however, agree on most important things — courage, family, loyalty, devotion . . . honesty? Sure, honesty when it counted the most. But I remember Doc saying, "Don't ever let the facts get in the way of a good story."